Beautiful Serenity

TORI ALVAREZ

W0006219

BEAUTIFUL SERENITY

TORI ALVAREZ

Published by
Eternal Daydreamer Publishing
San Antonio, TX USA

Paperback ISBN: 978-1-7343363-5-1

Cover Design: Maria Ann Green
Editor: Jacqueline Hritz
Formatting: Eternal Daydreamer Publishing

 Created with Vellum

** Content Warning**

This book contains some graphic violence that may make some readers uncomfortable. The heroine is recovering from a traumatic rape. The experience is relayed through memories and speaking with her therapist. This may pose as a trigger for some.

To every woman who has had to endure pain at the hand of another.
Remember you are strong.

CONTENTS

CHAPTER 1

JAVIER

LONELY WAS NEVER A WORD THAT CROSSED MY MIND. OUR house was always a chaotic hotspot. Everyone coming and going, talking, and wishing for more privacy. The lack of square footage here made for close quarters more days than not. But now…now, everyone is moving on and I'm the only one left living here. If it had happened over time, it might have been easier to adjust to it, but it all seemed to happen overnight.

Guela's house was the only safe place for three misfits to grow up in. My cousin Antonia, my older brother, Alejandro, and I ended up on her doorstep as young children and never left. Toni was the first to begin to move on. She was the one with book smarts and was able to go to college on a free ride. Then the dominoes continued to fall…Guela passed away, and my dad went off to prison. A woman finally got under my brother's skin, and whether he admits it or not, he is living with her.

A quiet house is not in my plans, so here's to another night of texting people to come over for drinks. I don't even really care for these people, but I refuse to spend another night alone in this house. A knock on the door announces the next round of drinking and hangovers.

———

"Wakie, wakie, sunshine!" a much too cheery voice yells through my door after knocking. "I hope you're decent. I'm giving you a chance to let me know if you have someone in there before I walk in."

I pick my phone up to check the time, 9:00 a.m. Why the hell is she here so damn early? Amelia stirs next to me.

"Lola?" Amelia whispers.

I nod my head. "I'll be out in a sec," I yell through the door.

With a slight headache, I sit up, not really wanting to leave the comfort of my bed but knowing if Lola is here, Alex is not far behind.

"I guess I should go." Amelia sits up, looking around for her clothes.

I feel like a creep for sleeping with Amelia last night. We were both in a bad place and didn't think things through. The last thing I need is her fucking boyfriend, or ex-boyfriend— you never know with those two—knocking on my door, pissed.

Amelia and I throw on our clothes, then stand quietly in front of each other. I wonder what thoughts are going through her head.

"Uh…" My brows pull together in question.

"It's fine. It is what it is." She shrugs, bringing her hand up and touching my cheek.

"Come here." I open my arms, and she tucks herself in my chest.

I have known Amelia since she was a kid. She was Toni's

best friend all through school. But now that Toni is engaged to Garrett and in graduate school, their friendship is strained. They aren't in the same place anymore.

"I better go. You know Lola will tell Toni I was here." She stands on tiptoes and places a kiss on my cheek. "Don't worry about me. I'll be good. I'm done with that asshole."

"You know you can call me if you need me." And I mean it. While Toni and Alex are flirting with normal-people life, I still live in the hood. It's the only place I know.

She smiles and walks out of the room, closing the door behind her. Not wanting to face the day yet, I crawl back into bed. A knock on my bedroom door reminds me Lola is waiting.

"Come in if you have to," I answer.

The door opens, and Miss Sunshine herself walks in and jumps onto the foot of my bed. Lola is my brother's girlfriend. "Judging by the empty cans and bottles, I'm guessing you're sleeping it off." She smirks at me. "And on a school night?"

"I'm sure you know the answer to that." I cover my face with a pillow.

"If you don't want Alex to know the debauchery you're partaking in while he is away, I would get up and help me clean before he gets back." She begins bouncing on the bed to annoy me.

"Where did he go?" I mumble, still allergic to the light.

"Tacos for me, of course. He dropped me off and said he would go pick them up." I feel the bed move as she stands. "I'll start cleaning, but you better get your ass up." She slaps the covers teasingly with me underneath.

I really don't want to hear crap from Alex right now, so I stumble out of bed, making my way to the bathroom.

By the time I make it to the living room, Lola has all the empty cans and bottles collected in a large plastic bag. I walk over to her. "Thank you."

"You're welcome." Her smile is genuine. "This is new for you…partying in the middle of the week."

"As you can see, I'm not working today." I shrug my shoulders in indifference. It really doesn't matter what night people come over, as long as I don't have to hear the silence of an empty home. But I will never admit that to her or anyone else. They each have their lives to lead, and I just need to figure out what to do with mine.

She hands me the filled trash bag, and I walk into the kitchen to pick up any remaining evidence of the night before, then walk it outside to the large trash can. Stepping back inside, I see Lola at the sink washing dishes. I step up to her and softly shove her to the side.

"I got this. You shouldn't have to clean up after me." I'm a little embarrassed by the state of the house.

She shoves me back, looking up at me. "I don't mind." She looks away, grabbing another glass from the counter and bringing it to the water. "All teasing aside, why the party last night?" Her gaze stays on the sink.

I take a deep breath, not wanting to admit my loneliness, but knowing she'll continue pestering me until I give her something. "I don't know." I grab a towel from the drawer and begin to dry the dishes she's placing on the rack.

"Really." Her worried eyes meet mine.

"I don't know. Really. Everything has changed, and I'm lost, I guess. Trying to find something."

She turns off the water and grabs a paper towel, drying her hands before wrapping her arms around my middle and placing her head on my chest. "What do you want to do?" Her voice is soft with concern.

My brother truly lucked out with this one. She is a genuinely caring individual. She can tame the unruliest beast, like Alex.

"I want to work on classic cars. I'm bored out of my mind

spot-welding and fixing crap. And the work at the garage isn't much better. I want to be able to rebuild or design."

"Then what are you waiting for?" She pulls back looking up at me again.

"Nothing. I've called a couple of places and even dropped off some applications, but those jobs are few and far between." I can hear myself whining.

She winks at me. "You'll find something. You just need to see yourself as the capable, amazing person I see you as."

Lola started out as Toni's friend, then became my brother's girlfriend. But since she has come into our lives, I have seen her as a wise little sister.

I roll my eyes at her, stepping back to the sink to finish up the dishes.

"You had people over last night?" Alex's voice behind me makes me jump.

Lola busts out laughing at my expense.

"Really?" I turn around to face him. "How in the hell do you already know?"

"You have to ask?" He's taking tacos out of a brown paper bag, placing them on the table.

Lola walks to the table and takes a seat, then grabs a foil packet and opens it. Alex takes his seat, placing a couple of tacos at an empty chair for me.

My brother has had his finger on the pulse of the neighborhood since he was in high school. It doesn't surprise me he knows, but I wish there was a way to have my own life. I have lived in his shadow for too long. I don't blame him, he protected me when we were little and has continued to do so. Growing up with an alcoholic, abusive father he felt it was necessary. But we are adults now and he doesn't know how to let go.

I take a seat with them at the table, grabbing a taco and wondering if he is going to ask me anything about last night.

We all take a few bites in silence before Alex decides to begin again.

"From what I hear, last night was quite a bit larger than what we did in the past." He doesn't look at me, keeping his gaze on the salsa he's pouring on his taco from a small plastic cup.

I don't want to lie because I know he knows the truth, but I don't feel like having this conversation right now. So I stay silent.

"What time do you have to go into the club tonight?" Lola asks.

"Same time I always go in…" He lifts his gaze to her, smirking, "You can stop trying to help Javie. He's a big boy and knows how to care for himself." Lola's eyes widen at being caught trying to change the direction of the conversation. He finally turns to look at me.

"What's going on? We have never let the crowd control us, and from what I hear, last night it almost did." Alex stares, waiting for an answer.

Fuck! I should have known better. This shithole part of town is too fuckin' small, and everyone is always in each other's business.

"Nothing was out of my control. I had it the whole time." If he's going to go there, I'm willing to push back.

"What about the fight I heard about?" He pushes harder. What does he want to hear? That I was too shit-faced and know better than to lose my edge around others? That I don't know why I lost control?

"You heard right. There was a fight, but I shut it down fast." A bit of an exaggeration since I had help and kicked everyone out after I realized I had, in fact, lost control.

"On your own." He knows everything and is wanting to see if I come clean.

"How in the hell do you know all this?" Lola speaks with her mouth full.

"I just know," Alex answers her, his gaze never leaving me.

I toss my taco onto the table, dropping my face into my hands and rubbing it roughly. There is no way to avoid this fucking conversation now.

"Fine. Fuck it. I lost control. I was too shit-faced to give a damn." I stand quickly, the chair falling behind me from the force.

"Hold up." Lola's voice trembles. "Alex." She waits until he turns in her direction. "Have you ever heard you catch more flies with honey than vinegar?"

His eyes narrow, and I can't help but stifle a laugh. She is his complete opposite.

"Instead of accusing and flying off the handle, maybe talk to your brother." Her eyes widen at him.

Knowing Alex is listening, I answer as honestly as I can right now. "I don't know what the hell I'm doing." I shake my head. "I'm just trying to figure my shit out."

Lola's lips pull out just a fraction.

"What are you trying to figure out?" Alex asks more calmly.

"Everything. Don't worry. I won't put us in jeopardy. I scared myself last night when I couldn't close things up on my own." I pick up the chair, sitting back down.

Alex nods, taking a bite out of his taco.

It's quiet for a bit before Alex drops the next bomb on me. "Are you going to tell Toni about Amelia?"

My head falls back, and I stare at the ceiling. "I wasn't planning on it. Are people talking about that too already?"

"No, but they will. Her car was in front of the house when I dropped Lola off," Alex huffs out. He really knows how far gone I was last night.

If I have learned anything, it is to never lose your edge around others. You can party and have a good time, in fact that's required, but never, and I mean never, be so out of it you can't control business if you need to. If trouble comes at you out of nowhere, you better be in the right state of mind to take care of it.

"She broke up with the jackass. I provided a warm bed." I try and make it less than what it was. Both of us clutching the last remnants of our previous lives. She has lost Toni, and I am just lost.

"I hope that's the case. Because you and I both know that jackass doesn't learn easily. He WILL come looking for a fight," Alex reminds me.

He has a point. Amelia's ex-boyfriend has a temper and has never learned not to mess with us. His ass has been beat one too many times, and he still comes knocking when he thinks he's been slighted. It was always Toni riling him up in the past. She never learned to hold her tongue—or knew she didn't have to with Alex and I in the background.

"I know." My shoulders slump as I pick up a taco, taking a bite in resignation. Last night was a huge fuckup. Now to clean up the mess.

RITZA

As much as it feels like my childhood room is closing in on me, I don't want to leave it. The protective cocoon is stifling, but welcome. I had too much freedom, got lost in it, and now I'm here. Scared all the time. I force myself to try and live a normal life, but it's all for my family. I don't want them worrying anymore. They have done so much already trying to take away the pain.

My phone buzzes on the nightstand. I pick it up noticing a text from my brother, Damian.

I need you in the shop this morning.

I've been working at my brother's body shop since I came home this past spring. This was the only thing I was able to do, knowing my older brother was always around. He rarely leaves the shop when I'm working. He's always been my protector, and I think he feels guilty he couldn't be there when I needed him the most.

OK. I'm getting dressed and will be there in about an hour, I respond to him.

My brother started this body shop a little over a year ago. This has been his dream for as long as I can remember. Mom and Dad made him prove himself before giving him the money to get it up and running. He worked at several collision places, learning the front and back ends of a shop so he could successfully run his.

His true passion is taking old cars and restoring them to new glory. Keeping the nostalgia of the classic car while adding all the conveniences of newer models. He figures out how to merge the past and present into something much better. He drives an eighties Mustang that he has completely restored. If you see it going down the street, you wouldn't think it's anything but an old car, but he has added current technology on the inside. For whatever reason, that's his favorite body style. Not mine, but I don't drive it. Actually, no one is allowed to drive his car.

———

I WALK INTO THE GARAGE, and Damian is in a group with the three friends who started this adventure with him. They are deep in conversation, so I stay at the door waiting for them to finish their business. Damian looks up and sees me.

"Ritza, we need you to pull any resumes we have received lately. We need help around here," he yells to me as the other guys continue talking, paying no attention to me.

"Okay. Anything else? Do you want me to start setting up any online job postings?" I yell back, not wanting to intrude in their meeting.

"No. Let's see what we have first before I get every Tom, Dick, and Harry thinking they can do this job." He shakes his head.

I guess they have finally reached the point in this business where they will have to open their doors to people outside of their small group. That's what they wanted, to build this as the go-to destination of South Central Texas to restore cars.

I turn around, walking to the office.

Damian was stricter on me than my parents. Knowing I had an older brother watching me like a hawk was probably the reason my parents didn't have many rules for me. They knew I couldn't really walk on the wild side with Damian insisting on being my protector. As much as I hated having him around, my girlfriends always drooled over him, and the guys idolized him. Cue eye roll.

I open the filing cabinet where I have placed all the resumes that have come in. We have never posted any openings, but some eager guys have dropped off resumes anyway, just in case we ever needed anyone.

I take a seat at Damian's desk and start to sort through them, organizing them based on their qualifications: office staff, specialty people and general automotive. Flipping to the next one, I am shocked this person even turned this in. His résumé is only his name, Javier Martinez, his phone number, and his specialty, welding. He added one previous job and nothing else. Not the typical resume. I wonder how old this guy is that he would turn in something so unprofessional. Should I toss it and not even waste Damian's time? I stare at it. To the stack of specialty jobs it goes. What gives me the right to be a snob? Some of these grease monkeys may not know better.

"What do we have?" Damian's voice startles me from my focus.

"You have a few to go through. More than half the resumes were women wanting a front-end job. Probably to try and gawk at you and the guys all freakin' day." I roll my eyes, shaking my head. He has the audacity to smirk. He has no shame. "I removed those from these." I point at the two stacks in front of him.

He looks down at them and raises a brow.

"This stack," I point to it, "are all the general automotive people." I point at the next stack, "This stack are people who specialize."

He grabs the stack of specialized jobs and begins flipping through them. "Anyone stand out?"

I shrug my shoulders, "Don't know. What are you looking for?"

"You know the guys and I have general knowledge, but we are needing a few more who can work on specific jobs. I need a couple of guys in the paint shop, I definitely need a welder who knows what he's doing for frames and body, and I really need someone to take over the seat interiors. I think we should grow a bit more before we add that portion. I can keep using Jack's place for that."

"There were only two welders in there and a few for paint shop," I answer from memory.

"Great. Call the two welders to come in. We have a sixties Camaro coming in that's in really bad shape. I know I'll need a guy who knows what he's doing for that project. One for Thursday morning and the other for the afternoon. I want to meet them separately. The painters can wait."

"Got it." He hands me the stack back and walks out of his office.

I begin to pull out the resumes I need when my phone buzzes. I grab it, looking at the text that just came through.

Happy hour tonight for taco Tuesday. See you at 5.

My other saving grace since I have been home is my best friend. I don't know what I would do without Cecilia. We have been friends since elementary school, so my brother trusts me with her. He hates letting me out of his sight, but if he knows she is around, he calms a bit.

Fine. I'll meet u there, I respond.

See u there, she answers right away.

It's been months, and taco Tuesday has been one of the only things I have consistently participated in. When I've tried to go out, Damian is of course by my side, but I haven't lasted past an hour or so. It's just a feeling that pops up—a slight numbness that starts from the top of my head and slowly cascades down. My body haywires somehow, because as the numbness travels, my heartrate picks up. And it's time to go. I need a bright room, weighted blanket, and hot tea before I crash completely.

Our weekly Tuesday dates are the only thing keeping me sane. Sometimes other friends join us, sometimes it's just the two of us, but each week I get to feel normal, even if it's only for a couple of hours. I have never had to leave early, always able to eat, talk, laugh, and have one margarita. There's safety in staying at that one table—no one jostling me in a crowded bar, no loud music, no fear of someone spiking your drink.

I take a quick deep breath. I can't think about it.

CHAPTER 2

JAVIE

I'S BEEN A COUPLE OF WEEKS, BUT THE CALL I HAVE BEEN waiting for finally came in! After sending my name out to different restoration body shops, I heard from one. There are only a few in town, so the competition is fierce, but I know my shit. I *will* get this job.

I walk into the office area of the shop, and no one is around. I stand at the counter, waiting for someone to greet me, wondering if I got the wrong day. I pull my phone out of my pocket to check the calendar and note I entered. Correct day.

"Hello?" I say loudly. I saw guys in the garage. Maybe I should walk out there instead.

"Sorry. I lost track of time." I hear a female mumble.

A beautiful brunette in a large hoodie and jeans comes out of an office. A hoodie in ninety-plus-degree weather?

"How can I help you?" she says, and I can tell she is chewing and trying to quickly swallow whatever she was eating, not really paying attention to me.

"Hi. I'm Javier, here for an interview." I extend my hand to her.

She glances down at my hand, but instead of taking it and shaking, she turns around and messes with some papers on the counter behind her.

"Sure, okay. I'll let Damian know you are here. You can take a seat." She turns briefly, waving her hands at the couple of chairs they have in the waiting area.

I take a seat as I watch the girl walk through a door. After a couple of minutes, she walks back with a guy—I'm assuming Damian—following behind her. She walks back into the office she appeared from earlier, and the guy walks around the counter and extends his hand to me.

"Javier, nice to meet you. Thank you for coming in. I'm Damian Fuentes, and I co-own this shop." He shakes my hand firmly then lets it go and crosses his arms.

"Nice to meet you," I respond.

"I am not at the place to offer anyone full-time status yet, so I wanted to let you know up front. If that's what you need, I understand if you don't want to continue," he says rather bluntly.

I'm somewhat bothered by this statement. What the hell am I here for then? Reigning my temper in, I ask, "Then I have to ask, what am I doing here."

"Fair question. I can offer some contracting jobs until my garage takes off. The guys that I do have here working for me do not have the expertise in a couple of areas that are crucial to the reconstruction of a classic car. Like welding. Those jobs we contract out right now." He pauses, watching me through narrowed eyes and tense body. For someone looking to hire, he does not seem to be wanting to welcome me. Is he is trying to intimidate me? He's probably just another guy thinking he's a big dog with nothing to back it up.

Lucky for me, growing up on the southside with a brother

who is a true fucking alpha has taught me how to deal with guys like this. Most cower when they can't intimidate. It's not in my nature to post up, but I sure as hell will pull the card when I need to.

"I'm guessing you have a car that needs some body work done. Show it to me," I answer, pretending to be bored with this conversation. I want this job, but I *will not* act like I need it or have to have it.

He nods his head. "Follow me."

He turns and walks toward the door he came through, and I follow him out to the garage. There are two other guys working on a car that is up on a lift. He stays silent as he walks to the third stall where there is a tarp-covered car. He grabs one corner and pulls it away.

Shit! An old Camaro that looks like it could be unsalvage-able. But here's the beauty. A place like this can bring it back to life. I go up to it, running my hand over the hood. It's rusted through in some areas; there's a huge dent in the door panel and lots of small spots overall that need to be reinforced.

"I'm in." I can't hold the smile back seeing this car and what it could be.

"What needs to be done?" he comes back at me, still no hint of congeniality.

"Why would I answer that without a job offer? If you need me, hire me. If not, then you're wasting my time." I shake my head, turning to walk away from the job. As much as I dream of working on a car like this, I will be no one's bitch.

I get a couple of steps away from the car when Damian says, "Fine. Let's talk numbers."

Damian walks past me, clapping me on the shoulder. "Follow me." He strides back toward the office the girl was in.

"Ritza, I need my office," he tells her.

"Okay, then I'm headed home." She stands up. "It's all yours."

"By the way, you don't have to come in tomorrow. The guys and I are going to take off early."

"I'll come in anyway, just so I have an excuse to leave the house." Her brows raise in question.

He shakes his head, but says, "Fine. But I wasn't planning on staying all morning."

"We'll talk later."

She walks around the desk toward me where I'm standing at the door.

"Guessing you got the job. Congratulations." Her lips pull out into a hint of a smile, but it doesn't reach her eyes. Her honey-colored eyes, filled with sadness, pull me in. I want to be able to take away the gloom that is stirring there.

"Thank you." I smile.

As she leaves the office, Damian says, "Have a seat."

———

I haven't been in Damian's shop since last week. This is only a part-time job, so I will have to work around my full-time schedule. I walk straight into the garage this time, skipping the office but wondering whether Ritza is here and why she looked so sad the last time I was here. She may be beautiful, but I know absolutely nothing about her. I need to stay away from that one. For all I know, she's Damian's girl.

First thing I notice is they have the body of the Camaro already lifted off the frame in the last stall. I walk around it, surveying it for real this time. Running my hand over the metal, pressing on spots to feel the structure, thickness, and stability.

"Hey. Glad you're here." I look up to see Damian and three guys flanking him. "We pulled it apart this morning so it would be easier for you to work on. Let me introduce you to everyone." He finally looks somewhat at ease.

"This is Mateo. He co-owns with me." He waves his hand to the guy on his right. "Enrique." He points to the guy on his left closest to him. "And Jaxson." He points to the last guy, who is the only one smiling.

"Nice to meet y'all," I respond.

They all come around the car, looking at the battered body of a classic car that was, in its day, a gorgeous piece of machinery.

"Is this one of y'all's cars or a client's?" I wonder out loud, not knowing if they would divulge and what information they would share with me since I'm only contracting.

"It's a client's car. I was able to catch a break on it because he didn't have a timeline for it to be done. We won't be under the gun for it." Damian answers. "But that also doesn't mean we are going to dance around and keep it in the shop longer than necessary." He points at Jaxson.

"What? It was a fluke accident that we missed the deadline on that Z71. And you have to admit, that wasn't the coolest car to work on." His loud, boisterous laugh fills the garage.

Mateo cracks a smile, holding in what I'm guessing is a laugh. "It was an old dude trying to reclaim his youth." His laugh finally leaves his lips.

"Aren't they all old guys trying to do the same with these cars?" Damian asks, still not amused.

"Yes, but some more desperately than others." Jaxson's laugh continues until he's doubled over holding his stomach.

Not in the know about that client, I can only shake my head and smile.

"I swear you fools never work." Ritza's voice breaks through Jaxson's laughter.

"Ah come on, Ritz. You know we do. Jaxson just reminded us of Z71 guy," Mateo says to her.

She rolls her eyes, and a genuine smile spreads across her face for a split second before she turns to Damian and says, "Mom said you have to come to dinner tonight. No excuses. And since I haven't had to answer the phone for any of your many female admirers, I know you aren't busy."

It's nice to know she isn't his girl, especially since she intrigues me. Why is she trying to hide her beauty?

"I could have answered my phone and accepted an invitation," he quips back right away.

"Sure, if your phone wasn't sitting on your desk." She turns and walks back to the office area.

"Go to your parents' house for dinner. It can't be that bad." Mateo claps his hand on Damian's shoulder.

"It can." Damian's head drops, and I wonder the story behind this conversation.

Wanting to break the uncomfortable silence that just fell upon us, I ask, "Can I get started now?"

"Sure. The MIG is behind you, and the rest of the equipment is on the left shelf."

I turn around, looking at his set up, satisfied with the equipment. I wasn't sure what welder he had. He only mentioned having what I needed when I was here last.

"I'm going to go get my helmet and gloves out of the car."

RITZA

I hate that everyone is still worried about me, but I don't know how to move past the fear. Nowhere truly feels safe. Another 'family dinner' where I make everyone uncomfortable talking about why I'm still scared and unable to take the next step.

"I'm here." I hear Damian's voice boom through the house.

I roll out of my bed, pulling on an oversized hoodie. I have raided my brother's closet and bought probably one too many online, but right now, they are the only thing I can wear. Walking down the stairs, I take each step as slowly as I can, even though I know I'm just prolonging my family's sadness and worry.

I creep around the corner quietly, and I hear hushed voices in the kitchen.

"She stopped seeing the counselor. She refused to enroll in school. She only goes to the garage unless it's Tuesday and she's at El Gran Margarita with Cecilia. She can't continue living like this. It's not a life. It's been over four months. I still hear her scream some nights in her sleep. But now she locks her door, and I can't go in to help soothe her back to sleep." My mother is trying hard to whisper, but I can hear her passion. She still calls my best friend by her full name, never mind that she's been Cici to everyone else since she decided to shorten it in high school.

"I know. I'm at a loss too." My brother sounds exhausted.

"You need to get her to go…" my mother continues.

"You know it's only because they worry." I jump and turn toward my father's voice, hitting my back against the wall. He is standing at the bottom step watching me.

I nod, embarrassed I was caught eavesdropping.

He takes the last steps to stand in front of me. "I didn't mean to scare you." He opens his arms to me. I walk in them as he envelops me tightly. "This too shall pass," he whispers in my hair. I refuse to let tears fall. Too many have been shed over this.

"Hey," Damian greets us, coming around the corner. "Dinner's ready."

I pull away from my dad and look up at him. My brother is almost a carbon copy of him. Tall and strong, with an intimidating presence. When I was in high school, I had such a hard time dating because once the guy met either my dad or my brother, they ended up shying away. After a while, I made my mom tell them to stay away. At least until I could decide if I liked the guy or not.

But now my dad looks tired. I hate knowing I've made him age a decade since the spring. He has constant dark circles and bags under his eyes and permanent lines between his brows from the furrow he wears every day.

We follow Damian to the table as my mom is setting the last dishes down. I know she plans on having a talk because she made my favorite meal, fettucine alfredo with shrimp and chicken, French bread, and a side salad.

Dinner begins pleasantly enough with my dad and Damian talking about the garage and business. My dad gave Damian the money so he could buy it with Mateo. It has been slow going, but Damian and Mateo don't want just any body-work, they want to reconstruct. Because of this, they have been selective on the jobs they have accepted. The Camaro they took in will be the biggest turnaround if they are successful.

My mind drifts to the new guy, Javier. I was amazed he didn't cower when Damian introduced the guys. Javier stood proud, just watching them. That is their usual, coming at new guys all at once to see what they are made of. Javier is the first to look bored with them. That in itself is strange, but his soft gaze when he looked my way gave me stomach flutters, which took me completely by surprise. All guys have given me the creeps since the incident.

I feel bad because I'm sure the majority of the guys I encounter are okay men. Immature? Sure. Flirty? Sure. Maybe push a little too hard? Some. But they wouldn't hurt a girl for their own kicks. I just can't get myself to move past the fear I have when a male is around.

I have avoided all guys since the incident, except my brother's friends. When Javier came in for the interview, he didn't gawk at me or try some cheesy line to get my attention.

It's amazing how many guys still try to hit on me when I am sans makeup and not dressing to impress. He was there for business and business alone.

But since Javier walked into the shop, my mind keeps floating back to him. He has a confident stature, but a calm demeanor. He was cordial, not overly friendly or flirty. Listened, and wasn't a show-off. And so, so easy on the eyes. His dark, wavy hair, probably messy from caps and the welding helmet that he wears. His dark eyes are somehow soft, not alarming. His five o' clock shadow competing with the goatee and the tattoos peeking out of his short sleeve shirt gave him an edge that was so contradictory to his peaceful presence.

My mom's voice breaks through my thoughts of him.

"Huh?" I look up from my plate, not really hearing her with my mind elsewhere. The change from my dad's and Damian's voices caught my attention.

"I said…are you going to apply for the spring semester?" my mom repeats her question, sounding a tad bit annoyed.

I don't want to answer because I know my answer is just going to start another round of disappointment. I know they are trying to be patient with me, and I do want to move past this never-ending fear. I just don't know how. The therapist wasn't any help because I. CAN'T. REMEMBER.

That's right. I can't really remember what happened. I was drugged. I blacked out. I may not have ever known what happened to me if I hadn't woken up naked in my living room. Let me repeat that. I woke up buck naked on the couch in my living room. My clothes were thrown about, and I was sore down there. I couldn't tell you how many men had fun with me. I couldn't tell you how long it lasted. I couldn't tell you what they sound like. Look like. Smell like. Nothing. I remember nothing except waking up sore and naked.

I guess that's stretching the truth a bit. I have flashes in dreams, but nothing I can hold on to. It's more about the feeling than what actually happened. Not being able to move. Having trouble breathing. Panicked. My therapist said that was a start. I may start remembering things when I'm ready to handle it, or when something sparks a memory. My brain has stuck to the one word—*may*. I *may* remember. No guarantees.

And I guess this is the reason I can't move on. Anyone on the street could be the person who violated me, and I would never know. I could walk right past them, talk to them in line while getting coffee, meet them at a party, and I would be the *pendeja* who is conversing with their attacker.

"Martiza," my dad says softly, breaking me away from the couple of memories that could send me spiraling, "I know you are still scared. But how about a baby step. You go to school here in town. You don't have to go back to TSU. One class. Just one class to try. If it's too much, drop the class. But at least you tried."

My dad's eyes are sad. His shoulders are slumped, like he's carrying the weight of the world. And I guess he is. He's carrying my weight. I know I need to learn to carry my own, but...

"Why don't you take a class that Cici is taking?" Damian pipes in. "An elective that won't really matter if you drop or fail."

I don't know if I can do this, but maybe, just maybe, if Cici is with me, I'll be able to get around campus. I take a deep breath, holding it and exhaling slowly, calming my heart rate, which had just picked up at the thought of being around so many people. My mom is watching me with brows pulled together, probably saying a silent prayer that I agree to Damian's idea.

"I'll give it a try." My hands are tingling, the numbness beginning to travel with the idea.

I start to rub them together, squeeze them, pop my knuckles, anything to keep the feeling in them and stop the irritation from moving.

"Oh, sweetheart, that's all we ask. Just try baby steps." A brightness I haven't seen in months appears on my mom's face. Her dull, tired complexion perked up with five words.

Damian's phone beeps, and he takes it out, looking at the screen.

"Can we please finish dinner before you start with that phone?" my mom scolds Damian like he's a teen again.

"It's business, Mom," he retorts quickly. "Ah, fuck," Damian mumbles while typing.

"Really?" My mom knows he won't stop cussing but still feels responsible for reminding him about his language.

"What's wrong?" I ask at the same time.

"The guys and I were taking tomorrow off. Heading down to the river to go tubing. But that new welder we hired says he can put in a full day. Since we have to work around his full-time job, we have to take what we can get. I guess I'll have to stay back and open the shop for him."

"I can open the shop for him," I blurt out without thinking.

My dad's head whips up from his meal, Damian's eyes come up from his phone, and my mom stops mid-bite at my statement.

"Uh…well…I just thought that I could be of help," I stammer.

"Are you sure? What happens if you have an episode?" Damian places his phone down on the table as his gaze bores into me, searching for more information.

Episode. A nicer way to say "panic attack." Damian is the one who has seen the onset of them. Since my parents don't go out with us, they only witness me when I get home.

"I'll call Cici or Mom." I shrug, hoping they don't ask

more questions. Wanting to see Javier again is strange, and I don't want to share that with anyone. What if this is a fluke?

"But if you have one, then what? How do we tell Javier that he needs to leave because there is no one in the shop?" Damian questions. "I'll just stay back."

"I'll go into the shop if she needs help. I'll take tomorrow off from work and get some errands in that I have been putting off. That way if she calls, I'll go in and let this guy finish his work while I'm there with Ritza," Mom says right away. I wonder whether she figures something is up or is just happy I volunteered to do something on my own.

"That works." I try not to look too excited. "Besides, it's not like I'm going to be around anyone. He'll be outside working, and I'll hang out in your office finishing up payroll and paperwork. The stuff you hate to do."

A chill makes its way through my body. I'm not sure if it is excitement or nervousness, but whatever this new feeling is, I kinda like it.

Dinner continues a little lighter after that. My agreement to try one class and volunteering to go into the shop alone has us having a more relaxed dinner than we've had in a long time. I also feel just a tad lighter.

CHAPTER 3

JAVIE

THE GARAGE DOORS AT THE SHOP ARE CLOSED AS I DRIVE UP, which surprises me. I let Damian know I was able to come in, and it's a Friday. I park and check my phone, making sure I read his message correctly last night.

Come on in was his response when I told him I ended up with the day off. I exit my car and walk up to the shop to check the front door. There's a post-it note stuck on the door —*Call the shop when you are here.*

I dial the shop's number, wondering why I'm calling the shop if he's not here.

"Fast Lane Auto Body and Collision, how can I help you?" Ritza's voice answers.

"Uh… It's Javier. I was su—"

Ritza cuts me off. "I'll open the door."

A few seconds later I see her walking up to the glass door. She turns the lock, pushing it open for me.

"Damian and the guys had plans today, so I told them I would open the shop for you to get some work done." Her voice quivers just a tad as she speaks, almost as if she's uncomfortable.

"Okay." I'm the new guy here, and I know beggars can't be choosers. "If you would rather, I can come in another day," I offer. She is gripping her hands together tightly, and I'm worried I'm doing something to make her nervous.

"No. Really, it's okay. I'll just be in the office anyway." She tries to smile, but it's forced and looks painful.

"Look," I place my hand on her shoulder, and I feel her tense, so I quickly move my hand away, "I'll just come back later. Tell Damian to text me when the shop will be open next week, and I'll see what I can do."

I can see it in her eyes. She's scared. She shouldn't have to be here alone with a strange guy if she doesn't want to. I turn to walk out, bummed I'm not going to get to work on the car but knowing it's best for her.

"No. Please," she announces loudly to my back.

I turn around, and her face has fallen. She's not even trying to hide whatever is bothering her anymore. She gazes into my eyes, then looks to the ground. Her arms are wrapped tightly around her middle.

"Uh...look...I'm sorry." Her chest expands as she gulps a huge amount of air and lets it out quickly. "I'm a mess right now. Just...I can't explain...but...I want you to work if you want to. I told Damian I would open. I need to."

She never looks up, speaking to the ground.

"You need to?" My brows pull together. I wait patiently for her to answer.

"Yeah." Her head starts to come up, and her eyes land on mine. "I..." She shakes her head.

She has nothing to explain to me.

"Okay. I'll get to work if you're sure," I tell her.

She nods her head as she pulls her bottom lip into her mouth.

I point to the door leading to the garage, letting her know that's where I'm headed. I may spook her if I make any sudden movements.

"I'll try and make it quick," I tell her so that she knows she won't have to stick around longer than necessary.

"Really. It's okay." Her lips pull into the forced smile I've seen before.

As I'm about to walk into the garage I turn back. "I'm going to open the last bay door."

She just nods her head as she stands in the same spot, frozen.

I turn on the lights and open the bay door so I can see the car clearly. I pull out the MIG before heading back to my car for my helmet and gloves. I want to start by removing the corroded, rusted-out parts of the body. With those out of the way, I'll have a better picture of how much I'll need to replace for body structure before I begin the acid treatment and sheet metal repairs.

I pull on my helmet and slide on my gloves before firing up the machine. This may not be a pretty job, but I like the freedom of it. It's just me and my machine. This used to be a great escape from the craziness of my life. The lack of privacy living in such a small house with too many adults. The whoosh of the torch is always the best part. As soon has the torch hits the metal, all I hear is the sizzling and crackling. My calming sound.

As I watch the torch cut through the metal, my mind drifts back to Ritza. Each time I've seen her, she says so few words and has a sadness wrapped around her. Her brother must know she's not happy. He would notice something like that, right? Why would he let her continue to live in such sadness and fear? Today, I saw fear. Does he make her feel like this? Did I just step into some weird, sick family shit?

She's gorgeous, even hiding behind large hoodies and no

makeup. The summer heat hasn't let go yet, and all I've seen her wear is hoodies. Ones that are so big, they almost swallow her. Hoodies and ninety-plus-degree weather don't mix, but for her, they do. Does she not want to be seen?

How am I supposed to see her like this and not do anything to try and take those feelings away? My brain is telling me, *don't get involved,* and my heart wants to save her from whatever haunts her. Alex would tell me to look away. Don't get caught up in things that don't concern me. I usually listen, but this time…this time—I don't want to.

I continue working, wanting to complete at least this portion of the job. I'm trying to keep track of time, so I don't overstay my welcome with Ritza.

"Hey!" I hear her yell above the sounds of crackling metal.

I turn off the torch and flip my helmet up, turning around to face her. She is standing several feet away, her arms wrapped around her middle again.

"Do you need me to finish up?" I ask her.

"Uh…no." She continues watching me as she takes a couple of steps toward me. "I was wondering…because I was going to call for food…uh…are you hungry?"

Wait. What? Her question makes my brain short-circuit momentarily.

"I can eat," I answer her, hoping she will sit and eat with me.

"Really?" Her brows rise and her arms loosen just a tad.

"Sure. If you want, I can take a break and go pick something up," I offer, wanting to make it easy for her.

"I was just going to place an order for wings and fries from the Wing Place down the street. They deliver. At least here they do because the guys order so often." Her voice is soft but isn't trembling anymore.

I pull out my wallet from my back pocket, sliding my debit card out.

"I like regular hot wings. Here's my card." I extend it to her, not wanting to move and frighten her again.

She shakes her head. "Don't worry about it. I'll let you know when the food gets here."

RITZA

I just asked Javier for lunch. I did that. Don't think about it too much. Not right now. If you do, you'll freak out, and he'll think you're a weirdo. Wait, I am a weirdo. What am I doing? My heart expands two sizes larger as it begins to pound against my chest. It's so loud, it's echoing in my ears. Deep breath. One, two, three, four, five…hold…one, two, three, four, five…exhale…one, two, three, four, five. Again.

I close my eyes, one, two, Javier's eyes, three, four, his soft smile, five…hold…his presence, one, two, three. I let all the air out slowly. My eyes are still closed, but my heart has slowed.

I sit at my brother's desk and place the order. I have about thirty minutes to compose myself before I'm in a room, by myself, with him. What was I thinking? I watched him as he was working. Gawking out the window to the bays is what I was doing. He took his time. I watched him as he walked around the car. I wondered what he was thinking. His hand would glide over spots. He was pushing in places. Scratching places with steel wool. Almost like he was studying it.

He was concentrating on what he was doing. He never once came inside. Most of the other guys that have done work for Damian have found stupid reasons to come in and ask me questions. Push a little too hard. Invade my space. Each of those guys was quickly corrected by Damian or his friends and never came back. I wonder if that's the real reason Damian hasn't expanded? I'm here, and he doesn't trust I can handle things yet. Am I a burden on his business like I am on him?

I can't let my mind go there yet. I'm here right now, and I'm doing okay. Maybe not great, but it's a start.

My phone pings a message from Cici. *How about taco Tues on a Fri?* This is her way of trying to get me to leave the house on a weekend night.

Nah…staying in, I reply to her. While I miss going out, I haven't been able to last without a freak out. I'd rather not tempt it again just yet.

Pleeeeeaaaassssseee!!!!!

She knows I'm at the garage by myself. I texted her earlier to be on standby if I lost it. I know my mother offered, but I'd like to give her a day to herself. Hopefully she's not worried. She thinks with this step, I can take another.

I promise, I'm working on it. This is the best I can give her. Little does she or anyone else know, I asked a guy for lunch. Huge step, if I do say so myself.

As I'm going through invoices, a knock on the glass business door announces the food's arrival. I grab it, handing the driver a tip, and bring it into the office. I quickly clear the desk of all the clutter so we can use it to eat. Nervous energy strums through my body. My hands are slightly numb but jittery at the same time. My heart still thumps hard against my chest but not suffocating me.

I'm repeating the phrase, *I can do this*, in my head over and over as I walk out to the garage.

"Food's here." I yell again to get his attention over the noise.

He flips off the torch, and the smile that greets me as he lifts his helmet sends a warmth to my face. He places the torch down and yanks off his gloves and helmet. He walks in my direction before stopping a few feet from me.

"You can bring my food out here if you want." His arms are by his sides; he doesn't move.

"I cleaned off the desk in my brother's office. We can eat in there." Maybe he did just want food and he didn't want to eat with me.

"You do realize I've been out here sweating in the heat and the torch." His smile is gentle, lighting up his whole face.

"It's fine." I begin biting the inside of my cheek. "I don't mind."

Flirting was fun—in the past. I haven't done it since— Well, I won't think of that now. I don't even know if I remember how anymore. All I can focus on is wanting to spend time with him and not have a panic attack while doing it. I don't know what it is about him. He radiates a calmness I have never felt.

"Sure?" His eyebrow cocks up in question.

I attempt a smile. "Come on." I turn to walk back inside, hoping he follows me. His booted footsteps send an excited shiver down my back.

I take my seat in Damian's chair and wait for him to sit across the desk from me before pulling the food out of the bags. It's quiet as we begin eating. Not quite uncomfortable, but not a natural ease either. Neither of us is squirming to find words to fill the void, but the weight of the silence is sitting heavy.

I know I have a voice; I just need to find it. I want to know more about Javier. I'm surprised by the calm I feel sitting across from him. I have not spent time alone with anyone other than family or Cici in months. It's nice, yet completely scary.

The chime of the front door announces someone's arrival. My eyes widen, and I wonder who could be here and berate myself for not locking the door as my heart rate begins to sky-rocket.

"Hey, sweetie!" I hear my dad's voice break through the pounding that had just began. I suck in air quickly, trying to get myself back to normal.

Before I have the chance to respond to him, he steps into the office.

"Oh!" His brows raise. "I came by to see if you wanted some lunch, but I see you're already eating."

"Uh, yeah…" I pause, not wanting to explain anything to my dad in front of Javier. "Dad, this is Javier. The new guy we talked about at dinner that is helping with the welding the Camaro needs. He was nice enough to take a break and eat with me." My eyes widen at my dad, hoping he gets the hint not to say anything.

"Nice to meet you, Javier." My dad turns to Javier, extending his hand out.

Javier stands quickly, wiping his hands on a napkin before taking my dad's hand to shake. "Nice to meet you, sir."

"I guess I'll see you at home then." My dad comes around the desk and kisses my cheek. "I will eat alone today," my dad adds, probably for Javier's benefit and not mine.

"Okay." I nod my head and give my dad a small smile.

He turns around and walks out of the office, and I hear the door chime again announcing his exit.

"I'm sorry you missed lunch with your dad." Javier says, picking up a fry and sticking it in his mouth.

"Don't be. I see him every day. I live at home," I say quickly, then regret having to admit I still live with my parents.

"I was living with my grandmother up until last fall when she passed away. We kept her house, but now I'm pretty much by myself there." He keeps the conversation going.

"Who's 'we'?" I ask, curious about his life.

"My brother and my cousin. My grandmother raised us since we were kids. Our parents weren't really around or responsible enough to care for children. But my cousin Toni hasn't been living there since she started college a few years ago. She just graduated this spring. And now my brother is practically living with his girlfriend, so that leaves just me in the house." He shrugs, taking a drink from his soda.

"Does it get lonely?" My head cocks to the side just a fraction.

He looks down at his food. "I guess. I always thought there were too many people in my grandmother's small house, but now that it's only me, it is lonely. I hate to admit that, but I guess I just got used to living in the chaos." He finally looks up, his eyes searching mine.

Is that sadness I hear in his voice? It's odd. This guy who I thought was incredibly confident seems a little lost now.

"I can imagine it would be. I had a roommate in the dorms. There was always something while I was living there, so I decided to live alone in an apartment last spring."

He takes a bite from his chicken wing, then adds, "You're in school?"

Crap. I admitted being in college, but I'm not. "I was. I'm home now," I answer quickly, hoping he doesn't ask any more questions.

"You graduated?" His soft gaze is waiting for me.

"Uh…no…uh…I came home to help my brother out here at the shop. He needed someone up front." I blurt out without thinking. Not entirely a lie, but not the whole truth.

"That's nice of you. A big sacrifice too. Giving up college to help build your brother's business." He takes another drink. "My brother, Alex, would die before he would let Toni leave college. It was a constant battle with those two." He shoves more fries in his mouth.

"Why a battle?" That's odd, his brother making his cousin stay in college. What if that's not what she wanted?

"Long story," he shakes his head softly, "a story for another time."

I think I may have hit a nerve. Silence falls over us again. We continue eating in silence, but it soon becomes too much for me. My mind struggles to find something we can talk about that won't lead us to topics we aren't ready to share yet. I shove fries in my mouth to stop any idle chatter that is sitting on the tip of my tongue.

"So, Javier, where did you learn to work on cars?" falls from my lips after too many quiet moments.

"Please, call me Javie. Everyone does. I took auto shop in high school. That's where it began. Then when I graduated, I've worked in a few different auto shops. Some of the older guys there got me into welding. This was a good side job to make a few extra bucks. Soon I realized I would make more welding than at the auto shops. That's why a place like your brothers is great. I can combine these two skills because I love working on cars. That's where my passion is."

He was upfront and honest in his answer. I hung on every word. His deep, yet soft voice surrounds me in a calm I haven't felt in so long. I don't understand how his presence can make me feel safe.

"How about you? What were you majoring in before you came to work for your brother?"

"I was a business major. I know I want to open my own business; I just don't know what that is yet. Since my dad helped start Damian's dream, he said he would help me with mine when I figured out what I wanted that to be." I smile remembering the conversation that seems like it was a billion years ago. Everything is now broken up into *before* and *after*. Everything before seems like it was in another lifetime, and after is a black hole of time that never changes.

"Wow! That's nice. Are you planning on going back to school to finish so you can start your business?"

I'm stuck on how to answer.

"Uh…eventually. I'll stick around here until my brother

doesn't need me anymore." Lies continue to fall from my lips. He never needed me.

"You are so much like my brother." His lips spread in a gentle smile.

"Like your brother?" I ask, needing clarification.

"Yeah. Putting others needs before your own."

"Your brother does that?"

"He's older than both Toni and me. With shitty parents, he has been looking out for us since we were kids."

"Oh…" Sounds like there is so much more there.

"Well, I better get back to work. Finish up so that you can do whatever you had planned for the day." He stands. "Thank you for letting me have lunch with you. It was nice sitting in A/C for a bit. Do you want me to take all this trash to the dumpster? That way it doesn't stink up the office?"

And he's thoughtful. "Yes, that would be great. And thank you for joining me." I can't help the stupid grin that takes over my face.

CHAPTER 4

JAVIE

THAT SMILE AFTER LUNCH WAS THE FIRST *REAL* ONE I HAVE seen on Ritza. It wasn't only real, but playful too. All her smiles before have been to cover the constant sadness brewing in her eyes. That trouble was still there, but there was a light that was able to shine through. I want to be able to give that to her again. But I'm the dumbass that left without asking her for her number.

I don't know how smart it would be to try and date the sister of the guy you want to work for, but there is something about her. Pulling me to her. Don't know why I'm worrying about it now; I don't even know when I'll be able to see her again, or if she is even interested.

Laying off the parties since Alex busted my balls for the last one, I'm sitting home alone. Everyone I know is here in the neighborhood, and I don't want to be around the same people again. Watching Toni and Alex begin to step away from this crap side of town, I want to be able to do that too. But where and with who?

My phone buzzes on the coffee table in front of me.

Come on over to the Billiard Room on Broadway. A text from Lola.

I type out a response. *A pity ask?*

She is as sweet as they come, and I know she is feeling sorry for me.

No. Just didn't want you and Alex to get into it again if you decided a party was a good idea <wink emoji>

Haha… I respond, not finding it funny, but true all the same. *I'll head that way.*

I give in. I don't want to stay home, and this is a better option than wallowing and thinking of Ritza, who is probably out having fun.

———

I WALK into the pool hall scanning the place looking for Lola and Alex. To my surprise, Garrett and Toni are with them. Fuck! She's made sure to lay into me every chance she gets for sleeping with Amelia, and I know she's not done yet. Hopefully since there are a few of their other friends around, she'll keep quiet. One can only hope. But since I made my bed, I need to sleep in it…again.

"Hey," I announce to everyone as I walk up.

"Javie!" Lola exclaims happily as she comes up to me and gives me a hug.

"Really, Lola." I watch as Toni rolls her eyes. Yup, she's still mad at me. "He does not need that type of greeting when he's been acting like a dog." Toni turns away.

Fuck! Why the hell did I come? First Alex and his fuckin' power trip and now Toni with her bitch-ass attitude. Nope, not going to happen. I would rather have people over and lose control than sit here and take this shit in front of their friends.

"Fuck it! I'm outta here." I kiss Lola's cheek and turn away.

Before I can walk away, Garrett places a hand on my shoulder, halting me.

"Wait," Garrett says softly, then turns toward Toni giving her a look and motioning her to approach.

I watch as her shoulders slump slightly as she rolls her eyes again. Garrett is to Toni what Lola is to Alex. My cousin and my brother can be Type A control freaks on a power trip. They are constantly battling, while I get stuck mediating. It has been that way since we were kids. Garrett and Lola are soft, kind-hearted people, but boy, they can take control and push back when necessary.

"You need to lay off now. You said your piece the last time. Amelia knew what she was doing when she decided to crawl in bed with Javie. They are grown-ass adults. If they want to fuck, let 'em," Garrett says softly, yet sternly.

"Ugh…" Toni groans. And after a short pause she says, "I'm sorry. I don't want you with Amelia. She will end up getting you in trouble. I love her to death, but she has been nothing but a hot mess, letting Eddie call the shots. You know she will get back with him, and then it's a shit storm for you. She will only drag you down."

I'm surprised by Toni's admission. She wasn't mad at me for the reasons I thought. She was worried about me. While I completely agree with her about Amelia and her on and off again unhealthy relationship with Eddie, she is a friend. And friends don't abandon each other. I know it's killing Toni to walk away from her, but her life isn't in the hood anymore. And if Amelia doesn't get out, the ridge between them will continue to widen.

"I know" is all that is left for me to say.

Toni steps closer, placing her hand on my cheek and looking up at me, "You deserve more than what she is able to give. You're too nice." She pats my cheek teasingly then walks away.

She said her piece, and I know this will never come up again.

"Come pour yourself a beer," Alex tells me. This is a rare weekend night off for Alex. I'm amazed he's out. Working as a bar manager at one of the hottest nightclubs in the city every weekend usually means, when you have one off, you want to stay home and sleep.

I grab the pitcher, pouring myself a pint.

"You got next round," Alex says before getting ready to take his next shot. I watch him as he and Garrett dominate the table.

I stand around watching everyone talking and laughing. I don't feel out of place, but I also don't feel part of it. These are their friends. Well at least Lola's, Toni's and Garrett's. I think Alex may still be getting used to his new life. I can't ever see him being comfortable enough to relax fully around others. It took him months to trust Garrett.

Alex hands me a pool stick when they win the game. "Javie is coming in for me."

A couple of games and a few beers later, I announce my good-byes. I'm surrounded by couples, and I'm feeling a little out of place now.

Alex nods his head at me, probably recognizing the struggle to assimilate to a new life. A life I never thought would be possible. Maybe, just maybe, the hood is not where I will stay either.

RITZA

All weekend long, all I could think about was Javie. He told me to call him Javie. That means something. People usually only tell people to call them by nicknames once they have gotten comfortable. Right? Or am I just being a stupid girl overthinking this? But it feels nice overthinking something other than the night that changed my life.

My dad is the best though. When I got home Friday afternoon, after my time with Javie, all he did was smile at me and pretend to zip his mouth closed. No questions. No badgering about why. No looks of worry. Just a smile and then he turned back to the TV and whatever show he was watching. He knows I need to do this on my timeframe. He knows I can't be pushed to do something when I'm not ready. He knows I'm trying, but stuck.

Lucky for me, the quicksand I felt like I was standing in disappeared after that lunch. Before, the more I fought to *be normal*, the more I felt like I was sinking. Being swallowed whole. Having the air sucked away. I finally took a breath. A real breath. One I didn't struggle with.

Which brings me back to Javie. I wonder when I will be able to see him again. I know he's not done with the Camaro, but the next time he's at the garage, Damian and the guys will be there. There is no way they will let him close to me, and I don't want *them* around while I'm testing my resolve to move forward.

———

I wasn't planning on coming into the shop today, but my room started closing in on me. That's the most effed up part of all this. I don't want to be around people, but the safety of my house begins to suffocate. I can't figure it out. I was fine before. They had to drag me out of my room and bed, but now if I'm there for too long, it's like I can't breathe.

As soon as I walk in, I notice a few boxes behind the counter. I set my purse in Damian's office to begin the process of inventorying all the new parts they ordered and adding them to the customer invoices. Just as I'm trying to lift a heavy box onto the counter, the door chime rings. Focusing on the weight of the box I'm trying to lift, I ignore the door until I hear, "Hey, let me help you."

Suddenly, the box is taken from my grip and placed on the counter. I look up into his soft, warm eyes.

"What are you doing lifting this heavy box? Why didn't you get one of the guys to do it?" Javie questions me.

I smile at his chivalry. "I didn't realize how heavy it was until I thought I was going to drop it." I shrug my shoulders.

He just shakes his head at me with his lips pulled out a fraction. "How was your weekend?" he asks.

My eyes widen just a tad; I never have tales to share since I'm now a hermit. And I don't want to admit that to him. "Uh…nothing exciting. Same old, same old…" I try and deflect. "How about you?"

"Same." A small frown mars his face like he remembered something unpleasant, which has me wondering what it could be. Fight with a girlfriend? I've been itching to spend more time with him, and I hadn't even considered whether he's seeing someone. SHIT! That could be the reason his expression changed.

"Fight with your girlfriend?" escapes my mouth before my brain has time to stop it.

"No." His brows crease. "Why do you ask that?"

"Uh…" Here I go again. I'm a blubbering idiot when I'm around him. "It…uh…" He continues to watch me. "Just, you frowned when I asked about your weekend. I figured a fight with a significant other would cause that," I say quickly, trying to save myself.

"Nope. No significant other to fight with." He winks at me. Winks! And my stomach does a damn flip as I feel my face heat up.

"Oh" is all I can muster, not wanting to say anything else to embarrass myself.

"Just family stuff. You know." He watches me.

The door to the garage opens and Jaxson walks in. He pauses a moment before his body tenses. Javie has his back to him and doesn't notice. Jaxson thinks Javie is standing too close to me. They all know I can't be around people I don't know. I know what's about to happen, and I won't stand for it.

"Javie helped me with this heavy box I almost dropped," I quickly say to Jaxson, who is standing ready to pounce.

Javie turns around to see Jaxson's tense body, and Javie's stance changes. His fists automatically clench. I step in front of Javie, trying to defuse the situation quicky before Damian gets involved. I would hate to cost Javie this job.

"Thank you for the help. I think I got it from here." I smile, hoping he relaxes.

I turn back to Jaxson, asking, "What can I help you with?"

"I was actually going to check the deliveries that arrived. I'm looking for a part we ordered."

Javie and Jaxson pass each other quickly, without incident.

As soon as Javie is out the door and in the garage, Jaxson questions, "Do we need to fire him?"

"No!" It comes out a little too loudly.

"Are you okay?" He is standing further away from me than Javie was because he knows how I've reacted in the past when someone got too close.

"Yeah. Surprisingly, I am." A sense of calm slowly washes over me, while I also begin to miss Javie's nearness.

"You sure?" His eyes narrow in question.

I nod.

"Okay." Lucky for me, he is the most lighthearted of my brother's friends.

He grabs a smaller open box I had already inventoried, looking inside. "Is this all that came in?"

"Yes." I point at the big heavy box on the counter. "I only have this one left to go through."

He looks at the label. "Not what I was waiting for." He walks back out into the garage.

I go to the window and watch as Javie and Damian talk. Javie walks out of the garage doors to his car. He strides back in with his helmet, gloves, and a long-sleeved shirt, heading toward the last bay. I hate that Jaxson interrupted us. I was hoping to talk with him a bit more.

I begin to wonder how I can finagle more time alone with him. It will be impossible here at the garage with the guys always around. And I don't go anywhere else. I flop down into one of the chairs behind the counter, frustrated with the situation I'm in. Why did some asshole have to take away my sense of safety? Tears collect in my eyes as my hands start shaking in anger and frustration. I'm tired of living this way.

A loud thud from a tool being dropped in the garage pulls me from the depths of despair I was beginning to drown in. I quickly stand, walking into the office to hide and collect myself. I don't need to have any of the guys asking what is wrong or thinking that Javie caused this. He did, but not in the way they would think.

I grab one of the garage towels from the pack my brother has in his office and make my way into the bathroom. I run cold water on the towel, soaking it. I squeeze all the excess water out, then place it over my face. The cool sensation helps calm the storm that had begun brewing. I take a few deep breaths.

Just as I'm about to walk out of the restroom, my phone vibrates in my hoodie pocket. I pull it out to find a text from Cici. *Don't forget, taco Tues is tomorrow.*

I'll be there.

The strange thing is I'm not dreading it like I have in the past. Each week has been a little easier. I began to drive myself about a month ago. But there was always a small lingering dread attached. But I don't feel it today. Today I am looking forward to it. I walk out of the restroom calm again.

At the window again, I watch as Javie works. All I can see is his back. The torch is lit as he stands next to the Camaro.

Taco Tuesday. That's where I can see Javie again. I just need to swear Cici to secrecy. I know she has been feeding Damian some information. He asks, and she spills. It doesn't help that she has had a crush on my brother since we were younger. Unless she's specifically told beforehand what is off limits to share, he can get any information out of her.

I pull out my phone and type out the message. *I'm inviting someone to taco Tues. and under no circumstances can Damian know about it. Swear.*

I hit send and stare at my phone, waiting for her response. The three circles appear, and I know she's going to ask questions.

Who?

How have I not heard of this person before?

Are you sure?

What's going on?

Question after question pops up, and I smile to myself. Maybe, just maybe, I can move on. I just surprised my best friend, and I never thought I would be able to do that again.

A new guy Damian just hired. He's sweet. Just testing the waters.

I give her something, but not everything. I'm still feeling all this out myself.

You're sure? she asks.

Yes. At least I think I am. I'm more ready for this than I have been for anything in quite a long time.

In the office, I go through the résumés, finding Javie's with his phone number. I realize this is unethical, and I should not be doing this, but it's the only way to do it without my brother suspecting anything.

Hi. It's Ritza. I hope you don't mind, but I got your number from your application. I was wondering if you had plans tomorrow after work. I was going to meet some friends at El Gran Margarita for taco Tuesday. Wanna join me?

I hit send and look out the window. He still has the helmet on and is working. I wonder when he will be done with what he is doing. Not wanting to be caught staring at Javie by the guys, or worse, by Damian, I go back to the large box of parts I never finished inventorying.

About an hour later, my phone vibrates on the desk as I am finishing up for the day. It is face down, and I'm nervous to see what Javie responded. Or maybe it isn't even Javie, and I'm getting my hopes up for nothing.

I grab my phone, and without looking at it, I go to the garage window to see if Javie is done working. Sure enough, he is sitting on a box with his phone in hand, looking down at the screen.

Swiping my screen, I open my messages to find Javie's response.

I'm so glad you decided to text. I kicked myself for not asking for your number after our lunch on Friday. I'll be there. What time?

I can feel my heart race with excitement with his message. *5:30…meet you there.* Send.

I look back out the window to watch his expression. Slowly he looks up toward the window, smiling, and just like that, a balm was spread over all my torn pieces.

"Fuck!" follows a loud clank, and I remember that the guys can also see me. I duck down before any prying eyes notice me gawking.

I type out—*Please don't say anything to my brother or the guys about us meeting up. I just don't want him in my business.* Send.

Not that I think Javie is a guy to go bragging or spreading gossip; I just want this for myself right now. And if Damian knows, my mom will not be far behind.

His response comes right away. *My lips are sealed.*

I peek out the window once more to see him with a cat-that-ate-the-canary grin. I roll my eyes and quickly duck back into the office before I get myself caught acting like a teen with a crush. Wait. Do I have a crush? Not ready to answer that to myself just yet, I toss the thought to the back of my mind. I can't think of that now. Not until I make more progress.

CHAPTER 5

JAVIE

WHO KNEW I WOULD BE SO EXCITED FOR TACO TUESDAY? IT'S so stupid. Taco Tuesday is probably just a saying white people made up to make themselves feel better about Hispanic inclusion. But I will gladly use the term if it lets me see Ritza again.

I wonder how many friends she has invited. Is this a test for me to get her friends' approval? Not that I care if they like me or not, but I really don't want obstacles getting in my way before anything even gets started.

I took off from work a little early so I could shower and change, then make it across town.

Walking out of my room, I smell food and notice Alex in the kitchen cooking.

"I didn't realize you were here," I say, wondering why Alex has been spending more time at the house than at Lola's apartment.

"I had some things to take care of and had to pick up some more clothes. Figured we'd stay here tonight," Alex says while cutting meat on the counter. "Going out?" he asks when he finally looks up and notices I'm dressed.

"Yeah. Headed to have dinner with some friends." I keep it vague. I'm not ready to share Ritza with anyone yet. Not that there is anything really to share. "I'll see you later." I turn away from him to leave.

It's odd not having anyone to talk with anymore. I knew without a doubt I could always go to Alex for anything growing up, but now he has Lola to take care of, and I need to figure out life on my own. Alex, Toni, and I have always been tethered together, each other's lifelines. But lately it's like the lines are fraying and we each must fend for ourselves.

———

I PARK at the oversized Mexican restaurant that is showy in the best and worst possible way. It screams *Mexican restaurant* with the loud décor, but it seems fun and casual at the same time. I've never been here, so hopefully the food is worth what I'm sure I'll pay.

I walk in, not sure if Ritza is already here with her friends or if I should wait.

"For how many?" the hostess asks me.

"Uh…" I pause, not knowing how to answer.

"Are you looking for someone?"

"Yeah. I'm meeting someone. Not sure if she's here." I run my hands through my hair to give me something to do.

"I got you." The hostess's smile widens. "I just sat a couple of girls. One mentioned waiting on a guy. Follow me." She smiles knowingly.

Now I'm curious what Ritza told the hostess about me. I follow her through the large dining area to the patio area, where I see Ritza sitting at a table with another girl.

"I think I found your friend." The hostess announces as she approaches the table, waving her hand back toward me.

Ritza turns around and as soon as her eyes lock with mine, her lips pull out. She's wearing the same type of oversized hoodie and leggings I see her in while working at the garage. Her friend is in a typical girl outfit—a strappy top and shorts. Even sitting next to her friend, who is dressed to attract, Ritza is gorgeous.

"Javie!" The joy in her voice saying my name hits me.

I take an open seat.

"Cici, this is Javie. Javie this is Cici, my best friend." Cici is sitting across from her at a square patio table.

"Hi," I say as the hostess walks away.

"So Javie, Ritza says you work at Damian's garage."

"Not quite yet. He just contracted me out for one job," I answer honestly.

"You know Damian, he doesn't trust anyone and isn't ready to expand yet," Ritza chimes in, her eyes widening at Cici sitting across from her. I wonder what that was about.

A waiter comes up to our table. "The usual?" He's looking directly at Cici.

"Yes, please," she says quickly.

I order a beer but wonder what Ritza and Cici are drinking since they seem to be regulars.

"They know your order?" My brows raise in question.

"This is kind of our Tuesday ritual." Ritza answers quickly, her fist clenching on the table. I notice Cici open her mouth like she's about to say something.

"Then you can tell me what's good." I smile, trying to lighten the mood, not wanting Ritza to drive back into that sea of sadness I've seen in her too many times.

"Well…it depends. This place is more for the atmosphere than food." She shrugs her shoulders. "But they do make a really good margarita."

"You should have told me that before I ordered a beer," I tease her.

"You can try mine and see if you like it. I never finish it." Her shoulders drop a tad, and I can see her relax a bit.

"So do y'all have a liquid diet on Tuesdays?"

"Nah. We eat too. Just know going in, these are not home-made tortillas." Cici laughs.

I begin scrolling through the menu because I am hungry. I skipped out on lunch today so I could get off early. Street tacos seem like a safe bet.

The waiter drops off a couple of margaritas and my beer.

"That's a brain freeze!" I tease her.

"Can I take your order?" he asks after placing all our drinks down. We place our orders and there's a short pause as we all take sips from our drinks.

"Are you from here?" Cici begins the interrogation. I was kind of expecting it but didn't realize she would start in right away.

"I am. I grew up on the south side." I tell the truth. I know Toni never liked to admit where she was from, but it doesn't make one hell of a difference to me where I'm from. I don't think Ritza will give a damn, but if she does, then I didn't have her pegged correctly.

"Really?" Ritza turns to me.

I nod, my brows come together at her surprised tone.

"My grandparents were raised on the south side. My grandfather worked his ass off so they could move to a better pa—" She stops mid-word.

"No worries. I understand. Everyone tries to leave that side. Not everyone makes it," I agree with her. My family is one of them. Alex and Toni have their way out; I'm just not sure about mine.

Ritza takes a long sip of her drink, her eyes cast down at the table.

"Way to stick your foot in your mouth," Cici chimes in jokingly.

"Shut up!" Ritza grabs the lime wedge off the side of her glass and tosses it at Cici, which makes Cici laugh.

"Just call it like I see it." Cici winks at me, and I notice Ritza's lips pull down in disapproval.

Ritza's leg shaking is rattling the drinks on the table. She's got one hand resting on the table, so I place my hand on hers. She takes a deep breath in and out, visibly relaxing, and her leg slowly comes to a stop. Cici watches me closely.

Cici looks at her smart watch and stands up, grabbing her phone. "I'll be right back."

As soon as she is out of earshot, I turn to Ritza, "Are you okay?"

I brush my thumb over her hand, wanting to fix whatever just happened.

Her eyes meet mine, and the sadness is there.

"Hey. It's okay. Whatever it is. Tell me, and I'll handle it." I don't know what's going on, but I will do anything to make her smile.

Her breaths are short and shallow as her gaze comes to me then scrambles around the room. She takes a long breath in, exhaling slowly. She swallows, then another long breath.

"It's fine. It's nothing, really. Just a bad memory popped in." She shakes her head. "I'm fine."

"Are you sure? Do you want me to take you home?" She's hiding something.

"No. No please. I'm fine." She gives me a hesitant smile.

I release her hand and take a long pull from my beer, not knowing what else to do. I want to protect her from whatever she's fighting, but I don't know what I'm up against.

Cici arrives back at the table, sitting down. "Ugh, I hate living in the same town as my parents! I have to go pick up my stupid little brother from practice. He got grounded *again*, and they took away his car. Stupid shit." She takes a huge gulp of her margarita, then slams the palm of her hand on her forehead.

Yup, she gave herself a—

"Brain freeze!" she groans.

Ritza full belly laughs at her friend's expense, and it's music to my ears.

After she composes herself, she slides her margarita to me. "Go ahead and finish it up. Can you get my food to go, and I'll meet you at your place later and pick it up? I'll send you the money in a bit." She stands quickly, leaving us alone.

"I guess I do get to take you home after all." The thought excites me.

"Not really. I drove here from the garage." She shrugs her shoulders, her demeanor much calmer than before.

Wanting to know what happened, but not wanting her to freak out again, I decide against asking her about it. I'm at a loss for conversation.

"So south side? How was that? You mentioned your brother and cousin the other day."

"Yeah south side. I know it doesn't have the best reputation, but I can't change where I'm from."

"I would never want you to. You talked about growing up with your grandmother. How was she?" A tentative smile pulls out.

"She was the best. For her to be able to raise the three of us and put up with our shitty parents. She was a saint." I gulp the last of my beer down, deciding to finish up Cici's margarita. I don't believe in letting a good drink go to waste.

"She took on a big responsibility. I love my grandparents. I'm lucky to still have them in my life," she says before taking another drink.

I remove Cici's straw from the glass and take the wrapper off a new one, placing it in the drink.

"So what do you think? Good, huh?" She leans back a bit, her body more relaxed.

"It's good. Don't really have anything to compare it to because I don't normally drink them." I smirk, leaning into the table.

"Then what do you usually drink?"

"I'm a beer guy. On the occasion there's a good alcohol, tequila or whiskey. I won't turn that down."

"I'll keep that in mind."

"Margarita drinker?" I cock an eyebrow.

"I'm a whatever-is-around drinker. Margaritas are usually only for Tuesdays."

"Then what would I be able to get you on a Saturday night?"

"Uh…"

"The asada street tacos?" a waitress asks, interrupting our conversation.

"Can you put the other asada street tacos in a to-go container? My friend had to leave," Ritza asks the waitress after she places our dishes in front of us. "Watch the green salsa, that one is really hot," she says as I reach for it.

"Did you already forget where I grew up?" I huff out a laugh. "I think I can handle it."

"Don't say I didn't warn you." She smirks, and now I'm wondering whether she is a weak one with spicy food or her warning is actually necessary. But I can't back down now.

I spoon some onto one of the tacos, take my first bite, and holy shit! That is not normal hot salsa. My eyes begin to water at the unexpected burn, but I'm trying not to show it. I take a gulp of the margarita with the food still in my mouth, hoping the cold, fruity liquid will help tamp it down.

Ritza watches me, trying to hold her smile but failing miserably. I quickly chew so that I can swallow and be done with this spectacle.

She shakes her head back and forth with a full-blown smile engulfing her face, letting her shine bright. "I told you," she says and a small giggle escapes.

"You did." I concede to her. And I would go through that torture again if it meant she would show me the smile she's wearing now.

Almost all her smiles are for others' benefit, not because she truly feels the joy a smile should convey. She fakes them. She places them on so that others don't ask questions. I want to ask but know she wouldn't answer truthfully. She doesn't trust me yet. I think Cici was here to test me. She would have stayed, or Ritza might have had an emergency to go solve, if I didn't pass whatever test they placed me through when I arrived.

"You got to mix it with this one." She points at the light green one. "It's an avocado crema something or other. When you mix them, that's where it's at." She nods knowingly.

"Remind me to listen to you next time." I wink at her, hoping she understands I mean so much more than just in food. I want a next time with her.

The dinner continues, and I watch as she takes only sips of her margarita, not even finishing half of it. She has relaxed considerably, not trying to hide in the hoodie like I've seen her do in the past. She'll pull the sleeves down covering her hands or tuck them under the bottom, pulling it out like she's stretching it to tuck her whole body in. I want to know why she feels the need to not be seen.

"Where did you park?" I ask as we walk out.

"I'm around the side." She points in the direction.

I grab her small hand. "I'll walk you."

Her fingers squeeze around my hand. I glance at her, and she is looking down like her shoes need her attention. As soon as we turn the corner of the building, I notice a black Camry I've seen at the garage and know it must be hers.

"Your keys?"

Her hand leaves mine unzipping the small purse she's carrying and pulling them out.

"You should always have your keys handy before walking to your car." I feel the need to lecture her, never wanting her to be placed in a situation that she could get hurt.

"I know. I usually do. I was…uh…" she says quickly.

We stop at her door. "Today you have me here. But when you are alone, always have them out." I place a finger under her chin lifting her head up to look at me.

All she does is nod, then quickly comes in and wraps her arms around my middle, hugging me tightly. I hold her while her sweet lavender scent fills my senses.

"Thanks." She pulls back, as the locks of her car click. She opens the door and jumps in.

RITZA

I'm tucked in my bed waiting for Cici to arrive as I ponder the huge step I took today. I don't know what's holding her up since I texted her at a stoplight on my way home. I left her food in my car because I didn't need any questions from my mom about why I have Cici's food if I was with her. She'll get it from my car on her way in.

I want to jump out of my skin, I'm so excited, nervous, and scared. I went out with a guy! I went out with someone who wasn't my family or Cici! I didn't freeze when he held my hand. I hugged him. What the actual—

My door opens, and Cici walks in with a tentative smile. "So?" she says a little too loudly before closing the door.

I widen my eyes at her, knowing my mom may be trying to eavesdrop.

She mouths *sorry* quickly, walking in and closing the door behind her.

She sits on the bed with me, and I instantly wrap her in my arms, quietly mumbling, "thank you, thank you, thank you…"

"Then tell me how it went." Her voice is low, as she pushes me back to look me in the eyes.

"It went so well. Thank you for sitting in your car for over an hour. Really, I can't thank you enough."

"I'm just happy we have TV apps on our phones. I caught up on a show." She rolls her eyes playfully. "You almost had a panic attack and I was about to abort the plan. What happened?"

"The nerves of being there with him started. Not that I didn't want to be with him, but I was scared I would freak out. So of course, I started to freak out thinking that I could. I'm so fucked up!" I groan.

"You aren't. Do you realize what you did today? I mean it. Really." She grabs my hand, squeezing it.

"I'll never be the same." My head falls, my chin hitting my chest as tears begin to collect in my eyes.

"No, you won't. I'm not going to lie and say you are. That's not what best friends do. But you will be able to live again." She scoots closer to me, wrapping an arm around my back and placing her head on my shoulder.

"How will I ever keep his attention? Look at you, and look at me," I say the words so softly, I'm not sure she can hear me.

"What are you talking about?" she asks.

"You can live carefree. You have always been a flirt. It comes so easily. You have the perfect flirty personality. Like when you winked at Javie. He'll lose interest with all my hang ups, which he'll never know about, and go for you or someone like you." I find my voice again. The elation I felt just a few minutes ago has disappeared, and the worries and what ifs begin to take hold.

"He likes you. He paid me no attention when I winked at

him. I don't even remember doing it. It just happens." She's right. He didn't get caught up with her, but it doesn't mean he won't. And I can't blame him. I'm damaged, and she isn't. Lots of other girls aren't.

I don't know what to say. Everything I say will be a pity party, and I would rather make that a party of one not two.

"Why did you just say he will never know about the hang-ups?" she asks quietly, still holding on to me. I'm grateful she is. Just when I thought I was mending, it feels like I'm crumbling again.

"I will never tell a guy I date about this. Can you imagine? They would probably take off running knowing how tainted I am. The pity. Wondering if I enjoyed it. If I asked for it. If I'll always be fucked in the head." The tears I had been trying to hold back fall freely now. I've tried so hard not to cry anymore. I've spent too many days and nights drowning in the salty liquid.

"Shhh…" She pulls me closer, rocking. "When you find *the* person, you'll be able to share this part of your life. You're just not ready right now."

She lets me cry it out for several minutes, and when I finally compose myself, I admit my biggest fear. "What if I can't ever have sex again? What if I never feel safe enough or it—"

"Stop. You don't know that. No one does." She pushes me back to look me in the eye. "We are going to take this one day, one date, one call, one text at a time. Javie likes you. You feel safe enough with him, which you never thought would happen. Step one. We won't even think about all the others. Just see how this goes. No expectations. Just that he's nice, he likes you, and you trust him."

"But he's a man. Men have needs," I remind her. I mean, hello, I was in college. It wasn't like I was a virgin when "it" happened. People date, and it leads to sex.

"Exactly! He's a man, not a boy. Men, honorable men, can control their needs." She cocks her brow at me.

I just nod. I don't truly believe it, but I have nothing else going for me right now. I will ride this as long as I can.

My phone vibrates on the bed, and Cici picks it up, swiping and smiling as soon as she sees the screen.

"You have nothing to worry about." She turns the phone around for me to read the message.

Thank you for inviting me to dinner. Can't wait until next time.

"He only sees you, my beautiful friend." She places the phone in my hand. "You and I are going to continue to take the steps together. Even if you stumble, I will be there to pick you back up and crawl until you can take a step again. You and me. Your parents and Damian won't know a thing."

I bring my gaze away from the phone and back to her. "Well, us and my dad. Remember, he saw me having lunch with Javie? He knows there's more now. But since he won't ask, he'll sit back and be ready to catch me if I fall, and I'm okay with that."

She nods, then adds, "Are you going to answer him?" She widens her eyes at me, smiling.

I bite my bottom lip in nervousness and elation.

I type, *Me too,* and hit send.

I don't think I'll be at the garage this week. I'm slammed at the other job.

I wonder why he's telling me why he won't be at the garage until the next text comes through.

When can I see you?

"He wants to see me again!" I whisper scream to Cici who is sitting right next to me, reading the texts with me as they come in. "How?"

"Want to try shopping with me?" She lifts her shoulders.

"What?" My brows pinch together.

"We say we are going to try shopping one afternoon. Meet

him for lunch instead. We won't be able to get you out at night without raising suspicions right now. We need to build to that."

"Oh. Yeah. That works. Can I do lunch somewhere I don't know?" My heart begins racing at the thought.

"If it's with him, I think so." She pauses. "He can calm you. But if you want, I will be behind you, catching up on more TV shows."

"Okay. One more time. I can't have you always sitting in parking lots waiting to be my knight in shining armor," I agree, taking a deep breath and trying to tame the uncontrollable thumping in my chest.

Can we meet for lunch this week?

The three dots appear right away.

How about Friday? Let me text you place and time tomorrow.

A warmth spreads down my body at the thought of seeing him again.

CHAPTER 6

JAVIE

Trying to figure out where we could meet for lunch was a bitch. Finding a place that was close enough to the neighborhood so I didn't have to drive so far, but didn't bring her into the hood was a chore, but I did it. I found this cool burger place, and she knew about it, which was a plus. I'll also be closing tonight instead of getting off early so that I can take a longer lunch than usual, but it's worth it.

I'm working the desk this morning so that I don't meet her stinking from sweat working in the garage. I know she's used to it, working in one herself, but I'd rather not remind her of it.

My phone vibrates in my pocket, and I ignore it until it vibrates again, announcing a phone call. I pull it out and see Amelia's name on the screen.

"Hey! What's going on?" I answer the phone.

"My car stalled. Can you help me?"

Seriously, this shit happens today. I look at the time; I'm supposed to meet Ritza in an hour.

"Where's Eddie?" I know her piece-of-shit boyfriend is not going to be happy about me helping her out.

"I don't know! He won't answer his fucking phone. Please!" she says, whining her frustration.

"Where are you?" I know I should stay away, especially after the talk going around about Eddie wanting to kick my ass, but I can't leave Amelia out to hang.

I hear car horns going off, then Amelia yelling, "My car won't turn on, motherfucker! Go around! I'm at the corner of Fifth and McAlister. In front of that old record shop."

"Okay. Give me a sec, and I'll be there."

I let my manager know what I'm doing and pack up the battery indicator and charger, figuring that is the problem, then I head to meet her.

I find her and park in the lot in front of where she stalled. I'm glad she had enough sense to get out of her car and stand in the lot to wait. I didn't even think of telling her to do that with my mind on Ritza and not wanting to be late.

"Hey," I greet her as I step out of the car.

"Thank you, Javie." She shifts from one foot to the other.

"No problem." I avoid her gaze. Guilt is eating at me. I didn't want to come and help her. I would have left her here sad and alone. That's not me. I pull out the equipment from the trunk of my car.

Her hazard lights are blinking strong. Doesn't look like it's the battery, but I'll check it anyway. Amelia follows me in front of the car.

"Stay off the street," I direct. "You should never be on the road or in your car if it stalls like this," I inform her for any future mishaps.

She just nods at me and moves back up on the sidewalk, watching me.

I pop the hood and hook up the indicator. Sure enough, the battery is fine.

"Keys?" I yell to Amelia.

She tosses them to me, and I get in her car, cranking it to listen. The engine is turning over...she ran out of gas. I look at the gas gauge, and it reads half a tank. She has a broken gauge.

I step out and meet her on the sidewalk.

"You ran out of gas." I laugh as I tell her.

"What? But it says I have a half tank." She's shaking her head at me in disbelief.

"Well, the battery is good. Your gauge is probably broken. I'll walk across the street and get you some gas. You should be good to go after that. I'll be back."

I place the equipment back in my trunk and kick myself for not bringing a gas tank. I'll have to buy one for her. The sun is pounding, and I'm sweating like a beast. This is the way I'm going to have to meet Ritza.

Walking back carrying a five-gallon gas tank, the only one they had to purchase, I see Eddie yelling at Amelia.

Amelia's gaze comes to me, and I guess he notices because he turns his head in my direction. He waits until I approach and decides it's a good time to lay into me.

"What the fuck are you doing here, *culero* (asshole)!?" Eddie postures up.

Not in the mood for this drama, I answer, "I think her car is fine. She ran out of gas." I place the gas can down, then stand up, not giving him an inch.

"*Diga me* (Answer me)."

I shake my head slightly. "I think you got it from here." I take a step back, not wanting to give him my back.

"Amelia." I nod at her to let her know I'm leaving.

I take a few steps backward, not trusting him not to sucker punch me. I learned early on not to trust others. Alex ingrained that in me, so I walk to my car with him in my peripheral vision.

I'll just make it in time for lunch now. I send Ritza a quick text to let her know I'm on my way in case I catch traffic and am late. I blast the air conditioner hoping some of the sweat dries before I arrive.

RITZA

I arrive at the restaurant early and am able to park close to the front. I'm hoping I see Javie so that I can walk in with him. When we thought up this lunch date, I didn't consider walking into a crowded restaurant alone. I don't do anything alone, and I can't have Cici walk me in and risk him seeing her.

"He should be here soon. He texted that he is on his way almost fifteen minutes ago," I tell Cici over the phone.

"Good. Just sit in your car and talk to me. He isn't late. Remember we just got here early to get comfortable. How are you holding up?" Cici says happily over the phone.

"Surprisingly well. Jitters, of course, but I can't tell if they are from fear or nerves. I can't wait to see him again." I swear if my smile gets any larger, I'll feel like the Joker.

A lighthearted laugh greets my ears. "You are amazing! Do you even realize it?"

"I don't. Not yet. Hopefully soon." I don't feel strong. I'm still scared more than I'm not, but right now I'm excited to see Javie more than I'm afraid of being out in the world.

"Hey, I just saw his car. Stay with me until I see him walk up."

A minute passes as I listen to the music in the background playing in her car before I see Javie. "Gotta go," I say to Cici before hanging up, not waiting for her to respond.

I step out of my car. "Javie!" I say loudly so he hears me.

He looks up from his phone, a warm smile greeting me. He walks faster.

"I was just going to text you to see if you were here yet," he says standing in front of me.

"I got here a couple of minutes ago. I was finishing my conversation with my mom before I got out." I lie for no other reason than to make myself feel better for being a coward.

"Let's go in," he says, and as I turn to face the doors, he places his hand on my lower back guiding me in. My heart stops a moment, and I stumble on my own feet. His other hand comes up to my shoulder holding me in place. "Are you okay?" His eyes search mine.

I'm comfortable with his hands on me. It just surprised me; I wasn't expecting it. My heart isn't racing at a personal touch. It's safe.

"Yeah. Just clumsy."

I start walking, and he follows close behind, his hand remaining on my lower back, until we reach the window to order.

I've heard of this place but have never eaten here. It won best burger in the local newspaper contest last year. Casual, with a wide selection of local beer and live music on the weekends. Looks like they also attract a nice lunch crowd.

He holds my hand as we walk around looking for a table.

"Is that one good?" he asks pointing to a table surrounded by several busy tables. I glance around quickly, hoping it's not our only option. I don't want that many people around me. I spot one that people are vacating in a corner.

"How about that one?" I point at it.

He nods his head once and pulls me in front of him and guides me to the table. Knowing he's behind me fills me with a sense of safety I haven't felt in a really long time. We pass a bus boy on the way, and Javie asks for the table to be cleaned. He stands us by the table, waiting for it to be cleared and wiped down before allowing me to take a seat.

"This one is better. Away from all that." He tips his head toward the crowd then takes a drink of his sweet tea.

"I agree. We lucked out they were leaving."

We are quiet for a moment, watching the crowd. I'm taking this moment to ground myself. I haven't figured Javie out yet. He seems so soft and caring, but he also has a strong presence. Like when he met the guys at the garage. He didn't shrink or back down with them. I've watched many guys falter when they encounter my brother. Not in what they say, but their body language. They shrink, their puffed-chest ego isn't quite as secure when they come face-to-face with an alpha-asshole like Damian.

"Have they done anything on the Camaro?" Javie breaks me away from my thoughts of him.

"Nah, they have been busy this week with a couple of wrecks and bodywork for newer cars. Damian hates to take those for business, but knows he needs to until he has the solid footing with the classics."

"Working on classics each and every day would be a dream. I know how he feels. Cars now are all computerized. Not much to take apart and rebuild."

"You sound like him now." I roll my eyes, shaking my head. Guys and their cars. "Any plans this weekend?" I wonder what he does when I can't see him.

"I'm actually working all day tomorrow so I can take the day off Monday to work on the Camaro."

"I get to see you on Monday then?" There's a flutter in my stomach knowing I'll be seeing him soon.

"You do. But at the garage." His lips pull down, reminding me about Damian and the guys not knowing we are spending time together.

"I know." While it's not ideal, it's something.

"What are your plans this weekend?" he asks me. I prepared for this. I figured the more time I spent with him, the more I would need to be ready with answers to harmless but loaded questions.

"Not much. A bit of shopping probably. I'm more of a homebody lately." I'm not exactly lying. I can online shop, and I am a homebody.

"You sound like Lola. That girl never gets tired of shopping."

"Who's Lola?" It flies out of my mouth, the green-eyed monster rearing its ugly head.

"My brother's girlfriend. She's become like a little sister." How can he make a smile innocent but sexy at the same time?

Wait...did I just say that was sexy? I'm so confused how he has begun to change so much about the way I was. The way I was stuck. The way I couldn't move. With him, I want to be able to move forward.

"Oh." My random thoughts and the instant jealousy that appeared have made all words vacate my mind.

He continues. "Technically she was Toni's best friend first. But I could see her and Alex's attraction before they even admitted it to themselves. It was actually kind of fun watching him fuck up." He huffs out a short laugh. "He thought he was god's gift to women until her. She cut him off at the knees, and that fucker fell." He's nodding his head, eyes dancing at the memory.

"You've mentioned your cousin Toni and brother Alex. And now Lola. Does Toni have a boyfriend?"

"She does. But technically Garrett is her fiancé now. They're both in grad school because they're brainiacs. He proposed when they graduated."

"Wow! That's so sweet. Was she surprised?"

"You could say that. I told you our grandmother raised us. That's because we have parents that are worthless. Not role models in anything. Toni was never going to marry. She didn't trust guys. But Garrett was able to show her he was worth trusting."

I'm left speechless.

"Tell me about your family. Is there a reason you don't you want Damian to know about us?"

This is the question I wasn't ready for. Cici and I thought about so many ways this conversation could go, but we never thought about the hiding. I drop my head, my chin hitting my chest as I take a cleansing breath. The only way I can go with this is the truth.

"He can be overprotective. I want to figure out on my own if someone is worth giving my time to. If they aren't, then it's a clean bye."

"Where do I stand right now?"

As soon as he asks the question, the food indicator begins vibrating on the table.

"Hold that thought." His smile is slightly cocky. "I'll be back."

He picks up the buzzer and heads to the window to pick up our order. I watch him as he strides confidently through the restaurant.

He comes back with a tray and places the two baskets on the table, then goes back to return the tray. As soon as he sits down, he says, "I'm ready to hear my fate." He grabs a fry and sticks it in his mouth, winking.

I roll my eyes at him and his jovial confidence. Somehow, on him, it's not annoying. He's not full of himself. He's teasing but assured.

I tuck my lips in my mouth to keep from smiling and encouraging his behavior. But I secretly want to experience more of it.

"For now...I guess you're doing fine."

"Doing fine, like we're going out again?"

I take a large bite of my burger so I don't have to answer

right away. I'm flirting. Suddenly, I'm overwhelmed with feelings of pride in myself. Another step. I'm taking another step.

"I'm waiting." His lips curl down, feigning hurt.

I chew slowly, torturing him playfully.

Holding my lips firmly, not wanting to smile too wide, I
reply as nonchalantly as I can manage, "I think you are doing
okay, so, yes, I think we can go out again."

"That's what I was feeling but wanted to make sure." He
mimics the big bite I just took, smiling the whole time.

"Cici and I have a standing happy hour date on Tuesdays
for taco Tuesday. It is the only thing that is a must. It's our
way of knowing that we will see each other at least once a
week. Wanna join again?" I extend the invitation knowing
that is the one place I know I can handle. Another date with
him, even if it is with Cici chaperoning.

"I hate to intrude on your time with Cici." His brows
crease.

"It's not always only us. Sometimes others join too. It just
depends on who's available," I quickly blurt out, not wanting
him to say no.

If I'm going to keep him a secret, at least for a little while
longer, I need to do my usuals. If I take on too much, my
mom will think I'm ready for school. And that is one thing I
know I'm probably not ready for. Too many excursions out,
and the questions will begin flooding in.

"If you're sure. Like I said, I want to see you again, but
don't want to intrude."

"I'm positive. Cici doesn't mind in the least."

Little does he know she is his biggest cheerleader
right now.

Lunch continues, and the conversation flows easily. He
tells me about the garage he works at and apologizes for
meeting me all sweaty, but he went out to help a friend who
had car trouble before meeting me. It's things like that. He

took time away from his job to help a friend in need. But too quickly it comes to an end as he announces he needs to get back to work.

We walk out of the restaurant, and he follows me to my car. Worried about physical touch I'm not ready for, I wrap my arms around his waist giving him a hug. *I chose this, so I can handle this.* Another new mantra.

I feel his arms come around like a protective shield keeping anything that can hurt me away. It's gentle, but firm. A safe space to hide. Instead of my heart picking up the pace like I just sprinted, it slows down. I take a deep breath, wanting to savor this sensation. I have been so consumed by the storm of fear, guilt, and hate—I have forgotten what it was like to just be.

His hand slides up and cups the back of my neck before I feel him place a gentle kiss on the top of my head. His arms loosen, and I know it's time for me to let go, even if I want this tranquil feeling to continue. I let my arms fall to my sides, taking a step back and looking up to him.

"I'll see you Monday, beautiful." He brushes the side of my face with his strong, rough hand.

He opens my car door, waiting for me to get in before shutting it behind me. He steps back and waits until I pull out before walking to his own car. As soon as I am on the road, I hit Cici's name on my phone.

CHAPTER 7

JAVIE

Saturday night comes after a very long day at the garage. I'm not in the mood to go out or see anyone. Well maybe not *anyone*. If Ritza were to call and ask to get together, you can bet I would be up and showered in five minutes flat. But since I know that is not going to happen, the couch, TV, and a greasy pizza will have to do.

I can't figure Ritza out. There's something she's not sharing. I'm missing pieces to this puzzle that are important for me to see the whole picture. Did she really just drop out of school to help her brother? She doesn't seem to go out much. She hides herself in large hoodies like she wants to blend into the background. Hoodies in winter I can see, but not in the sweltering heat of the end of summer. She is hesitant, cautious— or more like, guarded.

Her brown eyes, speckled with honey, say everything that her mouth refuses to disclose. Sadness and fear linger there. There have only been a couple of times have I seen joy—true calming joy.

Not having the answers yet, I push the thoughts aside as I scroll through the movies streaming, finally settling on one.

———

DRIVING UP TO THE HOUSE, I see Alex's car out front. I walk through the front door to him nursing a bottle of tequila and Lola nowhere in sight. This can't be good.

"Why are you here?" I ask.

"Cause I live here." He slurs just a fraction. And if he's three sheets to the wind, something went down he wants to forget.

"Technically, yes, but you have spent every day and night with Lola. Where is she?" I know I'm hitting a nerve, but that's the only way I'll get my brother to react.

I know how he works. I've watched him my whole life. I walk away, letting him think I won't push harder. I take my time in the kitchen, scrounging around for something to snack on. Letting him think the questions are over.

I walk back out into the living room, bag of chips in hand, ready to battle.

"Where's Lola?"

"At home," he says dismissively.

"And you're polishing off that bottle because?" I continue to push.

"No reason." He continues to look at the TV, avoiding my glare.

I call his bullshit. I know he's been up to something shady as hell, and that shit has caught up to him.

"Look at me, asshole." I wait until I have his full attention before adding, "What the fuck did you do?"

"Don't worry about it. It's none of your fucking business." He's sobering fast with my interrogation. The slurring has stopped.

71

"Fuck you. You made it our business when you decided to fuck a friend." I drop the chips, ready to post because I'm about to hit my brother where it hurts.

"Who I fuck or don't fuck is none of your business."

"Again, Lola is our business." The more I mention her name, the angrier I know he'll get. He stays quiet. He's trying to rein it in, so I continue, "Since you are evading the question, I know things aren't kosher. You fucked her and threw her out, didn't you? You treated her like you treat all the fucking whores around here. That's what you wanted? To treat her like your fucking whore?"

I knew as soon as the word *whore* came out, he would see red, and I'm ready for it. He's up faster than I thought he would be with the amount of tequila he's consumed, and his fist connects with my jaw. Fuck, the pain sears even though I expected it. I swing back connecting with the side of his face. He was only able to land one good hit in his drunken state. Fists are flying, but we soon end up on the floor wrestling when he loses his balance.

"WHAT THE HELL?" Toni's voice breaks through. "STOP THIS SHIT!"

We pause long enough for her to kick us both in the ribs.

"Shit, Toni, what in the hell was that for?" I ask, pissed, my adrenaline still pumping.

"For y'all being dumbasses." She watches us sit up, our anger still brewing, but tamed. "Why were you fighting like ten-year-old boys?" She has no trouble calling us on our shit. Even if this time it wasn't mine.

Alex looks like a statue, sullen, not speaking. Maybe Toni can get him to admit what he's done. "Ask Alex if he's still dating Lola."

She watches Alex as she takes a seat on the chair.

"Spill." She crosses her legs under her, getting comfortable.

Alex stays quiet. I watch them both. I'm usually the one trying to separate them when they are too bull-headed to admit their wrongdoings. I am the peacemaker, while these two stir up so much fucking crap. But not today. Today I'm letting Toni go at him with everything she's got.

Toni yawns, rolls her eyes, then pulls out her phone, touching the screen, and then I hear Lola's voice in her voice-mail greeting. Toni hangs up as soon as the voicemail begins.

"We broke up. Is that what you need to hear? I'm a fuckup, and it's over. My relationship is none of your fucking business, and that's all I'm going to say," Alex spews out angrily, storming in the direction of his room.

"You know…" Toni begins, and Alex pauses, not looking back. "You are the only one who can fix it if you fucked up. I know we didn't have any good role models in this department, but if you love her like I think you do, man up and fix it."

That's it? That's all Toni has. I have spent my life separating them, scared they would get too heated and say or do something they would regret. Now…now when I need her to go at him like I know she can, she treats him with kid gloves? What the actual fuck!

I'm out. I storm out of the house, knowing my brother is selling again. Why he's selling weed, I'm not sure. He wouldn't be doing this on his own, especially when he's in a relationship with Lola. He always said, *Don't let them see your weakness*, and Lola is his. And I'm pissed at Toni for…I don't know, not being Toni enough to get him to admit the shit he's in.

"Where the fuck are you going?" Toni yells to my back.

I turn around just to shoot her the bird before slamming the door behind me. All I wanted to do was sit on the couch and rest after working the past seven days straight, but instead I'm in my car driving with nowhere to fucking go.

I stop at a local taqueria, one of the few that sells beer. My jaw is sore, and I'm figuring I'll have a mark tomorrow. Great.

Perfect way to see Ritza. She's jittery enough, and now I show up with a bruised face. I wonder what she'll think or whether it will scare her away.

"*Estas listo para ordenar?* (Are you ready to order?)" An older lady stops by my table.

"*Tráeme un Lone Star y tres fajita tacos de pollo con guacamole. Por favor.* (Bring me a Lone Star and three chicken fajita tacos with guacamole.)"

Like I don't have enough shit to deal with in my own life, now I'm sitting here worrying about Alex and Lola too. I pull out my phone and send her a quick text.

Hey. Just wanted to check on you. Everything ok?

She didn't answer Toni, so I know she probably won't answer me, but I still want her to know she can come to us even if my brother fucked it up royally.

RITZA

I don't remember the last time I woke up excited for a new day. It was only a couple of months ago that I didn't want to leave the safety of my bed. Then when I did, I would grudgingly get up just so my parents would stop considering sending me to a mental facility. Each day I would robotically brush my teeth, get dressed, and throw my long hair up in a messy bun. I wasn't trying to impress anyone. Even less than that, I just wanted to be invisible.

But today, I'm excited because I get to see Javie. I know I probably won't be able to talk to him long, but just his mere presence is enough to fill me with joy. He sees me but is careful not to push. I've been wondering if he is doing this on purpose. Does he feel that I'm different? That I'm damaged? I don't ever want him to know my past. To know how dirty I am. To look at me with sympathy, or more likely, with disgust.

No. No. No. He will never know. Cici and my family, if it

ever gets to that point, will need to swear they'll never divulge what has happened to me. I can't have him see me any different than the way he sees me now. How his eyes smile when they look at me.

I tug a hoodie off a hanger and am about to slide it on, but stop. I think about Cici and her stylish wardrobe. The kind of wardrobe I loved to wear. Moisture collects in my eyes. I want so much to be able to look like my old self. I can't; I'm too scared to be seen. But I still secretly wish for it. I step into my closet again and brush my hand over those items—cute tanks, skirts, dresses, fitted shirts. All gorgeous and some even with tags still on them.

Small victories. I scan my closet and find an old graphic tee. I'll say *vintage*; it sounds better. It's too big on me, but it's better than Damian's oversized hoodie. Wanting to avoid questions from my mom, I slide the hoodie on over top to leave the house.

———

SITTING IN DAMIAN'S OFFICE, I can't concentrate on anything. I have looked at the same three invoices dozens of times. My brain is not registering what I should do with them. I keep getting up to look out the window to the garage. Javie has been coming in through the office before he goes out, but I'm so scared of missing him, I can't sit still. Back and forth I go. I'm just glad the guys are busy with a car that came in over the weekend and they aren't paying attention to me.

It's about to be nine o' clock, and he has not shown up. I'm considering texting him when I hear the door chime. I spring out of my chair to the front, and relief spreads throughout my body when I see Javie walking toward me. He has a baseball cap on today with a T-shirt and jeans. He looks a little different, more relaxed than he's come in before.

"Hey." I play it cool. No reason for him to know I was climbing the walls waiting for him to arrive.

"Hey yourself." His smile melts me.

Standing close to him, I notice his jaw is discolored and bruised. I place my hand on his cheek softly. "What happened?"

He shakes his head then leans into my touch. "Nothing to worry about. My brother and I had a disagreement. It's what we do. He doesn't look any better."

"Really?" Sounds reasonable because I know Damian has had his fair share of scuffles over the years, many with his own friends.

"I'm sure. Don't worry about it." He takes my wrist bringing the palm of my hand to his lips, kissing it softly. A warmth zings up my arm at this small contact. He lets go, and I instantly miss his touch. "I better get out there. We don't want any of the guys to walk in and see us." He winks at me, nodding his head with a playful pull of his lips. Before he opens the door, he turns back. "By the way, I like the shirt."

He noticed I wore something different today! I pulled it and tied it in the back to gather all the excess fabric. I watch him as he approaches the guys. They exchange a few words, and Javie walks to his car for his gear. It just dawned on me that he always walks in here empty-handed and makes another trip to his car for his stuff once he checks in with the guys.

Had he been coming in through the front to see me?

He returns to the last bay and places his things down. He takes the bill of his cap and casually flips it backward, and I almost come unglued. How can that simple move look so incredibly sexy? I'm in so much trouble. I want him, but I'm terrified of what will happen if I try to do anything physical with him. How long can I keep us in the…what are we in? Is this the friend zone? Does he want to be in the friend zone? Can I offer him anything more than the friend zone?

Life is so different than before. Friends with benefits was the norm. Hookups and one-night stands were spoken about casually. I took sex and intimacy for granted. I had no idea it could be stripped away from me so easily.

Taken from me and I still don't know exactly what happened. That's what hurts the most, the not knowing. It's always the same questions—in my drugged state, did I have the sense to say no? Did I fight back? Did I struggle to get away? Did my body betray me and enjoy the sensations? Did I give the wrong impression? Why me? It always comes back to that one. Why me? Was it what I was wearing? Was I overtly flirting with the wrong person?

STOP! Breathe in…. Hold…. Close my eyes… Slowly exhale… Repeat. I didn't ask for it. Breathe in… Hold… Slowly exhale.

The door to the bays clangs open, which scares me, and my eyes fly open. Damian is rushing to me.

"Are you okay?" He's bending down, grabbing my face in his large hands, bringing my gaze to his, his brows pulled in.

"Yeah. Sorry." I grab onto his wrists, bringing them down. I shake my head, take a deep breath, and exhale before answering. "I just let my mind run away with questions again. I'm sorry. I was able to bring myself down."

His eyes widen. "You brought yourself down?" he says just above a whisper.

My hands fly to cover my mouth and as my eyes widen as I realize what just happened.

"Hey, hey, hey…" Damian grabs my elbows, holding me steady. "You did it." His voice is soft and proud.

I nod my head, still stunned. I hadn't even thought or acknowledged what I've been able to do lately. Before when the questions came crashing through my thoughts, a full-blown panic attack would take over. As soon as one question popped in my mind, I would spiral. Fainting and hyperventilating were common, and I needed my family to watch over me as they guided me back to normal. I've been able to stay in control without going dark.

My hands fall to my sides, and he's still looking at me with narrowed eyes. "I did it." A small surge of pride hits.

"I'm gonna go back out. Okay?" he asks with hesitancy in his voice.

"Yeah. Go." I nod. I pull my lips in my mouth nervously.

Damian stands to his full height, looking down at me. I can tell he is struggling to leave me, unsure if I'm truly okay. I give him a shove, trying to ease his mind.

He turns around, and when I look out the window to the bays, Javie turns his back to me and Damian walking out the door.

I go back to the office and find a text waiting for me.

Are you ok? Javie did notice my episode.

I'm fine. I felt a little dizzy for a sec. It passed. I try and dismiss it because I don't want him to know what really happened.

Sure? Another text comes in instantly.

Yes <smiley face emoji> I add for good measure.

Then I quickly send another. *And I'll see you tomorrow after work, right?*

I wouldn't miss it

CHAPTER 8

JAVIE

THE BLANK LOOK RITZA HAD WHEN I TURNED AROUND TO look at her through the windows scared me. And I'm guessing I wasn't the only one it scared. The tone in Jaxson's voice when he called out to Damian, and how quickly Damian moved to get to her, tells me they all know something I don't.

As much as I want to know and protect her from whatever secret they are keeping from me, I want her to tell me. I want to hear it from her. I want her to tell me when she's ready. When she trusts me enough. Not before. I want to earn that honesty from her.

Only then will I know I have her. The way I want to be hers.

Her text dismissed the urgency the guys seemed to think was necessary. They all stopped what they were doing and pretended they weren't paying attention to her through the window. I, of course, followed their lead, not wanting them to suspect anything. But little did they know, my breath hitched, and I don't think my heart beat again until she looked up toward me.

Wanting her to know I'm here, I sent her the text. Even if she doesn't trust me yet, she will soon figure out she can lean on me. I can carry the worries she's trying to sweep under the rug.

———

I'm surprised to find a guy sitting at the table with Ritza and Cici at El Grand Tequila for their taco Tuesday. I wonder if she made Cici invite someone since she had invited me. And why invite me to her time with Cici? We can always do something on another night.

All these questions are for another time. I will continue following her lead because that's what she needs.

"Ladies." I approach the table.

"Hey!" Ritza turns, and when she sees me, the smile on her face settles some of the uneasiness I had still lingering from yesterday. Her eyes dance with excitement.

I place my hands on her shoulders and bend to kiss the top of her head. Her shoulders relax under my touch, almost like they had been tensed before.

Just like yesterday, she is wearing a T-shirt without the kind of large hoodie I was getting used to seeing her in. No body deformity or self-harm scars on her arms that I noticed. Just a couple of things that came to mind as I'd tried to guess why she would be wearing hoodies in the summer.

"Hi Javie. Meet Mark, a friend of ours," Cici chimes in.

"Mark." I nod my head, giving Ritza's shoulders one last small squeeze before taking my seat.

"How was work?" Ritza asks.

"Same." I watch as she twists her body to face me. "But I won't be by your brother's place anytime soon."

"What? Why?" Her eyes widen instantly.

"I finished the job on the Camaro. No need to go back unless your brother gets another car in that he needs help with." I shrug, disappointed I won't be able to use that as an excuse to see her.

"Really? Why'd you finish so fast?" Her lips pull out trying to smile, but a frown is threatening to take over.

"I thought about dragging it out, but then I didn't want your brother to think I couldn't handle the job." I lift my brow.

"Of course. What was I thinking?" She straightens herself quickly, turning back to the table.

"Camaro? What were you doing?" their friend Mark asks me.

"I'm a welder. I was doing the body work on the car to get ready for the paint job."

"Cool. I know Damian has done some great work on cars."

"Yeah, it's a great garage." I agree. I'm not sure how close this guy is to Ritza and her brother. But if she wants to keep us a secret, why would he be here?

"Can I get you something to drink?" A waiter stands by the table.

Thankful for the distraction and change of subject, I answer. "A Dos Equis draft, dressed please. Tajin on the rim." I don't feel like talking about Damian to this group.

I look around the table, noticing they already have drinks.

"Have y'all ordered your food yet?" I ask the table, not sure how long they have been sitting here. Long enough for Mark to be halfway done with his margarita.

"No. We were waiting for you," Ritza answers quickly.

Her drink, as usual, is still almost full, while Cici has made a dent in hers.

There are so many questions I have. Nothing quite

making sense except that I truly believe she is happy to see me.

"If you don't have Damian's garage anymore, what are you going to do?" Cici asks.

"I have a friend whose uncle owns a welding company. I'm going to be doing some work for them." I answer as vaguely as I can. No need for people to know more about me than I'm ready to share.

"So you won't be at the garage that you were working at anymore?" Ritza turns and asks quietly.

"Not for a while. This guy has quite a few jobs coming up and could use me full time. I'll go back when the work slows." I want her to know what I'm doing. I want her to know I'm not hiding anything from her.

"Makes sense."

"Enough about work. I don't want to even think about the real world after college. I don't want to grow up," Cici whines, making Ritza laugh.

"Of course you don't." Ritza rolls her eyes at Cici.

The rest of dinner goes by with casual conversation.

I walk her out to her car like always, her hand clutched firmly in mine. I've noticed she seems to need the connection. She clicks the button, unlocking her car door when we approach.

"Thank you for coming," she says shyly.

"If you invite me, I'll be there." I brush stray strands of her hair away from her face, letting my hand run down her neck and land on her shoulder. She inches a little closer, watching me.

I've never hesitated before, always knowing exactly the moment when a girl needed or wanted that first kiss. But with Ritza and her mixed signals, I'm at a loss. She acts like she wants friendship one minute, but the next, she seems attracted to me. She never overtly flirts. Never lays on the girlish giggles. Never initiates any contact.

"What would you say if I told you I wanted to kiss you right now?" I decide to show my hand. It's do-or-die time.

Pink tinges her cheeks and neck, like she's embarrassed, but she says just above a whisper, "I would say you should."

I don't waste any time. I move in, sealing my lips to hers. Her body trembles slightly. She moves closer to me, and I envelop her in my arms. Her kiss is cautious, and she pulls away, quickly tucking herself in my chest.

RITZA

The past couple of weeks have flown by. I'm filled with excitement just thinking about Javie's texts or calls, let alone the times I actually get to see him. When he's near, the casual way he touches me—on my lower back, my shoulders, holding my hand or running up my arm—has my body wanting more. The problem is I'm not sure how much more. That's a place I can't think about quite yet. Each and every one of his kisses thrills me. I have come to expect them now.

And now I said yes...*yes* to a date. He seems interested, and I'm not letting this go. I can't. When he's around, I find it so much easier to breathe. I don't know what it is, but he brings me peace. Cici and I figured out a way for me to get out of the house at night without too many questions—a movie night and sleepover at her apartment. I know my dad suspects something but has kept quiet and has let me do what I have needed to. I think my mom is just happy I'm trying to do more.

My phone pings as I'm counting down until the end of the day when I can see Javie tonight.

I'm sorry. Change of plans. A text from Javie.

Disappointment hits me like a punch to the gut.

My fingers are shaking as I try to figure out how to respond. Moisture collects in my eyes.

Are you at the garage? Another text comes in.

Yes, I answer quickly.

Are the guys still there?

I type, *They are getting ready to close.*

Can you stick around? I'll meet you there.

Yes

Tell me when they leave.

I look around the office and try to figure out what excuse I can use to stay and not raise Damian's suspicion. The chime of the front door has me jumping from my chair thinking Javie is already here.

I'm greeted by a delivery driver carrying several boxes.

"Hello. Can I leave these here with you?"

"Yes, of course. On the counter. Is this all of them?" I ask.

"Yup. That's it. Have a good day." He turns around and walks out of the door.

I rush to the boxes, opening them up and pulling out the invoices to each. Back at Damian's desk, I have the computer open in front of me with a stack of invoices next to it. I sit and wait until I hear the door to the bays open, then start working.

"Ready," Damian's voice calls out.

"Not yet. Go on." I try and sound as casual as I can while yelling to him from the office.

He pokes his head in the office. "What are you doing that can't wait until tomorrow? I'm ready to go."

"I opened the deliveries that came in, and I'm in the middle of entering them into the books and then on separate customer invoices. I don't want to lose my place."

"Ugh. Okay." He takes a step into the office as I hear the guys saying their goodbyes and the door chime.

"No. Go on. I've got this. It will take me like twenty

minutes tops. It won't even be dark outside yet." I need him to leave.

His brows raise and eyes narrow. "You sure?" His tone is skeptical.

"Yes. Now go so I can finish and get out of here too." I look back down to the screen and act like I'm working.

"I'll lock the door behind me. Do you have your keys?"

"Yes, I have my keys."

"Text me when you leave." He rubs the back of his neck roughly.

"I will."

I watch him as he turns around and wait for the chime and the click of the lock before I text Javie.

Everyone left. I'm here.
Be there in 5.

I pace in the front area, waiting for Javie's car to pull in. He's canceling on our date but is coming to see me. Is he canceling our date because he got a better offer? Is he tired of waiting? Does he want more than the hugs and quick kisses— the only thing I've been able to offer him so far? Of course he does. What twenty-something guy sticks around for that?

I'm on the verge of tears when he pulls in. He exits his car and strides to the door quickly as I unlock it to let him in.

He comes in and stands in front of me, not saying anything. I've never seen him this way. He seems larger than life, his face stoic. I can't tell what he's thinking or feeling. His eyes hold no answers. He takes a deep breath, bringing his hands to cup my face.

The tears I was trying to hold in betray me as one slides out. His thumb moves to wipe it as he exhales.

"I'm sorry I have to cancel. A family issue I don't want to talk about, or really can't talk about, came up. We're all getting out of the city."

"Are you okay?" His hands slide down to my shoulders as

he pulls me in close to him, wrapping me in his strong arms. I bring my arms to wrap around his waist. His hand is running lightly up and down my back.

"Yeah. I'm good. Nothing that we can't handle." His voice shakes a tad.

"We?" I'm wondering who exactly the "we" is.

"Me and my brother. We'll get through this too."

Get through what too? Seeing him this way, so different than what I've seen of him is eye-opening. His demeanor almost off-putting. I wouldn't think he wanted to see me if he wasn't clutching me to him.

"Where are you going?"

"To Toni's fiancé's ranch." His hand stops on my back, and he pulls away. He grabs his phone from his pocket and types something on the screen bringing it to his ear.

He's looking at the wall behind me, avoiding my gaze. I can hear the muffled ringing.

"Hey, Garrett. Is it okay if I invite someone with me tonight?" The wall behind me has his focus. "Yeah…uh huh…but don't say anything. I'll tell them." I listen to his one-sided conversation.

He brings the phone down and swipes at it before placing it back in his pocket. He finally meets my eyes.

"Only if you want, since it is about forty minutes out of town, but if you want to meet me out at the ranch to hang out for a bit, you're welcome to come." His brows raise.

"I would be meeting your family." He just said they were all going, and he has just invited me there too. Is he serious? I was worried he was going out with another girl, and he's inviting me to meet his family.

"Well, yeah." A small playful smile appears. Gone is the indifferent cover he walked in with.

"Okay. Tell me where I'm going."

———

DRIVING DOWN A TWO-LANE COUNTY ROAD, I'm shaking my head at myself for acting like a teenager, lying to my parents about where I'll be. Well sort of. I'll be spending the night at Cici's when I get back into town.

I hoped I wouldn't get lost, but it made me feel better knowing Javie would come get me if I did. I find my way to the gate, and I recognize the logo. I'm about to drive onto the property of a cattle beef company. His pinned spot on my phone's map says I'm at the correct location.

I drive about a mile up the road and find the house he told me about, where I see his car parked. I'm at the right place. I'm sitting in my car taking a few breaths to calm my racing heart. Racing because I'm nervous about meeting the people that seem to mean the most to him. A knock on the car window and his smiling face warms me.

He opens my door, extending his hand to me. I grab it and step out. He closes the door behind me and says, "Come on. Everyone is on the back porch just chilling."

Channel my past self. Channel my past self. Channel my past self. Another mantra. I've been full of them since meeting Javie.

I was never the shy one. I could talk up anyone, anywhere I went. That's what I need. I don't want to be seen as the awkward girl everyone wonders what Javie's doing with.

"Hi!" I paste on a big smile. "I'm Maritza. Sorry to crash your party." My mouth opens out of discomfort, and I don't wait to be introduced.

I clutch Javie's hand, hoping I can keep up appearances and I don't have an episode.

Javie taps my hand with his fingers, then gives it a small squeeze. He knows I'm nervous.

"Ritza, this is my brother, Alex, and his girlfriend, Lola." He points to a beautiful blond and a guy who resembles Javie but has a much harsher look. Javie wore that same look earlier at the garage.

Lola straightens, sitting up. "Hi, welcome."

Javie continues, "And that's my cousin Toni and her boyfriend, Garrett. This is his ranch we're crashing." Toni is gorgeous and serious. Her lips pull into a fake smile.

Garrett, a cute boy next door, smiles, shaking his head, almost like he's apologizing for his fiancée. "Hello. Not crashing, definitely invited. Did you find it okay?"

I nod, worried I'll begin nervous babbling.

Javie points at a patio chair for me to take a seat and pulls one up for himself.

"Are you in school?" Lola asks, smiling with a sparkle in her eyes. She seems so different than Javie's brother, who is sitting, emotionless.

"I was, but then my brother needed me full time at the garage, so now I'm just working." I give her the answer I gave Javie.

Between Alex's look of indifference and Toni's glare, I wonder how Javie can be so warm and welcoming. I never had trouble with people liking me, and now somehow I seem to be upsetting the people I want to give me a stamp of approval.

"Garage?" Lola continues the conversation.

"Yes, the body shop he owns. He's trying to build it up." My lips pull out as I try to cover up the awkward feeling.

"That's how you met Javie!" Toni exclaims loudly. "Is that the shop you want to work in full time?" She turns to Javie, eyes wide.

A laugh coming from Alex surprises me. Both Toni and Alex seemed to relax at that statement. Not sure why, but at least it helped break the ice.

"Way to play it cool, Toni. Thanks. But yes. That is the shop I want to work at."

With all the hiding I've made Javie do, and knowing he wants to work at my brother's shop, I feel grateful he has continued seeing me. He could have tossed me aside so as not to jeopardize his chances of being at the shop full time.

Thinking of this, I turn to Javie and kiss his cheek.

"My brother only has a couple of friends who work for him full time. He wants to get a bit more established before he takes on any more. He contracts out right now for the things he can't do, like interior seat work and welding. But he is very impressed with Javie's work. He just doesn't know about us." I babble like an idiot.

"I'm sure older brothers can be a pain in the ass when you're trying to date someone. Not that I have one, but the way these two are with her, I can only imagine." Lola quickly jumps into the conversation, pointing between Alex and Javie then flicking her head in Toni's direction.

"Like we could control anything Toni tries to do. She was and still is a pain in the ass who does whatever the hell she pleases." Javie laughs at his own dig at Toni.

Garrett is nodding his head slightly with a huge smirk on his face. Toni turns in his direction, and when she catches him, she swats his chest playfully.

His eyes widen at being caught. "What? Like he's wrong?" He smiles, and a dimple appears.

"Ugh. I thought this was rag-on-Javie time. He's the one that brought new meat." She shakes her head at Garrett, trying to seem unaffected by his charm.

After the ice was broken, the conversation continued more naturally.

———

I LOOK in the rearview mirror and see Javie's headlights behind me. He did not want me driving back to town in the dark by myself, so he's following me. He is driving into town and back out to the ranch to ensure I make it to Cici's safely. This is swoon-worthy movie shit. Really. This doesn't happen. Does it?

His family dynamics are interesting. This evening I couldn't help but watch how they interact with each other. Except for the one laugh from Alex, the rest of the evening he seemed detached. He doted on Lola, and his eyes softened anytime she tried to bring him into the conversation, but once he was done, his demeanor switched. He loves and adores her; I could see that a mile away. It's odd how different they seem though.

Once Toni relaxed, she seemed pleasant enough. Her relationship with Lola was fun to witness. As much as Toni tried to be nonchalant about things, Lola was able to get her to show her excitement. Hearing them talk about her wedding was fun. She wants it small and only close family and friends, while Lola wants her to go big. Not sure what all that talk was about, but Lola wants her to "show up" all those dang girls who love to talk. Lola is sweet, but she sure does have a sassy side.

I'm delighted Javie introduced me to them.

CHAPTER 9

JAVIE

Tonight went better than I expected. I was nervous Toni would do or say something to scare Ritza off, but Lola and Garrett were able to balance everything out. Ritza does everything to hide and blend. When you are the new person to a group, you are front and center. Toni and Alex can be a lot to take in, especially together, so I was worried how she would react to them.

Can she handle all my family crap? If I tell her what my family is really dealing with, will she run for the hills? I'll have to come clean soon because I won't be living in town anymore.

I had a feeling my brother was dabbling in his old business, but I was in denial. I didn't want to believe he was selling weed again for the neighborhood boss. I should have said something sooner. Maybe it wouldn't have turned into the shit-show it is now. His arrest and now the drive-by shooting at the house has made it impossible for me to continue living at Guela's. I'm pissed at him for getting in again, even though I know he did it against his will. He can't talk about it, according to his lawyer. Thankfully, Lola pushed back because that dumb-ass was willing to stay in jail after his arrest. But Lola didn't listen and got him a lawyer. He loves her too much to jump back into that business on his own. We were...are trying to leave that life behind.

But now that the house and our family is a target, I can't live at Guela's anymore. Garrett offered to let me stay at the ranch in the workers' house. At least it's better than Lola trying to get me an apartment like she wanted to do. I can't take Lola's money. I'll start looking around. Even if it's a dump, it's better than living off of her. I know she means well, but I need to do this on my own.

Ritza parks her car in a spot at Cici's apartment complex, and I pull up behind her. I click on the hazard lights and get out of my car to walk her to the door. She turns around to look at me when my car door slams shut. She stands by her car, waiting for me to approach.

"Thank you for following me home." A small smile appears.

"What kind of guy would I be if I let you drive at night back into town on your own? Especially on a road you're not familiar with." I don't want her to feel like she can't take care of herself. I know Toni and Lola would put up a fight about that kind of comment, but something tells me that she needs to hear that.

A short giggle leaves her mouth before she answers. "Probably a jerk."

"And I definitely don't want to fall into that category." I cup her cheek with my rough hand and a sigh escapes her lips.

She wraps her small hand around mine and pulls it away from her face but continues to clutch it tightly in her hand.

She exhales then is up on tiptoes. Her hands come up to my neck, and she pulls me down placing her lips to mine in a gentle, quick kiss. The one I've become accustomed to. But instead of curling herself in my chest as she always does, she watches me then comes in again, her lips meeting mine, and her body relaxes. Her lips linger on mine, a kiss filled with emotion. She pulls away after several long moments, and her arms rest on my shoulders as she curls into my chest. I place my lips on the top of her head and wrap her in my arms, cupping her head to my chest. The need to protect her grows stronger every day.

After a couple of minutes, she pulls away, kissing me once more, "Good night, Javie." Her face is calm, not the usual tense smile she shows the world.

"Good night. Go on, I'll watch you until you get inside." I nod my head toward the building.

"Okay." She smiles and walks away.

I WAKE to the sounds of my family in the kitchen making breakfast. I slept like the dead last night once I got back to the ranch house. I'm not sure if it was the stillness of being out in the country versus the constant noise of living in the barrio or the fact that I know Ritza is beginning to trust me. Last night's kiss may have been PG rated, but I could feel how much strength it took for her to initiate it, but it also felt like so much more. I *will not* take that for granted.

"Are you ever getting out of bed?" Toni yells through the door while pounding on it.

Since all the workers on Garrett's dad's ranch were gone this weekend, I'm not sure what room I'll get when they get back. At least I have this room for one more night. I'm not sure how many workers live here; guess I better ask Garrett. Two of the rooms have a couple of double beds, and this room is set up with twins and a couple of bunks. I have a feeling this is where I'll be with other guys. Sucks, but it's only temporary.

"I'm up!" I yell back, stretching my arms above my head before sitting up.

I join everyone in the kitchen after washing up. I take an empty chair, grabbing a biscuit from the center.

"Ritza was nice." Lola begins. "Quiet, but nice."

I bite my tongue knowing that Alex and Toni are dying to question me about her.

I grab the butter and the jelly for my biscuit, not speaking.

After I'm done buttering and placing jelly on my biscuit without a word, Toni finally breaks. "Seriously, you're giving us nothing!"

Garrett chuckles at her outburst, and Toni turns around quickly to give him a death glare.

I take a large bite of the biscuit, smiling.

Alex raises a brow, his eyes narrowed. "This is not the best time to be bringing someone in the mix."

That one comment has me seeing red. I stand pounding my fist on the table, "Fuck you! You made this fucking mess, and now you want to dictate who I can see. This is all you *culero* (asshole). You were the one dancing with the devil, so maybe it's not the '*best time*,'" I air quote with my fingers, "for you, big brother, to have Lola with you."

My fists stay clenched. Fuck him if he thinks I'm going to listen to him when we just went through a drive-by shooting because of his sorry ass.

His lips turn up, and he nods his head once. "You'll need to learn to control yourself when it comes to her."

I shake my head. "What?"

"That girl has gotten under your skin. When they do that, it's harder to control your reaction when someone messes with them. Cool and controlled…plan the attack. You know the drill."

"Mother fucker…you were testing me." I sit back down and grab the biscuit I dropped in my outburst.

"Just returning the favor." He winks. Paybacks are a bitch. I did the same thing with him regarding Lola not too long ago.

"So you like her…really like her…" Lola chimes in with a sing-song voice.

I roll my eyes at her and her antics.

"What? Be mad at your brother, but I want to hear about her," she continues.

"What do you want to know?"

"EVERYTHING!" She exclaims loudly. I should have known.

"You know we met at her brother's garage. I don't know… but there was just something about her, like she's trying to hide from the world, but I saw her. She couldn't blend into the background for me, even though she tries." I grab the bowl of eggs and a few pieces of bacon, serving myself as I speak.

"What do you mean she's trying to hide?" Toni asks.

I take a bite of eggs, finding the words to explain.

"She's quiet. Doesn't draw attention to herself. She had been wearing large hoodies and jeans, in summer… The hoodies drowned her. I would bet she's wearing Damian's clothes."

"Girls don't need to flaunt their body to be seen," Toni says with a huff.

"No. That's not what I'm saying. I saw *HER* in the hoodies. I just told you that. But there's something. The only places we've been are restaurants. She's twenty-one, and she has not asked to meet at a bar. To go out anywhere other than restaurants. Nowhere to meet up with friends."

"Maybe she doesn't drink?" Lola shrugs.

"But she does. Ritza and her best friend, Cici, go to this restaurant every Tuesday, and they have margaritas. Ritza never finishes hers and shares with me, but she's still drinking. And there's a sadness and fear in her eyes. She's gone through something." I take a bite from a piece of bacon.

"She wasn't wearing a hoodie last night," Garrett states frankly.

"She has been wearing them less lately. Lately it's been T-shirts and jeans. But I did notice a hoodie in the passenger seat of her car. Almost like a security blanket." I'm speaking with my mouth full. I am finally able to talk about her to my family. The past few weeks have been hard on me, not being able to speak with my family.

"Be careful with that one, brother. You are already in deep and know nothing about her," Alex says.

"It'll be fine. I was in deep with Toni and didn't know her either," Garrett counters. Thinking back, Toni did hide who she was from him until Guela passed away and our world crumbled.

RITZA

"You are going to need to give me something before you go home!" Cici is jumping on the bed, waking me up. She let me come back to her place and didn't push me for information on my date last night. She knew I needed to process the night before I could openly talk about it.

"Can I at least brush my teeth first? And have coffee?"

"Brush your teeth yes! Dragon breath is not attractive. But you better be drinking the coffee and talking at the same time!" She's still bouncing on the bed. "I'll make coffee while you brush. I expect you out in the kitchen in five minutes." She moves off the bed and toward the bedroom door. "And ONLY five minutes." She turns back looking at me pointing a finger.

I laugh at her dramatics, but I do need to talk to her. She

has been great at helping me break down my progress and not letting it overwhelm me.

In the kitchen she is sitting at the table scrolling through her phone.

"Where do I start?" I ask sitting at the table with her. She places her phone down, full attention on me.

"Anywhere you want." She also knows I may not tell her things in order. I talk about what weighs the heaviest first.

"I kissed him. Kissed him, kissed him!" I launch the grenade and wait for it to hit. Her eyes widen as her mouth falls open slightly. I've left her speechless.

"Uh…you…uh…" She licks her lips and closes her mouth still staring at me.

I nod at her and smile.

"You took the initiative?" She is finally able to spit out.

"I did. I was scared shitless, but I wanted to. Have been wanting to, if I'm honest." Suddenly, nerves prickle up and down my arms, and my heart rate picks up. Panic attack. I'm squeezing my hands together.

"Breathe!"

Cici breaks through the white noise in my ears. I inhale deeply, filling my lungs until I can't anymore, and I hold it for…five…four…three…two…one…exhale slowly. I close my eyes and repeat a couple times more.

"Better?" Cici asks when I finally open my eyes and look at her.

I nod, still taking deep breaths.

"Are you ready to talk about it?" Her voice is soft and soothing.

"Yeah, I think. I don't know what brought that on. It was weird. I was excited about it, but then my mind went back to… I should be scared and…"

"You should not be scared. Not anymore." She grabs the hand I placed on the table and squeezes. "Cautious? Yes. But not scared. Not with that boy. You have him wrapped around your little finger." She gives me a naughty smile while picking up her other hand wiggling her pinky at me.

I can't help but laugh at her, and it feels good. It helps lighten the heaviness that had just landed on me.

"I don't understand how." There it is. I finally spoke my new fear out loud.

She shrugs her shoulders and shakes her head. "Life works in mysterious ways. Now go on. The kiss?"

"It was sweet. He let me lead like he knew I was…uh… figuring…uh…needing the time. He stood there waiting patiently for me to…I don't know. Everything about him is calm and controlled. He is a silent protector I didn't know I needed."

"Gah!" Cici dramatically leans back in her chair, "It's like a damn fairytale! Where's my Prince Charming?"

A giggle comes up, and I try swallowing it down because it will only encourage her behavior.

"I will say, his family is intense. His brother is scary. Not gonna lie. And I thought Damian was intense, but Alex takes the cake. But the way he is with his girlfriend, Lola. So sweet. It was odd to see this scary guy doting on this cute, tiny petite girl."

"And his cousin?" She prompts me to continue.

"She seemed like she was going to be a bitch, but once her and Lola got to talking, she wasn't so bad. They are a tight-knit group. Toni's fiancé was super sweet. I guess Javie's family needs sweet to balance out their…I don't know…their hardness."

The coffee pot beeps, announcing the bitter goodness to begin our day.

Cici gets up and pours two cups bringing them to the table where she already has the creamer and sugar.

"Is there more?" she asks as she drowns her coffee in sugar.

"Not really. But I wonder if it's almost time to tell my parents what I've, or we've, been up to. I want to be able to see Javie without all this sneaking around."

"Are you ready?" She cocks one eyebrow.

"Honestly, I don't know. I just know that if Javie is around me, I'm okay. He quiets the noise."

CHAPTER 10

JAVIE

THE WORKERS' HOUSE IS NOT THE MOST IDEAL PLACE TO LIVE, but it will have to do. Driving back and forth into town sucks. It's impossible to go back and forth from town to the ranch and back again to meet Ritza for a date. That's why I'm here at Lola and Alex's place, finishing a shower so that I can meet Ritza for another Tuesday happy hour. That is the only constant I know. Every Tuesday without fail, I have seen her at the restaurant. A couple of times with others but mostly, it's her and Cici.

A pounding on the door comes before someone says, "I'm home now, so don't think about walking around naked!" Then a giggle.

I roll my eyes; Lola would laugh at herself.

I dry off and dress quickly because I'm already running late. I texted her that I got stuck at work later than I wanted.

I walk out into the living room, where Lola is sitting on the couch scrolling on her phone.

"Where's Alex?" I'm curious where my brother is since he doesn't have a job right now.

"He went to speak with one of Garrett's dad's friends. He didn't waste any time setting up meetings with them. You know your brother; he'll go stir crazy not being able to work. He needs a job and hopefully a recommendation from Mr. Anders will help him get one."

"Good for him. I was beat after yesterday and packing up the house. I really didn't feel like going into work today after all that."

"Didn't feel like work, but not too tired to go meet *her*," Lola chimes, her eyes sparkling in mischief.

"HA...HA," I roll my eyes as I pick up my keys, wallet, and phone from her table.

"Seriously, she was nice though. But don't you want to know more about her?" Lola inquires.

"I do but I also know I can't push her. She'll open up. It may take time, but I have faith."

"But—" Lola starts.

I interrupt her. "No buts. I gotta go. I'm late already." I open her front door, my backpack and things in tow. "Thanks for loaning me your shower."

"We're talking about this later!" she yells to me as I close the door.

She is like a dog with a bone once she sets her mind to something.

———

"HEY! SORRY I'M LATE," I announce to Ritza and Cici after giving Ritza a quick kiss. I take a seat.

"No worries. But I'm gonna get going now that you're here," Cici announces. "Here." She pushes her drink my way.

Guilt about my tardiness is stuck in my throat. "You

should have texted me not to worry about coming if you had to leave." Guilt about my tardiness is stuck in my throat.

"It's fine. Cici has to go, but I'm good. She was just waiting with me so that I didn't sit by myself while waiting for you," Ritza says as Cici races off waving.

"Have you eaten?" I ask Ritza once we are alone. If she has already eaten, there is no reason for her to have waited for me.

"Nope. I was waiting for you." A smile that could light the whole room appears.

"I'm so sorry I was late. You shouldn't have waited." I'm taking in her smile, committing it to memory.

"I wanted to see *you*. I wanted to spend time with *you*." She raises her brows as her bottom lip gets sucked into her mouth.

"Well then, let's get you fed." I wink at her, knowing it colors her cheeks in a blush.

I look around for wait staff so we can place our orders. She has been sitting here for over thirty minutes.

"Was work crazy today?" she asks as I'm still trying to wave down someone to take our order.

"It was. And it didn't help that I took Monday off." I answer her as a waiter approaches our table.

"Ready to order?" the waiter asks.

"The tacos Norteños please. With beef," Ritza answers him.

"Make that two," I say when he looks at me. "And a Dos Equis dressed please."

"Anything else?" he asks.

"That's it," I answer.

As soon as he walks away, Ritza asks, "You took Monday off?"

I guess it's now or never. I was going to have to tell her about my family's troubles, though unsure how to approach it.

"Yeah… It had to do with why we were out at the ranch

and why we stayed out there all weekend." I start. I take a large gulp of the margarita that Cici left behind, buying time to think of what to say so that it doesn't sound as shady as it is or could be.

She watches me, waiting; her brows come together when I stay quiet for too long.

"We were out at the ranch because something happened at the house last week. The day I asked you to come out there." My mind is reeling, not wanting to admit what we are dealing with. Knowing it isn't quite over.

"What happened?" Her eyes narrow, and I see her breathing pick up. I've just scared her, and I haven't said shit yet.

"Hey. It'll all be okay. Just some things had to change," I start, then take a cleansing breath before continuing. "We had a drive-by shooting at the house while Lola and I were there. My brother and I have done some shit that we're not proud of. Things that we had put behind us, but somehow—"

I'm interrupted when the waiter places my beer on the table. Right on time.

"Can I get another?" I ask the waiter before he walks away.

As soon as he is a couple of tables over, she says, "Continue."

"My brother got involved with that crap again. I don't know why, and I know he was somehow forced into it, because he's with Lola and he wouldn't jeopardize that. He was arrested for selling weed. Not that they found anything when they searched the house, but...anyway, Lola bailed him out then the shooting happened. That's all I can really say. His lawyer doesn't want him discussing it with anyone. So that's all I can tell you about what happened," I rush through the explanation not wanting to admit it was once a part of my life too.

She takes a couple of deep breaths, looking around the room. I give her the time she needs. She may not want anything to do with me anymore.

"What does that have to do with you taking Monday off?" She looks at me again.

"We closed up the house. Got the window that was broken fixed and moved anything with some value out. I moved out to the ranch for now. I'm staying there until I can find an apartment for myself."

"I'm sorry." Tears begin collecting in her eyes.

"Hey, hey, please don't, *bonita*." I swipe her cheek with the back of my hand, just wanting to feel her.

Her lips pull out tightly, then she rolls her bottom lip into her mouth. I grab her hand on the table, enclosing it in both of mine. Will she be walking out now? I watch as her chest fills yet again.

"Are you okay? Why didn't you tell me that night?" Her voice shakes.

"We were all still processing. Alex was freaking out because Lola was in the house with me. She was really shaken up, and we were all making sure she got through it. She's pregnant."

Her eyes widen at that bit of information.

"And to be honest, I didn't want to share it with you. I didn't want you to think badly of me." I shrug my shoulders at that admission.

"But this wasn't you. You didn't do that." She pulls her hand out of mine and grabs mine with both of hers, squeezing. "You had no control over what happened. Please be honest with me about things."

I nod once. I'm biting my tongue because I want to tell her the same thing. I know there's things that she's not telling me. But knowing that I didn't scare her away is good enough for now.

"I'll start looking for apartments this week. Two days and I'm already tired of the commute back and forth from the ranch."

"That's a ways to go every day. What part of town are you looking into?"

"Not sure, but I guess since I spend most of my time with my family, I was thinking of looking close to the university, since that's where they are."

"Makes sense." She nods, taking another sip of her margarita.

"Any interesting new cars in the shop?" I ask, trying to change the subject after a couple of quiet minutes.

"Nope. And the guys are all grumpy about it. Lately, just car accidents. They hate taking in those cars, but that's where the money is. I don't know what's going on, but they are actually swamped."

"Really? Do they need any help?" I'm hopeful they'll call me back for anything. For one, I'll be able to see Ritza more often, and two, that is the place to be when they are able to move solely into reconstruction.

"Probably, but they are too much of whiners to admit it. They would rather grumble around the garage like toddlers throwing temper tantrums." She giggles with what I'm guessing is a memory of them. I hung around there enough to know their ways.

"Maybe you could throw a hint out to your brother about me."

"That's actually a great idea." She gives me a small smile. She pauses, then continues, "Changing subjects, how far along is Lola?"

I shrug. How would I know?

"When is she due?" She changes the question, but it still means nothing to me.

"To be honest, all I know is that she's pregnant. If she or

Alex mentioned those other things, I zoned out." I shake my head, suddenly realizing there's probably so much more to being pregnant than just carrying the baby.

"Men!" Ritza exclaims dramatically, rolling her eyes at me.

"What? It's not mine so..." I shrug while laughing.

"She's probably very early on since she isn't showing at all," she informs me. "The first trimester."

"Even if that baby wasn't planned and is a complete accident, it couldn't have happened at a better time. Alex may have fought Lola harder to stay away from him if she wasn't carrying his child. He's a stubborn bastard and thinks Lola deserves one of those prick assholes from college."

The waiter drops off my second beer. I take a long pull from the first he dropped off, now more settled and relaxed with the hard part of our conversation over.

"Why does he want her with someone else if he likes her?" Ritza inquires.

"He doesn't just like her. He's madly in love with her. He would take a bullet for her. And that's the reason. I've told you a bit about my family. We came from nothing. The only stable part of our lives was my grandmother. Alex didn't graduate from high school. He dropped out and ran with a tough crowd in the neighborhood. He, or we, haven't always been upstanding members of society." I roll my shoulders back. By relaying Alex's truth, I'm admitting my own. "Lola comes from money. Lots of money, according to her. Alex felt that she needed to date and marry someone from her circle. What he failed to see was Lola needs more than just a man with money to marry. She needed a protector. Someone who could catch her if she fell. And that's my brother. It took her being pregnant for him to see that."

"A protector," she whispers. I wonder if she meant to say it out loud. Her eyes glaze over in deep thought.

I let her stay there, processing what she needs to, before she is startled by a glass dropped and shattering at a nearby table.

"Where'd you go?" I dare ask, wondering if she will tell me something.

"What do you mean?" Her eyes dash back and forth from me to the table.

"Just a second ago. You were deep in thought," I whisper, like I'm approaching a caged animal.

"I was." Her face crinkles up in discomfort.

I nod.

Her shoulders fall forward as she takes a sip of her margarita. "I guess it kinda reminded me of…oh, gawd…it's stupid." Her eyes roll as she shakes her head and bites the inside of her cheek.

"Tell me." I smile, trying to relax her.

"Sorta like a fairy tale. The prince she wasn't looking for appeared to save her. Or catch her, like you said." Her gaze fixates on the table as she speaks.

"I guess so. Although my brother would never, ever describe himself as a prince." I shake my head, laughing loudly.

She looks up at me, her eyes wide.

"I told you it was stupid." A red tinge is creeping up her neck.

"No, no, it wasn't stupid at all. I'm laughing at my brother. You've met him. He's the furthest thing from a prince you can get."

"True," she agrees before the waiter appears with our food.

RITZA

On my drive home, I couldn't get the idea of Prince Charming out of my head. While I understand all the arguments about girls needing to save themselves, it's also nice to know you can fall and someone will be there to catch you. I'm not sure what Lola needing saving from, but what's so bad about the 'right' person being there to help you through? That's what Prince Charming was—the Right Guy to come along and save her. Doesn't have to mean it stays that way. They could walk beside each other and take turns carrying the load. But guys get crapped on when they try to save the day.

Why am I debating myself? But on another note, he called me *bonita*! He gave me a pet name. That means something. Right?

I park my car and walk into the house, distracted with my thoughts.

"How was dinner?" My mom asks as she comes around the corner to greet me. She stops in her tracks, and her eyes widen when she sees me.

Shit. Shit. Shit. I forgot to put my hoodie back on after dinner. Now that I have been taking them off more, I don't know how in the world I wore them in this heat for so long. The questions are coming. I'm wearing one of my old, somewhat fitted, concert T-shirts.

"It was good. The same as every week," I answer, knowing the flood gate of questions is about to open.

"You aren't wearing a hoodie?" Spoken very slowly, her statement comes out as a question.

"I'm not…" I pause, knowing I can't get away with just those two words. "It was really hot when I got in my car after dinner."

I'm crossing my fingers, hoping this explanation will appease her.

"Oh. Yeah." My mom nods her head, lips pursed.

I'm waiting for her to say more, but she turns around and leaves me. My expectation of her grilling me is obliterated. I'm confused, but grateful I don't have to lie to her.

I climb the stairs to my room and fall into bed. And I'm back to thinking about the knight in shining armor. Can a guy save you even if he doesn't know he's doing it or why? Javie's commanding but subdued presence is good for my soul.

Everything and nothing continues to swirl until I hear a knock on my door.

"Come in." I sit up.

"Your mom told me you were home already," my dad says as he walks in and sits on the side chair.

I nod, not having anything else to say.

"Wanna talk about it?" His fingers dance on the armrest.

"About?"

"You know what." He drops his head to the side, and I hear his neck crack. Damian reminds me so much of him right now.

"I don't know. I don't even know where to begin." My gaze drops to the bed as I pick at a loose thread.

"How about tell me about the lunch I saw you having at the garage. With the new guy?"

I wonder if my dad really doesn't remember his name or is just acting like it.

"Javie. I had lunch with Javie."

"Javier. That's right."

"There's not much to say because I don't quite understand it myself. There's just something about him that doesn't creep me out, scare me, or make me feel uncomfortable. In fact, it's just the opposite. When he's near, I calm. I've almost had a couple of panic attacks when he was around, but somehow, when I hear his voice, I can pull myself out. It's strange."

When I look up, my dad has a huge smile plastered across his face.

I widen my eyes at him. "What?"

"There's not much to say," he laughs the comment out.

I cock my head to the side, not understanding what he's getting at.

"If you've almost had a couple of panic attacks around him, that means you have been around him more than just the lunch I saw you having." He smirks at his correct assumption.

I drop my head backward, the ceiling becoming the most interesting thing in the room. My dad stays quiet knowing I need to gather my thoughts.

My head rolls to the side until my focus is on the comforter again. "I have been seeing him, but he doesn't know anything about—" I stop, not able to speak of the incident.

"He doesn't know what happened in the spring," he finishes for me.

I nod, taking another moment. "Correct. We have been hanging out. As friends, I guess. He has a standing invitation to join Cici and I every Tuesday. That is where it all started. I figured if I could be with him at the restaurant with Cici, I could try more things. And I have."

"What have you tried?" His voice is cool and controlled, not surprised like I would have imagined.

"Mainly going to other restaurants. Cici has been helping me. The first time she followed me and sat in a parking lot close by in case I needed her to come save me. Now I'm able to meet him at any restaurant. I never go in without him. I stay in my car talking with Cici until he arrives, and he walks me in. As long as he's near, I'm okay."

"That's a huge step. Why haven't you told us?" His voice shakes.

"I don't know. I guess I wanted to do it on my own. If I failed, or it didn't go well, I didn't have to admit it to anyone." I shrug.

"You know we are only trying to help you. We want you to enjoy your life again." His voice cracks.

"I know. And I'm sorry I've done this to you. Make you worry." Tears flood my eyes. This is all my fault.

My dad jumps out of his chair and comes to the bed, hugging me. "I don't want to hear you say that again. You have done nothing to us. Some asshole, yes. But never you." He's squeezing me tightly.

He rocks me until I calm.

"Dad?"

"Yes?"

"Can we not tell Mom about this yet? Please. I know she wants me out and about. And I am. I've told you I am. But I need to do this my way. Please." I'm speaking into his chest, where he has me in a bear hug.

"I will keep it from your mom for now. But we will need to share it with her soon. Okay?" He agrees but has me beginning to get ready to share. "I really think that if she knew you were trying to get out, she would back off some. Her heart's in the right place. She just wants to see you as the lively person you once were."

"I don't know if I'll ever be that person again," I answer flatly.

"You're right. You will *never* be that person again. But you can find joy again. And that is what I should have said. We both want you to enjoy your life." He corrects himself, knowing an experience like mine can and will change a person forever. "You know, if you want to talk, I'll listen. It will be hard, but I will."

I shake my head in his chest. My parents know the most basic details of what happened to me. I won't ever share the small pieces that I remember. Waking up naked. A torn shirt and busted bra hanging off me with no shorts or panties. Painful throbbing between my legs. A pounding so hard in my head, I thought it would explode. A skinned knee. A sore arm. A swollen ankle. A missing wedge-heeled shoe.

Nightmares of men laughing. Having trouble breathing. My body won't move. It hurts. Faces. Several faces. They're blurred. *Look how wet she is.* Who's wet? Why is my body betraying me? *Pinch those pretty, pink nipples.* More pain. Mumbled voices. More laughing. No more. I can't take anymore.

"Ritza, *mijita—*" I hear my dad. "Shhhhh...I've got you." *I'm squeezed tightly.*

Oxygen. I can't breathe.

"Mijita, take a deep breath for me." I'm home. I pull away, looking at my dad, the confusion slowly melting. Another anxiety attack hit.

Breathe in...one...two...three... How many times will I have to remember to breathe? How long do I have to live this way? Each time my mind goes back to that night, those jumbled pieces of memory, body aches, a simple bruise, I get lost again. I can't let them win. Four...five... My lungs are empty.

Normal breaths now. I'm fine. I'm safe. I'm at home.

"Better?" My dad watches me, his brows pulled so close together, the lines around his mouth more pronounced over the last few months.

"I'm back. I'm okay now." I fill my lungs once more for good measure, letting the air leave my body slowly before continuing. "Just your offer to talk about it had me thinking about it. I've ignored it for so long lately that just those few thoughts had me spiraling."

"Mija. That is why we want you to see a therapist again. You can't live that way. Always scared an old memory will come up and you are on your own. You *need* to talk about it."

"I'll think about it." A slight concession. If I continue with Javie, I can't have this happen around him. He can't know.

"Do you want me to stay with you?"

"No. I'm going to call Cici." I want time for myself now.

He nods his head and makes his way to the door.

"Find a therapist you like. Hop around if you need to until you find one that you are comfortable with." He walks out, shutting the door behind him.

CHAPTER 11

JAVIE

Finding an apartment that's reasonably priced close to Alex and Toni turned out to be more of a chore than anything else. I can handle the price for a tiny studio, but it's all the damn money they want up front that's stopping me. I can't afford anything here. The barrio is where I belong. It's what I can afford.

I walk into Garrett's apartment to find him and Alex playing video games. Alex was never one to play, but I guess with all the extra time on his hands, video games have become his thing.

"Hey." I walk to the fridge, helping myself to a beer before coming back and taking a seat on the side chair.

"Hard day?" Garrett glances at me quickly in the middle of their game.

"You could say that," I start. Breaking it to Alex that I will be moving back into Guela's house won't be easy. We just found out yesterday that the neighborhood boss and his son were arrested. Alex won't say much about it except that it's over. All charges against him have been dropped. And if so, then I guess it may be less of a risk for me to go back.

Garrett pauses their game of war, turning to me and asking, "What happened?"

"Where are the girls?" I don't want them walking in while we are having this discussion. Especially Lola because she'll just try and give me money.

"Shopping," Alex answers me. "I think Lola is stress shopping after everything that has happened. Or at least that's what Toni said she's doing." He shakes his head. "So, what happened?"

"Nothing big. Just apartment hunting isn't going so well. Everything is too much for me to handle at the moment. I can get a small place, but the first month's and last month's rent along with the deposit are above me," I start. "Since Jefe got taken down, I thought I would move back into Guela's house."

I slide it in quickly, then take a long swig of the beer.

Alex is already shaking his head back and forth, not agreeing with me. But I'm a grown-ass man, and he has no say in where I live.

"You will not move back to the hood," he says with finality.

"Since I'm an adult and I can make my own decisions, I say I will be moving back." I push back. I rarely do; we've never been in opposing corners.

"There are still too many of Jefe's guys around there for you to go back. It's not safe."

"Well, there is no other choice. I can't stay at the ranch forever. I come into town every day for work. It isn't like when you were there and lived and worked there all week." I stand by my decision.

"I will pay for all the upfront money. Use the money you found in the shed." The infamous shed money, code for the money he made while he was working for Jefe, the neighborhood boss. Our hiding spot when we were dealing. This is the reason I know Alex was dealing again. There wouldn't be any 'shed money' if he wasn't. "You wouldn't be having to look for a place to live if it wasn't for me, so I should pay for that."

He does have a point, so I don't argue. "Thank you. That will help."

"Which complex?" Garrett asks.

"The Regency. They are one of the only ones over here that have a small studio." Not my preference, but until I can get better full-time job, it will do.

"I'll get you the money tomorrow. Will you be at the ranch?"

"Where else would I be?" My first weekend at the ranch with workers there.

"How has it been?"

"Dinner every night is good. But sharing a room...eh," I answer Garrett's question.

"I've spent many a drunk night in that room." A small, devilish smile appears. I'm figuring he has been drinking out at that house since way before his legal age.

"Come into town and we'll go by that place to leave your application and whatever deposit."

————

I'm stuck again. Can you pick me up? A text from Amelia comes through just as I was heading back to the ranch after turning in my application and deposit money.

Where are you? I respond, not wanting to. But I won't leave a friend hanging.

Downtown. The Blue Room

On my way

I wonder what she's doing at The Blue Room. It's a

brand-new, upscale bar. The only reason I'm aware of it is because Toni and Garrett went a couple of weekends ago to meet a few of his frat brothers.

As I get closer, I text her so she can meet me outside. She's waiting on the sidewalk as I pull up, looking tired and frustrated.

I stop the car, clicking on my hazards. The way she throws her purse and plops in the car seat, I know she's not in a good mood. As soon as she closes the door, I drive off. We go a few blocks before she acknowledges me.

"Hey, Javie. I'm sorry I had to call you again." Her voice shakes, so I turn to look at her and tears are collecting in her eyes.

"What's wrong?" Concern for her fills me even though I know she brings half of the crap she deals with on herself. Like staying with that douche of a boyfriend.

"Nothing. Same old shit, different day." She roughly wipes the tears that have fallen with the back of her hand.

"Why were you at The Blue Room?"

"I was working. What did you think? I could afford to buy fifteen-dollar cocktails?" She rolls her eyes, clearly pissed about something.

Not wanting to upset her more than she already is, I stay quiet. I'll drop her off and let her process her issues on her own. We drive in silence for several minutes. Tears have continued to fall, and each time she brushes them away.

When I hit the exit to the barrio, she finally speaks. "I'm sorry. I'm pissed and am taking it out on you."

"Who or what are you mad at?"

"Life, I guess." She shrugs as she leans her head on the headrest, closing her eyes.

"What did life do now?" We don't have it easy living on this side of town. Not enough money to escape. I'm barely able to able to crawl away with help.

"My car is a piece of crap that won't start again. Eddie thinks it is the alternator. I rode the bus to work. It took me over an hour to get there. *Over an hour.*" She stresses those last three words. "We live less than twenty minutes away. I didn't feel like wasting another couple of hours riding it back. Eddie was going to pick me up but decided he would go into work at The Hole early. He could have waited until I got off, then went in, but he went in. No doubt to drink before it got busy."

"I'm—" I try to apologize, even though nothing is my fault.

"And Toni has turned into a stuck-up snob," she continues the complaints. "Did you know she was at The Blue Room a couple of weeks ago?" She doesn't wait for me to answer before continuing. "And all she did was acknowledge me with a small wave and hello. She couldn't be bothered to talk with me. Paying attention to those stupid stuck-up snobs."

"Don't," I say sternly, stopping her rant.

"What?" She turns to me, "You know it's fuckin' true. She's turned into another person."

"*Stop!*" I say loudly, wanting to shout at her but refraining.

Her eyes widen at my outburst just as we pull up to her apartment complex.

"Sorry." She opens the door, jumping out before I have fully stopped the car.

I get out following her, knowing Eddie isn't home.

"Why are you following me?" She begins bawling.

"I'm sorry for yelling, but you know better than to bash family." I grab her shoulders and pull her into a hug.

"This sucks," she mumbles against my chest.

"What does?"

"My life." She hiccups.

"It doesn't have to." I squeeze her. "You know you should have dumped Eddie a long time ago. Toni has been telling you this for years. You should be back in school. Why did you quit? Your mom said you could live with her if you were taking classes. You chose to live with Eddie instead." I drop the truth, reminding her that she has made these decisions.

I rub her back, wanting to be able to help her, but I know she may take me down in the process.

She finally pulls away, looking up at me. The desperation I see is too much.

"Let me take a look at your car." This is something I can help her with that won't get me in trouble.

She pulls the keys from her purse and hands them to me.

"I'm going to change, and I'll be back out," she tells me as I go back to my car to park it properly before looking at hers.

———

"BAD NEWS?" she asks when she comes back out. She changed her clothes; now she's wearing a pair of short shorts and a tiny shirt, her cleavage spilling out. She also freshened up her makeup.

"Nah. Eddie was right. It is the alternator. But I'll go by the pick-and-pull to find you one tomorrow. I can switch it out."

"Thank you." She takes the couple of steps closer to me, letting her breasts brush against my arm. "You're like Superman, always saving the day."

"Nah, just helping a friend." I stress the word friend.

She comes in closer, her shoulders pushed back as she brushes her chest against mine. "We could be more, though." She licks her lips seductively.

I take a small step back, knowing I'm walking on dangerous ground. I've slept with her. I knowingly let myself get caught up, but she never gave up Eddie. It might have been different if she had.

"You have a boyfriend," I remind her.

"I don't have to have one," she purrs.

"No, you don't, but you do. You chose him. Even after we got together."

"I'm sorry. Lola got there, and you had me leave. I was scared to be on my own," she begs me, grabbing my arms and pulling herself closer to me.

"I can't. I'm seeing someone," I say, even though that's kind of a stretch. I have no idea what Ritza and I are, but I do know that if some guy was on her like Amelia is on me, I would kill the motherfucker.

She steps back quickly, eyes wide. "What? Who?"

"Not that it's anyone's business, but her name is Ritza, and I met her at a garage I did a job for."

"Really? A garage bunny. You're better than that." She rolls her eyes, coming in closer.

I place my hands on her shoulders to keep her away. "She's not a garage bunny. She's not hanging out hoping to pick someone up. Her brother owns the place, and she works for him."

"Oh my gawd! You're so trusting. She probably picks up half the guys that go in there." Her laugh irritates me.

"No, she doesn't. End of discussion." I hold out my hand with Amelia's keys for her to grab.

"Sorry," she says robotically. "But I need you more. And you know we can be good together."

"I guess. Maybe we could have. But you went back to Eddie." I jingle the keys in my hand so she will take them. "It was never our time. You chose Eddie, and he can't even bother to help you fix your car." That might have come out harsh, but frustration has set in. "But here I am, the *pendejo* (dumb ass) always coming when you call. Let me know when Eddie is at work so I can come by and switch out your alternator, then we're done. I can't keep doing this with you."

Her eyes instantly water. "You really don't want me to call you anymore?"

"I don't know, Amelia." I place the keys on the top of her car since she has not grabbed them. "I won't mess up what I have with Ritza. I can't."

I turn to walk away. I feel guilty leaving her alone and upset, but nothing good can come of this.

RITZA

Talk to a therapist. That has been on my mind since talking with my dad. I've googled people and offices. Judged how they would be based on how they look. Do they look judgmental from their picture? Will they even be listening to me, or will they be focused on their own inner turmoil? Will she be strong enough to hear the dirtiness I remember? I thought I had decided against speaking with a male, because, well…they are male. But all those pictures and names have me second-guessing myself.

I scanned the rape crisis website. There are a couple of male therapists at their location. That's where I was referred to in the beginning, but I refused to go. I chose my own counselor and went a handful of times, then decided it wasn't working. Can I really go and speak with someone?

I'm going to the rape crisis center. Can you be on standby? I text a quick message to my dad. He's the only one I trust to tell right now.

Sure. Can they see you right now? His response is immediate.

Yes. I called.

Next, I type a message to Damian. *Not going to be there until later.*

OK. He doesn't care when I'm in the shop. All he cares about is the paperwork getting done and that he doesn't have to do it.

I can do this. I can do this. I can do this. I keep repeating it in my head over and over as I drive to their offices.

———

"HELLO. I'm Ritza and…uh…I uh…called about an hour ago." I stumble over my words. I cross my arms across my chest protectively.

"Hi! I'm Jennifer." Her smile is soft and her voice calm. I guess they want anyone who walks in to feel safe. "Follow me. Josh let me know you were coming."

Follow…where? My heart rate picks up, and I'm frozen to the spot.

She takes a couple of steps, then turns back, realizing I haven't moved.

"Ritza? Give me a moment. I have an idea," she says just above a whisper.

I'm breathing, which is a start. I stand in the waiting area for just a couple of minutes when Jennifer, a gentleman, and another woman walk in from the hallway Jennifer left through a few minutes earlier. Jennifer opens a door to a room behind her desk, and the other woman sits down where Jennifer was.

"This is Josh." Josh gives me a tentative smile and walks into the room. "We can get acquainted in here," Jennifer says, waving me in.

I look around and know in my brain that this is a safe space. I take one deep, cleansing breath and follow Jennifer into the room.

Once I'm in, I see a comfortable setup with one couch and several chairs in a circle.

"Please take a seat where you feel comfortable."

I avoid the couch, taking a seat in the chair furthest from it.

"Hi, Ritza. I'm Josh, and I have been working here for

about three years. I want you to know that we are here to help you. Jennifer is my supervisor, but if you feel more comfortable speaking with a woman, I completely understand."

I nod absent-mindedly.

"Would you like me to stay for your first session?" Jennifer asks.

I look around the room at the neutral colors with pale blues scattered about. Blue is the color of calm. At least that is what I think I read somewhere. The ocean. The sound of the waves. Maybe that's why blue is the calming color. What else is blue that can be relaxing? The sky. The clouds moving so slowly, creating pictures.

"Ritza?" Josh saying my name pulls me from my thoughts.

"Oh. Sorry." I shake my head. "It's fine. I can talk with Josh."

Safe space. Remember safe space.

"Okay. I'll be around, so if at any point you change your mind, Josh will call me." She turns to the door and walks out. Josh takes a seat across the circle from me in another chair.

"How would you like to start?" Josh begins.

I shrug, shaking my head. "I don't know."

"Can I ask you questions?"

"I guess." I'm not sure I want to answer.

"Were you raped?"

My eyes fly open with the impact of those three words.

"By your expression, I'm guessing yes." His tone is gentle. "When did it happen?"

My arms tighten around my middle. "Spring semester."

"Is this the first time you are speaking to someone about it?"

I shake my head. "I saw a therapist before, but I was still having nightmares and not leaving the house, so it wasn't working. I stopped going after a few visits."

His lips pull out. "Unfortunately, counseling isn't a magic

pill. It takes time. The experience may never leave you, but we will work toward trusting and living again."

We continue with a few more basic questions about why I decided to come in, but I've avoided the main reason—Javie.

"Has there been any progress, or have you still been in the same place since the last time you were seeing someone?" he inquires.

"Yes…uh, yeah…I guess I've made some progress." I pause, unsure what I think is progress is what he is thinking of. "And that's why I decided to try again." I focus on picking the fabric balls off my hoodie, the ones that form when you've washed something one too many times.

"What progress have you made, or do you feel you've made?" His watchful eye is not uncomfortable.

"I met someone and…uh…I guess…I want to feel like I can be myself again." I say. But I know that is not possible, so I correct myself. "But I know I'm never going to be myself… but I still want to…um…" I stop my words. Thoughts and feelings so difficult to express.

"Tell me about this person you met."

"He's been different than everyone else…from the moment I met him. He sees me." How does one explain a sense? "Since, you know, I've tried to hide. I don't want people, but especially guys, to notice me, see me, flirt with me. It makes me feel dirty. Creepy. Seen. I didn't want to be seen at all." Times in the shop when guys tried to talk to me, I just about freaked out until Damian or his friends stepped in.

"But when Javie looks at me…it doesn't feel intrusive somehow. He sees me or…he sees more than a girl. I'm not explaining well." I shake my head and roll it out, hearing my neck crack. "But I can say I'm not scared."

"You came back to counseling for a guy?" he says just above a whisper, his eyes narrowed.

I roll my lips in my mouth, my gaze drops to the wooden

floor. Is that wrong? Wanting to get better for someone else? It's also for my family. They have had to deal with my ups and downs since…

"There is nothing wrong with that. I'm sorry. It just surprised me. That is usually not the most common reason."

"Oh."

"You trust Javie?"

I nod. "Yes. He's the only person I trust other than my family and my best friend, Cici." I tell him all about my recluse behavior and what I have been doing since meeting Javie. What I have been able to do by myself.

"It's just I'm scared of losing him. He's a guy. And I'm not normal. Not anymore. I want him. I do want more with him, but what if I can't give him what guys need? How long will he wait? What if someone else gets his attention? Look at me! I live in jeans or joggers and hoodies. Well at least I've been able to wear some T-shirts lately. But still. I'm not dressed like the typical college girl." Word vomit commences when I begin thinking about him moving on to someone who catches his eye.

"What do you mean, how long he will wait?" Josh says this as his brows pull together.

"You know… I know guys have their needs. So how long will he wait for me to be comfortable with myself and with a guy again?"

"It should never be about what he wants or how long he will wait."

I know this. Logically I know this. But emotionally, no, I don't. All I know is I like the way I feel when I'm with him, and I don't want to lose that.

We continue, getting to know each other. He doesn't ask any questions that feel too intrusive, and I'm relieved. I wasn't ready to talk about memories or the lack of them.

———

"How was it?" Cici asks me as I'm talking to her on the phone on my way to Javie's.

"Not bad. We really didn't talk about it. I think he was letting me get comfortable first. That was nice," I share. She doesn't know what happened or what I remember either. Those memories I've kept in a locked vault. No one should be subjected to them.

"Will you share everything with him?" I can hear the hesitation.

"I guess. Maybe. I don't know." I thought about it every time he asked me a different question. I had resigned myself to breaking down if needed, but don't really want to.

"Can I ask why you're okay telling a stranger what happened and not sharing with those closest to you?" Does she think I don't trust her?

"I'm considering sharing with a stranger because I don't have to see him all the time. I can't share that ugliness with those who will look at me with sadness and pity in their eyes. Y'all already see me like that, and I haven't even shared the ugliest parts of it." I hope the explanation makes sense.

"Maybe you see that because we don't know. Because we don't know what ugly is. If we knew, our minds wouldn't wonder anymore. We would know, could file it away and move on. But we don't know. All we see is you having trouble moving forward. That scares us."

All I thought of was the mental picture they would have.

"I hadn't thought of that." I admit, a little embarrassed I had only thought about myself. "I'll think about it," I add for good measure. And I will.

"That's all I ask."

It's quiet for a few moments before she asks, "Where are you going now?"

"I'm going to go see Javie's new apartment. He just got a new place, and he said he and his family would be moving him in today. For future reference, if it ever comes up, I was with you."

"Got it! Have fun. Bye," she says, hanging up.

I pull into the apartment complex he told me and begin driving around to find his building number. I see the rental moving van and his brother in the parking lot before I notice the building number. I park my car, excited to see Javie.

I step out of the car and hear Javie's voice. "Hey! Come on up."

I look toward the moving van and see him carrying one side of a couch and his brother on the other.

"Hey," I yell to him, walking in their direction.

"Ritza," Alex says and nods his head at me. I follow them up as they make carrying the couch up a flight of stairs seem so easy.

"Place it right here." I hear Lola's voice from inside the apartment.

"What if I don't want it there?" Javie jests back, clearly trying to annoy her.

"Just place it where I said. You'll thank me later," she says more firmly.

I walk through the open door, watching Javie and Alex placing the couch exactly where Lola instructed them to. Toni is in the small kitchenette area, and Garrett is stacking some boxes in the corner.

"A few more boxes and the dresser. That's all that's left in the van," Javie says as he comes up to me. His lips spread as he places a hand on my cheek and kisses my forehead before he says to the guys, "Come on."

He winks at me before he and Garrett follow Alex out the door.

"Hey, Ritza," Lola says to me, smiling. "I know, this place is tiny, but we'll make it work."

I guess she caught me looking around. It's one room…one room for everything. The kitchen is sort of separated by an island type of counter that I'm guessing will be used as a table. There are two doors along the wall across from his bed, which I'm going to guess are a bathroom and maybe a closet. I've never been in an apartment this small before.

Toni turns around, smiling. "Hey again. Javie talked you into helping too?" She rolls her eyes playfully, turning back around and grabbing a couple of glasses from a box before placing them in a kitchen cabinet.

"Hi. I respond to them," then add, "I volunteered."

"Aren't you nice. He bribed us with food," Lola jokes back. "And lately, I feel like I would do anything for more food."

Lola picks up a box from the floor as I ask, "What can I do?"

"There is a bucket of water in the kitchen. Can you wipe down the shelves in those other cabinets please? I'm committed to getting his kitchen done. Then he or you," a sinful smile spreads on her face, "can worry about the rest of the apartment."

I can feel my neck and cheeks heating up. I just shake my head and avoid the comment.

"What in the— Put that box down now!" Alex's voice and angry tone startle me.

I turn around, and he's scowling at Lola as she happily takes a step away from him. He quickly places the box he was carrying down and goes to Lola, taking the one from her arms.

"See! It wasn't that heavy," she tells him.

"I don't care. I told you I don't want you carrying any boxes." His voice calms as he speaks to her. "If you refuse to listen, all you will be able to do is sit on that damn couch and supervise." He cocks a brow at her, almost challenging her.

Javie and Garrett walk in and place boxes down in a corner.

She shakes her head at him. "I'm pregnant. I can do things. If all I do is sit on the couch and 'supervise,'" she air quotes with her fingers, "this whole pregnancy, with the way I'm eating, I am going to get to be as big as a house. Will you still love me then?"

He places the box down, and steps up to her. "*Te amo para siempre*." And he places a soft kiss on her nose.

"Can y'all not!" Javie laughs.

"I hope whatever he said meant he would love me, because if not, Houston we got a problem," Lola jokes, slapping him playfully in the chest. "Now pick that box up and place it on the counter over there. Ritza can help unload that one."

Watching them, I feel like I'm intruding. I've tried to look busy, getting the rag from the bucket of water, and not gawk, but how freakin' cute are they? Alex doesn't look like the nicest guy around—tall, dark, tattooed, with a permanent scowl. Meeting him in a dark alley would probably scare you. But Lola tames him.

I get busy wiping down the shelves of the cabinet, hoping no one noticed me staring.

"When Alex said to supervise, he didn't mean you could put Ritza to work," I hear Javie say.

"It's fine," I chime in, smiling.

I love the way his eyes dance with amusement.

"Come on, let's finish this, and we can return the truck and get something to eat," Garrett says to the guys.

Alex places the box Lola was carrying on the counter in front of me. Then I watch them walk out of the apartment again, leaving me with the girls.

It's tight in this small area with all three of us in here. We work, unpacking the kitchen items as the guys unload the last of the truck. They leave after the last load to drop the truck off and pick up some food.

"When are we having your engagement party?" Lola whines after we are done with the kitchen and are sitting around waiting on the guys to return.

"I told you, I don't want one," Toni responds, not looking up from her phone and whatever she's scrolling through.

"Shouldn't she have an engagement party?" Lola turns to me.

I pull my shoulders up to my ears, shaking my head. "Uh…I don't want to get caught in the middle of this." I smile knowing I'm the new one to the group and shouldn't be taking sides.

Lola childishly pouts at not getting her way with an exaggerated, "Ugh." She makes a quick about-face, though, and turns back to Toni, "Your future mother-in-law wants to throw you one. It's her only son, and I'm sure she wants to show-off." She shimmies her shoulders.

"She does not want to show off. Have you met Garrett's parents? Besides, you just got engaged. Why don't you throw yourself one?" Toni replies, bored.

"Yes, she does. She may not like the glitz and glamour on a normal basis, but when it comes to showing off her son, I bet you my trust fund I'm right." Lola's eyes widen. "And you know why I'm not having my own, so let me live vicariously through you."

Toni finally looks up at Lola, biting her lip. "She has asked me about an engagement party a few times. But she's never pushed. Just letting me know if I change my mind, she would love to throw one."

Lola nods her head. "I'm telling you."

"Fine!" Toni's head falls back as Lola begins clapping and dancing in her seat.

Lola picks up her phone and begins, "We need, what… like maybe six weeks to plan properly?"

"Ugh…what did I just agree to?" Toni mumbles without lifting her head.

"I wonder if my stomach will grow by then? I don't want to look fat in your pictures. I'll probably have to wait for the last minute to get a dress. Okay, venue, flowers, food. I'll call Mrs. Anders tomorrow—" Lola begins talking to herself.

"Can I tell his mom myself first?" Toni interrupts Lola's monologue.

"Oh, yeah. Sure. Sorry. Just got excited." Lola is still wiggling in her seat like a child who has had too much sugar.

Their talk about this party and all of Lola's ideas keeps them busy, which I'm grateful for. The more they talk about their own things, the less time they have to question me about my life. Then it dawns on me. I'm with new people. Alone. And I'm fine. At least I think I'm fine. Am I fine?

My breathing picks up just a bit, but I'm unsure whether it's a panic attack coming or the surprise at this revelation. I didn't even think about it when Javie left and said he would be back. Just then, the door opens, and the guys walk in with bags of food.

JAVIE

"I wanted pizza, but the pregnant lady demanded Chinese," I announce as I walk through the door. Ritza is sitting on the chair, and all the color has drained from her face. It doesn't seem like she is focused on anything. I quickly place the bag I'm carrying on the kitchen-table area and walk over to her.

I don't want to bring attention to her, so I crouch down in front of her and whisper softly, "You okay?" I let one hand graze the side of her face while the other slides over her wrist, gently bringing her back to me.

"I'm good. Why?" Her eyes focus on me.

Her secret. The one that takes her away sometimes. I can feel it and see it in her. She carries a pain she doesn't share.

"I don't know. You seemed uncomfortable," I whisper, not wanting the others to hear, knowing she wouldn't like it. I give her a gentle kiss, letting my lips linger. When I pull back, I see her chest rise and fall gently. She brings her head forward letting her forehead lean against mine.

"Come and get it," Garrett says to the room.

"Me first. I'm starving." Lola jumps up, practically dancing her way to the food. I'm amazed at how much she has been eating lately.

"Promise you're good?" I ask quietly.

Ritza closes her eyes, nodding her head slightly.

"Come serve yourself, Ritza," Toni calls out. "You want to get a plate before the guys clear out all the dishes."

I stand, offering my hand to help pull her up.

Ritza sits back down in the same chair after serving herself a plate. Wanting to be next to her in this much more relaxed environment, I sit on the floor, leaning against the chair. She is sitting with her legs crisscrossed in front of her, so her knee is sticking into my back, but I don't mind. She is here. It feels much more normal than sitting at a restaurant every week.

Everyone has settled in and has begun eating when Lola announces, "I talked Toni into having an engagement party!"

I look to Garrett for his reaction, and he just shrugs.

"I thought there would definitely be more enthusiasm for a party," Lola whines with food in her mouth.

"Amor, I think these parties are more for the girls than the guys in the relationship."

Lola just rolls her eyes, frowning at Alex.

"Have you told my mom?" Garrett looks in Toni's direction.

"No. She just persuaded me while y'all were gone." Her tone is as bored as Alex's. "I was thinking of heading to the ranch to tell her in person. I guess I'll take Lola with me so that they can start their planning." She rolls her eyes and shakes her head when she looks in Lola's direction. Lola shimmies in her seat while taking another bite of her noodles.

"I promise I'll eat before the party so I don't make a fool of myself shoveling food in my mouth the whole time," Lola announces with humor. "I swear I must be carrying a mini-Alex in here," she pats her stomach, "because I am always so hungry. Only guys can eat like this."

Ritza laughs. "Sorry. That just reminded me of my mom complaining about my brother and his friends. She swore she was grocery shopping at least twice a week because they would finish everything." She giggles to herself. "We never had to eat leftovers though because Damian would always finish them before anyone ever had the chance."

"I knew it!" Lola quips back. "We are having a boy with the amount of food this kid is consuming. How did your grandmother keep up with two boys?"

I look to Alex to see how he's going to answer. There is no need to bring the mood down with our story of poverty. We ate, and we usually ate well, all Guela's home-cooking, but there were times when I went to bed hungry.

"We managed." Alex keeps it simple.

"How is the job hunting going?" Garrett asks me.

"Same. I'm still pulling some hours at the auto shop and the welding job is starting to cut hours. I just don't want to give up cars, at least not yet." I shrug, taking another bite.

"Why had I not thought of this before?" Lola exclaims, her eyes wide.

"What?" Alex asks her.

"Why don't I open a business, and you and Javie can run it. Auto body, restoration, whatever. It's yours. You build the business. I'm just the seed money. I can ask my grandfather for real-estate suggestions."

"That's a great idea, but they still won't be making a salary until they get it up and running," Toni interjects.

"Sure they would. It would all go into the business model. I'm not just throwing money into this. We would need to make the plan, take it to my grandfather for his input before we begin. He does have the experience and can help."

I want to yell at Lola, *YES, let's do this*, but she's saving Alex with her money again, and I don't know how he feels about that.

Alex looks at me. "What do you think?"

"Honestly, I like the idea," I answer, treading carefully, not wanting to start an argument between them.

He nods back. "Me too."

I'm shocked he agreed so quickly. It makes me think his job hunting isn't going very well. I make a mental note to ask him about it when we are alone. Make sure we are on the same page.

Ritza squeezes my shoulder. I wonder what she's thinking about all this. The evening continues with more casual talk before everyone announces their departure. That is, everyone but Ritza. I'm amazed that she has stayed as long as she has.

I sit on the couch Toni and Lola vacated, letting the quiet settle in. The same quiet that I was having trouble with when I lived at Guela's, but somehow, it's different. It's welcome. It doesn't feel stifling. I don't feel the need to fill it with people or commotion.

"What are you thinking about?" Ritza's soft voice breaks through my thoughts.

My lips pull out at the sweet sound of her voice in my space. "Nothing. Just enjoying the silence."

"You enjoy it?" She stands up and moves to the couch, sitting next to me.

"I didn't before. But now...now it's different, I guess." I answer vaguely, not wanting to admit my previous behaviors.

"Why?" Her eyes narrow.

"More settled maybe?" I shrug.

I grab her hand and pull her a little closer. I'm dying for more with her but know she will initiate what she wants when she's ready. I want to know what happened to her and why it's affected her this way.

She comes to me willingly, tucking herself into my side.

"Want to watch a movie?" I ask.

She looks up at me. "Sure. Let me just text Cici that I'm staying here. I was thinking of chilling out at her place but—" She stops, color filling her cheeks.

"But?" I drag out the word playfully.

She drops her gaze to her lap.

After a few moments of silence, I say teasingly, "I'm waiting."

"But I think I would enjoy myself more here," she says just above a whisper.

"I agree. I *am* more fun than Cici." I can't contain the devilish smirk that appears. I cup her chin pushing it up just a tad to place a kiss on her lips.

A sigh escapes her as she burrows into my side. She's like the puzzle piece I was missing, fitting perfectly into me. She picks up her phone, typing out a quick text and placing it back down next to her.

"What do you want to watch?" I ask her.

"Whatever. Do you have Netflix?"

"Sure do." I bring it up on the TV and scroll through the different trending movies and shows.

"How about that one?" She perks up at what looks to be a

romantic comedy. Not one I would have picked, but if it will keep her here, I'm in.

"We found a winner." I click the movie for it to begin.

The evening was going along well, side commentary about the cheesiness of the movie, more snacks and drinks, and of course, laughter. It felt good to have her relaxed. There's been no sign of her usual state of masked tenseness.

While she didn't stay tucked in my side, she was always touching me in some small way. Her hand holding my arm, her head on my lap. Right now she is sitting on one leg while her other is draped over my lap. The inevitable sex scene in rom-coms is on the screen, and I feel her leg tense just a fraction. Is she uncomfortable?

CHAPTER 12

RITZA

I HAVE NOT HAD THESE URGES AND FEELINGS IN SO LONG, I HAD forgotten what they felt like. Sure, all the time I've had with Javie has had my stomach stirring with butterflies, and my heart would flutter, but true desperate arousal had not happened, until now. I didn't even know if I would feel it again or if I was doomed to just go through motions.

I keep touching him because I can't seem to get enough of him. He's safe and sweet and…so incredibly sexy. He has the perfect balance of cute guy next door with bad-ass hardness. Not too guy next door to be boring and not too harsh, which can be a turn off. His sweet smile with his half tattoo sleeve that peeks out of his shirts is…*argh*— I need to stop these thoughts because I feel like I want to jump his bones, and what if I do and then panic? How freaking embarrassing.

And this scene is not helping matters—*at all*. Why, oh, why did I choose a rom-com? Eyes on the screen and do not look at him. If I do, I don't know what I'll do.

He squeezes my leg, which causes me to look at him.

"What's wrong?" he asks, lips pulled down.

"Uh... Wha—," How could he possibly know I was at war with myself?

"Your leg tensed, and it felt like you were about to take it away," he explains when I can't formulate any words.

I nod my head slowly a couple of times.

"What's going on in that beautiful head of yours? Because I'm not asking for anything except this." He lifts his hand off my leg and waves it between us on the couch.

How does he always know? It's like he has a sixth sense or is living in my brain, which I know is not possible or he would run for the hills.

"I know." Two words. That's all I have. Because I know I'm safe with him. I have watched him interact with Cici on Tuesdays, and I see how protective he is with Lola and Toni.

Can I go further? Do I even dare?

"Are you going to share with me what's going on?" He persists; his eyes narrow.

No words. There is nothing I can say. My lips pull into the automatic smile I have mastered over the last few months, and I shake my head. "It's nothing. Stupid really." I bring my leg around and lean into him, placing my hand on his thigh and squeezing it softly.

"You know you can talk to me, right?" His voice is soft, like he's talking to a skittish animal.

"I know. But it was nothing," I say, trying to make it seem like it is no big deal.

Tucked into his side, I can't see his face, and I'm glad for the reprieve from his questioning gaze. Lucky for me, the love scene on the screen is gone. I take a deep breath. His arm hugs me a little tighter, and the small gesture has my heart exploding. I want to be okay. I want more. I want to be able to do things, sexual things, without worry about freaking out and having a full-blown panic attack.

His hand is lazily grazing my arm, and tiny goosebumps explode all over my body with this friendly touch. Tingles of excitement begin to flood my body. The slow spread of waves that are flowing through my body rouse the need. The thrill is beginning to become too much. I squirm, trying to calm myself until I figure out what I want to do.

My gaze comes down to his leg I have my hand on. His shorts have ridden up slightly while we have been sitting here, and more of his firm thigh shows. I let my fingers graze from his knee upward and back down again. Up and down. His leg tenses under my touch.

"How far up you going?" he teases, placing his hand on top of mine. I hadn't realized how high my hand was.

I sit up, looking at him. No words. An embarrassed, sly smile spreads across my face, and all I see is gentle patience. I close the distance between us and kiss him. Slowly. Tentatively. I want to feel him. I want to feel safe again. Normal again. Like a woman again.

The feel of his lips on mine has my whole body burning for more. I move to his lap, wanting to feel more of him. I snake my arms around his neck, pushing my breasts into his chest as I run my fingers through his dark-brown, tousled hair. The kiss becomes desperate. Hungry. I feel his dick come to life under me. I squirm a bit, enjoying the feeling of turning him on.

His hands come to my face, slowing the kiss, then pushing me back, prying us apart. I miss the feel of his body against mine. His lust-filled gaze is all I see.

"Are you sure?" he says in a husky but calm voice.

"I think so" flies out of my mouth before I think.

"Then nope. Back to the movie we go." His hands fall from my face as he leans back into the couch.

Panic. He doesn't want me. I quickly move off him, scooting to the other side of the couch, and he turns to me.

"Where are you going?"

My eyes water, but I refuse to cry here. Not in front of him. I feel like a deer in headlights. I don't know what to do or say.

"Hey. Come here," he coaxes me.

I'm frozen to my spot.

He turns and brings his hands to my waist and moves me back to his lap, tucking my head beneath his chin and wrapping his arms tightly around me.

"We will not be doing anything until I know you are sure you want to go further. I'm not taking a chance with an 'I think so.'" His arms squeeze me just a smidge as he kisses the top of my head.

"But I do want to kiss you. I'm just not sure about—" I whisper but stop, not knowing if I can even say the word *sex* out loud.

"Having sex?" he asks.

I nod my head on his chest, not wanting to admit it. My mind races for an explanation for why I'm not ready for that step. What twenty-one-year-old hesitates?

JAVIE

Damn, I'm so turned on right now. I've been waiting for her to give me a signal she was ready to move forward. The kissing is great, but I'd be lying if I said I didn't want any more than that. But I *will not* go further with an 'I think so.' I know there is pain and hurt there. I know it has to be significant for her to be as squeamish as she is.

The past couple of weeks, my mind has come up with the most horrid of scenes she might have experienced. I don't know which is correct or if any are, but I do know some asshole guy broke her. That much I am certain about.

"Hey," I whisper as I try and move her away from my

chest so she can see my face. I have to tell her I'm in this with her. We will work through this together, whether she talks to me about it or not. Eventually I'll ask.

She uncurls herself from me and sits up straight. I see the unshed tears and the look of defeat.

"You are in charge here. I will do anything you want and anything you are comfortable with. But you need to be really clear where those lines are. I'm not crossing one until I know you've called *go*."

Her lips twitch upward, then she rolls her bottom lip into her mouth, wetting it before sliding it out again. Her chest rises and falls.

"I like kissing you. I want to kiss you," she says cautiously.

"Kissing is definitely a plus." I smirk, trying to lighten the mood and bring her out of the funk she fell into.

"And…uh…" She looks down between us. "I…uh…want to do more." She pauses, and I wait for her to tell me what she's thinking. "But how…uh…um…do I…uh…tell you where the line is?"

"Baby, what is more? That's what I need to know."

She shrugs her shoulders, "I'm not sure. I just know not sex." She pauses then quickly adds, "Not yet."

"You know there is so much more between kissing and sex." I run my fingers down the side of her face. She is having such a hard time talking about it.

She nods.

"So, you understand my dilemma." I smile at her, wanting her to feel comfortable talking to me about this. If she can't talk about it, I doubt she's ready to do it.

She nods again.

I raise an eyebrow at her in question.

"How about a high school make-out session like your parents are in the next room," she says as a genuine, nervous smile brightens her face.

Since I never had one of those growing up in the hood, I'm going to guess my way through it and hope TV shows are accurate enough.

"High-school make-out session it is."

She hugs me tightly before pulling back with an expectant look. I close the distance between us, meeting her lips to mine, moving us to lay side-by-side on the couch. Her body is relaxed as I run my fingers over her arm and down her back.

Her hand is roaming over my back and shoulder, and I know the little man is coming to life again. I know she will feel him harden with our bodies pressed tightly together.

The kissing, the rubbing, the hands roaming on every part of the body we can reach in this position except for crotches, butts, and breasts. We continue until the credits begin to roll.

I can't remember the last time I was this turned on with no release. A cold shower and a rub out will be in my future tonight.

Ritza tucks herself into my chest as I hold her. How do I tell her I can see she's scared? Living in fear. That I want to protect her.

"I guess I better get going. Let you finish your unpacking," she says without moving.

"I think it would bother Toni and Lola more than me if I lived out of boxes," I respond honestly. Not a bad idea really. If I don't unpack, maybe they'll do it for me.

Her soft giggle soothes some of the worry I've been carrying when it comes to her. She pulls away, rolling herself to sit up, and I follow her lead.

She stands, picking up her keys and phone. "Walk me to my car?"

"Of course."

———

I'M SITTING in my new home, scrolling through TV shows to watch, when my phone chimes.

I had Johnny tow my car to the shop. Can you fix today?

Amelia. I wasn't sure if I was going to hear from her after our last encounter, but I had gone to the pick-and-pull to find an alternator for her in case.

Heading over

That's all I need to say. At least it will go quick at the garage since I can use all their tools instead of make-shifting the shit I've been able to buy and collect for myself. I'm nervous on the drive over, not knowing how to act with her after the last time.

I get out of the car and walk through the partially open bay door, heading straight for the last bay, which is rarely used. I find her car tucked inside. The garage doors are closed. The door to the small waiting room opens, and the clicking of heels on concrete follows. Amelia is here.

"Thank you for doing this," she says as she approaches. "Johnny said he's closing up. Just finishing some paperwork inside and to let him know when you're done."

She is wearing a very short mini skirt with a tight strapless top, no bra. I have full view of her nice, large breasts through the thin material. Any man would appreciate it, and it doesn't help that I've been taking cold showers lately. I know those breasts personally. I pull my gaze up to her face, and she gives me a look of triumph. She knows I was staring and that she succeeded in getting my attention.

I refuse to fall into her web. "I'll be done in about an hour. You can do what you need, and I'll text you when I'm done."

"I have nothing to do. I'll stick around and help you. Just tell me the tools," she purrs the word *tools*, "and I'll get them. Like a nurse for a doctor."

I lift the hood to begin. I look over at Amelia. "Bring me the ratchet and socket set."

She turns around and bends over, legs spread enough to give me full view of her ass and pussy—there are no panties in sight. She's slow and seductive in her movements. She stays bent over and turns her head with the ratchet in hand. "This one?" She wiggles her ass slightly.

My dick jumps to life, not having gotten any action lately except for my right hand.

"Yes."

She licks her lips, and she places her other hand between her legs, rubbing between her folds. "She's wet and waiting." Her voice drops an octave.

My cock pulses, aching to plunge deep into her wanting core. I'm frozen in place. The ring of the shop phone breaks me from my pussy trance. It's a good thing Amelia is hidden behind her own car or Johnny would have a free show.

She takes her time standing back up and strolls to me, ratchet in hand.

"And the socket set?" I tell her when she stands so close our chests touch.

"Want another peek of what's yours later?" Her voice gravelly with need.

I gulp down what little saliva I have, as my mouth turns dry. She turns around, taking a couple of steps away, then bending over and shaking her ass side to side. She picks up the socket set, turning around and sitting on a toolbox. She spreads her legs, her pink folds glistening. She pulls down one side of the strapless top taking her breast in her hand, cupping it, and pinching her nipple until it hardens, then taking the other breast out doing the same. Hardened nipples demanding my attention.

She slides her hand down spreading her folds apart, dragging her fingers over her wet center. "The sooner you fix my car," she brings her hand to her mouth sucking her fingers and popping them out, "the sooner you can taste this."

My phone vibrates in my pocket, and Ritza comes to mind. The reason for the cold showers. My right-hand game strong. Her face. Her fears. Her timid smile. My dick deflates. A pang of disappointment hits. Disappointment in myself. Why did I let Amelia grab my attention?

I take my phone out and a text from Ritza greets me.

Can I come over tonight? I'll bring food.

She is what I want.

Yes. I'll text when I'm home. At the shop now.

"Are you fucking serious? You're going to get distracted by a text over me?" Amelia huffs.

I look up at her, and she stands, angrily pulling her top up.

"Amelia, you are beautiful, and you know you are fuckin' sexy. But I told you last time I was seeing someone."

"I broke up with Eddie. I heard you moved out of your Guela's house. I thought maybe…we could…you know, move in together."

"I'm seeing someone," I stress to her again.

"But I thought we could try being us. I thought you liked me." Her eyes begin to tear.

"I do like you. As a friend. But I'm seeing Ritza."

She takes a couple of steps, standing right in front of me and placing her hands on my chest. "I need you. We are good together. I'll go back to school. I should be with you." Tears are flowing down her face.

"You don't need me. There is no us. There has never been an us." I step away. "Let me finish your car and you can be off. Wait inside?" We don't need to be around each other anymore.

Without a word she turns and walks to the door that leads to the waiting room.

CHAPTER 13

RITZA

Another session with the counselor. My second one this week. He mentioned today would be harder. Each session brings more questions. More memories stirred. He was right. The nightmares have been nightly now. They had become infrequent, but now I'm living the hell over and over. A hell I still don't quite remember.

"Have the nightmares changed? Anything that you feel we should talk about?" Josh asks.

I'm tucked in an oversized chair, my legs pulled up close to my chest with my hoodie pulled over protectively. "Mainly the same. But cigarettes or some kind of smoke. Which is odd right? We can't smell in our dreams, can we?"

"No, we don't smell in our dreams, but the memory or figment is so strong, you believe you smell it."

"Tell me about the smoke smell."

"I can't see anything. It's black, and I'm listening to a song that's not familiar, and it stinks of smoke. But it's a weird smoky smell." I pause. "In my dream, I'm not scared yet."

"Maybe it's part memory or maybe it has nothing to do with the rape," he says, shrugging his shoulders. "How are things with Javie?"

"Good. Well, as good as they can be."

"Why do you say, 'as good as they can be'?"

"Because we are grown adults, and I'm acting like a teenager sneaking out of the house to see him. 'Making out,'" I air quote with my fingers, "but never going further. Don't get me wrong, the make-out sessions are nice, and I'm glad he's sticking around for them, but what if I'm never able to move forward? Move past this point? I can't ask him to stick around with a girl who's forever broken and damaged." My voice increases with each word until I'm almost yelling.

"You aren't broken. You aren't damaged. Did something horrific happen to you? Yes. Yes, it did. But you are still you. Just with a tragic story mixed into all the other things that happened to you in your life. There are good, sad, and ugly things that happen to everyone. This, the rape, is an ugly one. That's it."

Tears I hadn't expected stream down my face. I grab a couple of tissues from the table beside me wiping them away roughly.

"How long?"

"How long what?"

"How long will it take to move on and forget this? I just want peace and calm. To not be hyper-aware of losing it or being on the verge of losing it."

He takes a moment, hand sliding through his hair. "I can't answer that. Everyone is different. Everyone processes at their own speed. We can't place a timeline on your recovery."

"But it's been months. Over half a year! I just want to be normal again," I huff.

"It has. And part of it was your avoidance of it. You thought you were okay by ignoring it, but the feelings were always there. The fear. The anger. The confusion. They never left. You suppressed them. And because of that, they could creep out at any time."

"So you're saying I did this to myself?" I drop my head on my knees, hot, angry tears spilling.

"No. You were doing what you thought you should. How could you know? You didn't and couldn't. No one knows how to process this. It's something no one should go through. And I'm here to help guide you to where you want to be."

I wipe my nose and grab more tissues to wipe my eyes. The tears are still flowing, but the surge of anger that had welled up has passed.

"Why don't we talk about what you have been avoiding."

"We're going there today?" I clench my hands into fists, rubbing them forcefully over my shins.

He nods his head. "You have avoided this question. I think it's time. What do you remember from that night and morning?"

I close my eyes, filling my lungs with air to buy time. "I went to a club with friends. We had done it so many times, I didn't think anything of it. We would go, dance, pick up guys. I wasn't a virgin. I had done the walk of shame before…" I confess.

"You can do all the walk of shames you want. Your body, your right. If you consent, then you never have to feel bad about the 'walk of shame.'" He air quotes with his hands. There is such a certainty in his voice.

"What if it was karma? I could have caused this. Brought this on myself. I was probably flirting with whoever did this. I invited it. Led them on. I've been black-out drunk before. I've had sex with someone I met the same night. I teased and kissed random guys for fun." My airways tighten, and my stomach is cramping.

"You have the right to have a good time. You did nothing

to cause this. No means no, and you definitely did not give consent."

"But—"

"No buts. You have the right to say yes or no to sexual pleasure. End of story." He takes a breath. "You did not bring this on yourself. Some guy—"

"Guys," I interrupt.

"Guys?"

"I think so. Everything is foggy and dreamlike. I think I heard different voices. Laughs that didn't sound the same." I drop my head sideways, leaning on my knees, letting myself relive that night and morning. "I remember being in pain. Having trouble breathing, but I'm not sure why."

I pause, and Josh waits for me to gather myself. I take a couple of minutes to build the courage to share the morning after.

"When I woke up, my head was pounding. I had never experienced a hangover like this. I really thought my head would explode. When I was finally able to sit up, that's when I noticed I was naked. I was on my couch. My shirt and bra were torn but still on my arms... My privates were sore. I had a couple of large hickey-looking bruises on my breasts."

More tears begin to form.

"At first I was confused. I tried so hard to remember the night before, and nothing came to mind... I had to pee, so I walked to my bathroom and when I wiped myself after..." I close my eyes, seeing the toilet paper again, "it was red with blood, and I wasn't on my period."

The room is eerily quiet; I can hear my blood pumping through my body. "I just wanted to forget, so I turned on the shower, ready to wash away everything, but then... I don't know... I thought, 'What am I washing away if I don't remember anything?'"

Tears fall, and I don't bother wiping them away.

"I turned off the water and sat on the toilet. I don't know how long I sat there, but I didn't know what to do next. I finally got up and looked at myself in the mirror. I didn't look like me. I know it was me, but…" I shrug, not knowing how to explain. "Finally, I thought about my phone and my keys. I threw on a large T-shirt and some joggers to look for my keys and phone. I found my phone in the couch and my keys were on the kitchen counter where I had left them. I didn't drive to the club."

It was like opening a dam. The story of the morning after continued to flow out of me. I must have been coherent enough to get the guys the hidden key for my front door. Anytime I would go out and wouldn't drive, I would leave a key out for myself to get back into the apartment. Why would I help them find the key? The guilt of bringing this on myself spikes again.

I considered calling a friend to go with me to the emergency room, but I was too embarrassed. I didn't want anyone to see me like that. The only saving grace at the ER was the wonderful trauma nurse. She was graceful. Her movements fluid and slow. Nothing to surprise or scare me. Spoke so calmly. Always informing me of what was going to happen before it did. Taking the time to make sure I was ready.

Nurse Lynn was finally able to convince me to call my family. I didn't want to see my parents. I was ashamed. I called Damian instead. I thought he would be pissed and that would be better than my parents' sadness and disapproval.

The sadness in his eyes when he walked into the room a couple of hours later broke me. I wanted him to be angry. I needed him to be angry. I needed that anger to break through the numbness I had shrouded myself in during the examination and questions. He rushed to me, wrapping me in his strong arms, and cried. He hugged me, rocking back and forth saying, *I'm sorry, I should have protected you* over and over.

I couldn't go back to my place. Damian called his friends, and they packed up my apartment. I moved back home.

Once it all came out, I felt empty. The cramps in my stomach were gone. The internal pressure that was always lingering had somehow evaporated with each word, almost as if they were holding space inside my body. The tears that had been flowing freely, dried.

"How are you?" Josh asks. He had sat quietly through the whole story. He nodded, but never interrupted, letting me take all the time I needed.

"Surprisingly, okay." I pick my head up, dropping it from side to side, stretching my neck. I drop my legs, and it feels as if I hadn't moved in days. I reach up, lengthening my back.

"We have gone over time, but I felt like you needed to let go of all you were holding in."

"I'm so sorry. Is someone waiting?" I stand quickly.

"No, no. I just wanted to let you know. You did really good work. I hadn't been scheduling anyone right behind you. I was waiting for us to have a session like this. Now I think the healing will begin."

"Really?"

"Maybe. You sharing all of this was huge. It showed your willingness to take the next step forward. You had been stuck. I can't say for sure, like I said, everyone's different. But I'm proud of the work today."

My lips spread widely. "Thank you." I pick up my keys and phone, my steps lighter than when I came in.

In my car, I send a quick text.

Can I come over tonight? I'll bring food.

I'm drained after today's session but want to see Javie. He is what I need to help me after the emotional couple of hours.

———

I RUSHED to pick up pizza and headed to Javie's as soon as he texted that he was on his way home. I'm always excited to see him, but today…today feels necessary. Some of the extra weight I had been hauling around day in and day out has lifted. I feel just a bit freer.

I knock on his door, stopping myself from bouncing on my toes. The deadbolt turns and Javie is standing in front of me, shirtless, hair wet, wearing only a pair of athletic shorts. The sight of a shirtless Javie sends a zing through my body that hits right between my legs. His firm chest peppered with a bit of hair and that V traveling down. This feeling is coming more frequently lately.

"Hola, *hermosa*." His lips spread into a knowing smile when my eyes come up from his chest to meet his. "Let me help you." He grabs for the box I'm holding.

JAVIE

Ritza's gaze stuck on my chest, and her cute red cheeks at being caught is just what I needed after my encounter with Amelia. While I care for Amelia, I can't be around her anymore after the spectacle she made today. She has no respect for me, acting that way, especially after I told her I was seeing someone.

She is consumed with herself and her needs, never thinking about consequences or others. She can be loyal to a fault, and that is what Toni needed growing up. Someone that she could depend on other than me and Alex. But Amelia's inability to mature and move forward has caused the rift between her and Toni, and now between her and I.

I walk to the kitchen, placing the box on the small counter.

"Want to eat here or in front of the TV?" I ask Ritza.

"We can eat here," she replies quietly.

She's standing midway between the door and the small counter that doubles as a table, watching me.

"Let me get a shirt on before we eat." I smile, hoping she moves from the spot she's frozen in.

"Yeah…okay." Her gaze drops to the floor as she takes a step toward the counter.

The apartment is miniscule, so it's not like there is any way to avoid looking at the other. Unless the floor becomes interesting.

I move to the opposite side of the room, pulling a T-shirt out of my dresser. I slide it over my head and catch her staring at me again. The only thing is, she is expressionless.

As soon as I catch her staring, she does a miniscule shake of her head, turning to the counter and opening the box.

"I brought pizza. Not sure if you've had it since you were craving it the day you moved in." Her back is to me now, so I can't see her beautiful face, but her remembering what I wanted to eat from before is thoughtful.

"I have not, and thank you." I come up behind her, wrapping my arms around her waist. She stiffens for a moment, like I had somehow startled her, but when her back hits my chest, her body relaxes against mine. I place a kiss on the top of her head, squeezing her just a little tighter.

She places her hands on top of mine, pushing herself into me.

"Is everything okay?" I ask, knowing she is still holding back from me. Maybe, just maybe, she will decide today she will share her secrets.

"Of course." She tries to pull away, but I hold her.

"I've got you. You never need to worry with me." I pause, then whisper, "I've got you."

She turns around laying her cheek on my chest. Her breaths are deep, but ragged.

"Why?" She says it so quietly, I almost missed it.

"Why what?"

"All of this? Why bother with me?" Her body stiffens, but she doesn't try to leave my embrace. "I know I'm messed up, and I'm pretty sure you know it too," she whispers, voice shaking.

"I know no such thing. But I'll tell you what I do know." I pause, before continuing, buying myself some time to figure out how much I want to say. "You are beautiful without trying. Inside and out. You are kind, thinking of others. Like with dinner tonight. You are real. You don't try to show off or be something you're not... But here's the thing. I know there's more to you. Part of you that you aren't showing me. But I want to know it. I want to know all of it. When you're ready."

I want her to know I see her internal battles. I don't know why, but I know pain resides there.

"Why do you think I'm not showing all of me?"

I kiss the top of her head again, bringing my hand to cup the back.

"Because I see it in your eyes. I feel it in your touch. There are moments when you leave me and are somewhere else." My fingers run up and down her spine softly. "You don't have to share now. I'm not asking you to. But know I'm waiting."

Her head nods against my chest. I'm not sure what she's agreeing to, but I can't force her to tell me.

Her stomach growls loudly, cueing us to leave this moment and eat. I was worried if she knew that I was waiting for her to be honest with me, it would backfire.

"Food. And TV. That's all we need to worry about tonight."

She pulls back, looking up to me. "Okay." She comes up on her toes, sliding her hands up my chest wrapping around my neck as she pulls me down for our lips to meet. She pulls away. "You didn't kiss me hello."

"It will never happen again." I bring my lips back to hers,

deepening the kiss, pulling her flush against my body. My body protests when I pull away from her.

"Let's eat."

———

WE ARE LAYING on the couch watching TV, but my mind is not focused on the screen at all. Her back is tucked into my chest, and our legs are tangled together. My hand rests on her hip. The floral scent of her shampoo is invading my senses, and it's taking so much effort to keep my dick soft. Her plump ass is pushed against me, and every time she moves to change positions, the friction wakes him up.

Before I realize what I'm doing, my hand is grazing up her waist, down to her stomach and up again, sliding down her hip. Back down the dip from her hip to her waist. That's when I realize what I am doing. I splay my hand on her stomach over her shirt. I had to place it somewhere and focus on calming down.

"Why'd you stop?" Her voice shakes.

"Because you haven't given me the go."

"Go."

"You know the deal. Tell me how far."

"Above the clothes. If I need you to stop, I'll say so."

"Promise?"

"Yes."

She moves, her butt brushing against my dick yet again. I breathe her in. I brush her hair to the side and place a few small kisses on her neck as my hand runs across her side along her ribcage, to her waist, and up her hip. I follow the curve of her hip and let my palm slide across the side of her buttocks.

Her breaths are deeper, stronger.

"Tell me what you want," I whisper in her ear.

She shakes her head slowly.

"I've got you. Tell me what you want." My hand continues to explore just her side.

She places her hand over mine and she glides it back to her stomach, coming up toward her breasts but stopping right under.

"Do I go higher?"

She nods.

I palm the bottom of her breast and give it a gentle squeeze.

A soft moan leaves her lips, and my dick instantly hardens. She glides my hand down back toward her stomach until she reaches below her belly button and stops again. She bends her knee opening her legs.

"Lower?" I kiss and suck her neck softly.

She nods again, taking her hand off mine.

I let my fingers stroke the area for a few seconds before I move my hand just a bit lower. Stroking. Kissing her neck. A little lower. She begins to squirm, rubbing her ass against me.

"I've got you," I whisper again. I will say it over and over again until she believes it. I've got her emotionally and physically—in any way she needs.

A soft whimper is my undoing. I slide my hand between her legs, and it is warm and inviting, even over her clothes. Her tight yoga pants let her enjoy the pleasure. I apply a small amount of pressure, and I'm gifted with another soft moan. She squirms, and I continue until she comes undone. Her chest heaves as she squeezes her eyes shut.

I wrap my arm around her middle and squeeze her softly. Today is for her. For her to begin to move away from whatever torment has been controlling her.

When her breaths return to normal I whisper, "Turn around, please."

She shakes her head.

"Then tell me what's wrong." I keep my voice low, knowing she is processing our experience.

She shakes her head again.

"You can trust me. That I promise. I've got you. Whatever you need. I've got you."

Wetness hits my arm she's laying on. She's crying.

I kiss her shoulder, softly holding her to me.

"Why?" I barely hear her say.

"Why what?"

"Why bother with me. I know I'm not normal and may never be. I can't talk about why. I may never want to." She tries to pull away from me, but I hold her. "Javie, you don't understand. I don't want to talk about it. Especially with you."

Those last three words hurt, and I move my arm, letting her go. She sits up and stands.

"I should go." Tears are flowing.

"Please don't." I stand next to her. I place my hands on her shoulders. "Talk to me or don't, it's up to you. I'm here. I'm staying here. I don't want anyone else. I don't mind waiting." I place a small kiss on her forehead.

"And if I can't reciprocate?" She's shaking her head.

"I'm not worried about that now. We will get through it together, whether or not you share what's behind all this."

"Are you sure?" She looks down to her shoes.

"Positive." I pull her to me and hold her. Her body relaxes as soon as she's tucked close to mine.

CHAPTER 14

RITZA

THE DRIVE HOME IS FILLED WITH CONFUSION AND ELATION. HE knows—maybe he's known for a while—I've been hiding something. He has stuck around even though I'm hiding it. Or trying to. Can I really do this with him knowing there's an elephant in the room each time we are together? It all feels like too much and not enough.

I walk into my home, still shaking with uncertainty. Today has been filled with breakthroughs and so much emotion. Sleep is probably the best thing right now.

———

I CAN'T BREATHE. Why can't I breathe. I open my eyes and everything is blurry. I can't focus on anything. Pain. I can't move.

"Wake up, baby. You're dreaming. You're safe." I sit up too quickly, and I feel dizzy.

My mom is sitting on the side of my bed. I see the fear

and sadness in her eyes in the dim light coming in from the window.

"When will these nightmares go away?"

"When you're ready." She comes in and hugs me. "You are working on you right now. Dredging up so much from that experience. It makes sense the nightmares would come back." She gives me a soothing smile. "And you have been doing and growing so much. I see it. I know it's hard, and you are doing it." She kisses my cheek. "Good night."

She walks out of my room, closing the door behind her.

I lie back down, bringing my blankets up to my chin and wondering when maybe, just maybe, I'll have a normal life again.

———

SITTING IN DAMIAN'S CHAIR, sorting through inventory receipts, I hear a crash in the garage and Jaxson cursing out loud. They have a new guy out there to help with the load for the next couple of weeks. A multi-car accident on the freeway has brought Damian great business, but he's moving away from his dream of restoring older cars. I keep telling him this is where the business is. I'm looking over his books, keeping his accounts, and the numbers don't lie.

I leave the comfort of the office to see what happened in the garage and if anyone needs anything as loud voices begin arguing.

"Fuck, man! How hard is it to hire someone full time! This shit ain't cutting it." Jaxson waves his hand in the direction of the new guy whose name I haven't bothered to learn. Not that he's a bad guy or anything, kind of boring really, but I knew he wouldn't make the cut for full-time employment. He shrank around the guys and their testosterone-filled presence.

"We'll discuss later!" Damian shouts at Jaxson. "Let's just finish the week." He claps No Name on the shoulder.

Jaxson shakes his head, throwing his dirty rag on one of the toolboxes, and storms in my direction.

He stops in front of me. "Can you convince Damian to finally hire someone good and full-time? Please."

I nod my head at him, giving him a small smile.

"I need a break. Can I take the office for a bit?"

"Go on." I pat his chest.

Growing up around the guys during my teens years was difficult, but fun. My girlfriends always wanted to hang at my place to ogle Damian and his friends. I didn't complain about it too much because every girl crushes on at least one of their brother's friends, right? But them always treating me like a little sister and scaring away my dates got old fast.

Damian comes in and walks over to me with some papers in his hand.

"We are going to need to hire. We can't keep this up," he says quietly.

"I know." I raise an eyebrow, wanting him to finish what I know he's holding back.

"Are you going to be okay with a guy or two more around here?" He keeps his voice low.

My first reaction is fear, but then I stop myself. Why? Why fear? What do I need to be afraid of? And a thought comes to mind.

"What if it's a girl?" My lips spread, thinking about a female busting their ass in here. Now that would be a sight to see.

Damian's lips pull out as he shakes his head. "Maybe. So, is that an 'I'll be okay'?"

"Yes. I think I'll be fine."

"Think." His eyes narrow.

"That's the best I can do. I'm moving on, but still have some trouble. I work through it, of course. I just want you to know I'm working on it, and I won't hold the garage back anymore."

He grabs my shoulder and brings me in, kissing my forehead. "Thank you."

"Maybe you can hire that guy who did the welding job on the Camaro," I slide in for good measure.

"Why are you so interested in who I hire?"

"I'm not." I shrug and turn away so he doesn't see the blush in my cheeks I get by just thinking of Javie.

I pull out my phone, sitting in one of the waiting-room chairs to scroll social media. It's not as hard as it was before to do nothing and scroll. Before it would hurt to look at everyone having fun in their lives while I was stuck in a dark abyss I never thought I would leave. Javie is a blessing in my life that I can never be grateful enough for.

Jaxson comes out of the office after a few minutes and comes to sit in the chair next to me.

"Whatcha doing?" His voice is silly.

"Nothing. Scrolling."

"Can I tell you something?" His voice is still playful, and he's wearing a shit-eating grin.

"Sure." I'm wondering which guy's gossip he's going to let me in on. He's always been the jokester spilling the guys' secrets to me.

"I saw a certain someone having a meal with a guy." My mind goes to which friend he's about to rat out, and I wait for him to continue. Is one of the guys gay and I didn't know? Why would he keep it a secret?

When he doesn't continue, I ask, "Who and with who?"

He's practically jumping out of his chair with excitement. "Hmmmm..." He drags the suspense out. This has got to be good if he's making such a spectacle for it.

"They were with that guy Javier who did the welding work for the Camaro." He winks at me knowingly.

My heart sinks. He knows I've been out of the house, out of the garage, out in public without the safety of Cici or my brother and his posse. Jaxson is not known for his secret keeping; there's no telling who he has already told.

My head drops at the worry of other people knowing. Their lofty expectations of what I should be doing. Tears fill my eyes.

"Hey. What did I say wrong?" he whispers.

I shake my head, not knowing how to explain.

"You're worried about my big mouth, aren't you?"

I look up; his brows are pulled together. I nod.

"I've kept it to myself for weeks and weeks now. I think I can manage a few more."

"Huh?" Words seem foreign with all the scenarios running through my mind taking up all my brain power.

"It's been forever since I saw you having lunch with him at that burger joint. He was even still working here at the time." He pauses. He brushes a tear that has escaped with his thumb. "Your secret is safe with me. I watched you from afar that day. Made sure you were good. You're different around him. I'm not gonna say you are your old self, but you have an energy around him. I watched you watching him here at the garage when you thought no one was looking. The way your eyes lit up when texts came through. Not all texts though." He winks, his playful grin back.

"I saw you becoming stronger. And when Damian mentioned a couple of weeks back that you were venturing out with Cici more but never mentioned Javier, I figured you have been keeping him a secret."

I nod, not knowing if I was that noticeable around Javie or if he is just perceptive.

"I'm able to see things others don't because they don't try

to hide things from me. They think because I can't take things seriously sometimes, I'm not watching." A sly smile spreads. "But keep that to yourself."

"Thank you." I reach out to hug him. Knowing that he will keep my secret settles the nerves that had begun to prick.

"You have my number if you need it. You know that right?" he whispers in my ear.

"I do. But with Javie, I don't need it."

He gives me a satisfied nod before standing up and returning to the garage.

————

I'LL BE SPENDING another night over at Cici's because Javie insisted on driving to the restaurant-slash-bar-slash-outdoor-event-venue. If he's picking me up from somewhere, it has to be Cici's since he can't pick me up from my house. Not while I'm still trying to hide him from everyone.

But back to this venue. It is a huge place with food, several bars, an outdoor stage area for live music, and games everywhere. It's massive and overwhelming. Walking in, my breathing starts to pick up, and I stop. Javie's hand slips out of mine as he continued to walk.

He turns back to me. "Hey. Up here."

My gaze had fallen to the asphalt below my feet. His feet come into my view as his hand cups my chin, bringing it up to meet his gaze.

"Do you want to go somewhere else? I'll text Alex and let him know we changed our minds, and we can go anywhere you want."

His lips pull down as he caresses the side of my face.

I can't do this to him. He was so excited about us meeting his family for food and drinks. He was going on and on about how Lola had chosen this place since she calls the shots, because apparently pregnant girls get dibs on food and fun since alcohol is off limits.

I shake my head. "No. Don't do that. I'm fine. I've just never seen a place like this," I try and explain away my fumble.

"It is pretty crazy. Garrett and Toni love it. They have come out a few times with friends and suggested it to Lola so she can have fun playing games. Ready?" He holds his hand out to me.

I place my hand in his and let him lead the way. Large Jenga and Connect Four games, cornhole, and a small putt-putt area fill the large outdoor space. The only thing keeping me composed is Javie's hand in mine. I know I'm squeezing his hand as we walk through the crowds of people, but it helps me. Knowing I have a grasp on safety is helping me settle with so many bodies surrounding me. The space is large enough that they aren't crowded together, but it's still more people than I have been around in months.

I'm watching all the people laughing and talking as we walk past. So carefree. Having fun. Not a worry you could see. That is the life I want again.

"Yay! We can order." Lola exclaims seeing us walk up. They are sitting at a large, hexagonal picnic table shaded by a couple of large umbrellas.

"Hello to you too," Javie teases her.

"That was my hello. Pregnant-lady talk." She points at Javie. "Now go get me food." She looks to Alex, raising a brow.

He kisses her forehead. "Anything else, mi amor?"

She shakes her head, slapping his ass. Garrett follows him as Toni and Lola stay sitting.

"Hi, Ritza! Sorry for the manners. I'm starving. I'm always starving." Lola laughs. "Come sit." Toni waves at me patting the bench next to her.

I still don't want to let go of Javie's hand, even if my palms feel clammy and sweaty.

"Ritza has never been here before. We want to go check out the place and menu." Javie chimes in before an excuse for not letting him go comes to mind.

"Well then hurry up and go," Lola responds.

"Hangry much?" Javie responds, then laughs as Lola flicks him off.

We get in a long line with Garrett and Alex.

"What's good?" I ask Garrett.

"So far everything we've had is really good. Toni wants the chicken sandwich, and I'm getting the burger. We'll start off with some fried pickles. The brisket sandwich is legit, and so are the sausage wraps."

"Now I can't decide what I want," I joke.

The guys start catching up, and I listen to their conversation, feeling like an intruder in their inner circle. I stay quiet, having nothing to contribute.

The line moves fast, and we are back at the table with drinks.

As Lola dips a chip into the salsa Alex brought back for her to munch on, Toni exclaims, "Are you going to share?"

Alex had placed the basket of chips and salsa right in front of Lola. As a joke, I'm guessing.

"Oh…yeah…sure." She places the chip in her mouth with one hand and pushes the basket in the center of the table with the other.

Toni rolls her eyes, smiling while grabbing a chip for herself.

Sitting at the table in our own area, away from the crowd, the tightness that had been squeezing my chest receded. I stayed present, never losing sight of where I am, and no panic attack starts. I'm able to control it with Javie's help. Even if he doesn't know he's helping.

"How's the engagement party planning going?" I ask as everyone has now begun to pick at the chips and salsa.

"Great!" Lola exclaims, her eyes lighting up as Toni exclaims, "Urgh!" dropping her head.

Garrett laughs. "Sure, start with an easy topic, Ritza."

"But seriously, it's not all that." Lola waves her hand in Toni's direction. "She's just complaining to complain." She giggles at Toni's dramatics.

"It's not that bad." Toni rolls her eyes. "I just wish I didn't have to invite my mom."

"I already told you, if you don't want to invite her, don't. Who the fuck cares about what's socially correct. If you don't want her at the wedding, she won't be. We'll go elope somewhere and only you and I will be there," Garrett tells Toni.

"Correction! Y'all and me too," Lola adds, clapping. She's hilarious.

"I would never do that to your mom. You know that. I'll suck it up for an evening. If she behaves at the party, I guess she can come to the wedding too," Toni says as her fingers tap the table.

Garrett places his hand on top of hers. "Whatever you want." He picks up her hand and kisses it.

"Since we're talking wedding stuff, Alex, will you walk me down the aisle?" Toni looks toward him.

A small smile forms as he nods his head. "I would be honored."

"And since he's busy with Toni, Javie, will you be the best man?" Garrett asks.

"Hell yeah," he exclaims excitedly, a huge smile spreads across his face.

Alex and Javie may be brothers, but watching them together, their differences are so apparent. I've never seen Alex relaxed except for with Lola—the way he talks to her and showers her with love and attention. But his look of indifference seems to be a constant with everyone else.

"I'm waiting!" Lola shimmies in her seat.

"For?" Toni asks her.

"Really. You're so mean!" Lola juts her lip out, pouting.

Toni laughs. "Fine. Will you be my maid of honor?"

"Yes, I will." She nods her head.

It's easy being around Javie's family. They are all so different, but like puzzle pieces, they seem to fit together perfectly.

The conversation continues, and our food arrives. It's easy to forget that I'm sitting in a huge venue because we have our own space, and they keep the conversation flowing. From school to the ranch to party planning, they never stop talking.

"We're meeting with your grandfather tomorrow?" Javie asks Lola nervously.

"Yup. Y'all are ready," she responds happily. "Besides, Alex needs to get busy. He is going stir-crazy in the apartment, and there's only so much house hunting we can do. Besides, I think we found our house."

I want to know more, but know it's probably not my place. I'm not even Javie's girlfriend.

"The location we found is great. Really centralized. Start small and expand, just like you talked about." Lola says reassuringly.

"We're good. I should be more nervous than you. I knocked-up his precious granddaughter and was arrested recently. If he's going to murder anyone, it will be me," Alex says flatly.

Lola leans into him, placing her head on his shoulder.

"Whatever, lovey-dovies. Who wants to play Jenga?" Toni asks the table.

"Me." Lola stands up.

"I'll play," I announce, surprising myself.

A low stand is set up a few feet from the large table with 2x4 planks cut up and stacked.

"Rock, paper, scissors who goes first?" Toni says.

Lola and I nod; we each get our hands ready.

"One, two…" Toni counts as she and Lola each hit a fist on an open hand.

"Three," they say in unison, spreading their hands in different shapes.

"Rock beats scissors!" Toni says smugly to Lola. "Ready?" She turns to me.

I smile and get my hands ready. One, two, three…

"Scissors beats paper," I say, smiling.

Toni rolls her eyes smiling and shaking her head.

"Don't pay attention to her, she always likes to win," Lola says, bumping Toni's shoulder with her own playfully.

"Y'all better play nice with Ritza. Y'all are both crazy," Javie yells to us.

They both raise their hands and flick him off. The guys start laughing and go back to their conversation.

"After you." Toni waves her hand at me.

I feel a couple of the boards looking for a semi loose one to start the game. We continue taking turns laughing and teasing each other.

I turn around and notice Javie and the guys are not at the table anymore. I look around and don't see him anywhere. My breathing becomes shallow as I continue to scan the area.

"Your turn," I hear, but it sounds like it's far away.

A hand on my shoulder brings me back, but I am slightly light-headed.

"Anything wrong?" Toni looks around the venue as she places her body in front of mine protectively.

"Uh…no. Sorry. I just spaced out people-watching, I guess." Her willingness to shield me from danger sends a warm feeling throughout my body.

I turn around, back to the game, and start feeling the boards. My hand is trembling, so I fear I may drop the tower.

"Back with more beverages, ladies," Garrett announces loudly.

"Thank you," Toni chimes.

I turn around to Javie standing behind me. "Miss me?" He smirks.

He has no idea how much and what could have just happened. I step into his chest breathing him in to help center and still my nerves. His arms wrap around me.

"Javie, let her go. Save that for later. We've got a game to play."

His arms loosen, and I step back. He hands one of the beers he's holding out to me. This one is sitting in a koozie.

I grab it looking at the logo on the koozie.

"I bought you one so your beer won't get hot too fast." Another thoughtful gesture.

"Thank you."

JAVIE

Watching Ritza last night talking, joking, and getting along with Toni and Lola made everything I've been worrying about ease a bit. I knew she was hiding something before she confirmed it. When she admitted she never wanted to tell me why she's tormented, it made me think she would pull away. Leave so she never had to reveal her truth. A truth I so desperately want to know, but she locks it away so tight.

I know she lives at home, but when I pick her up to go somewhere, it's always from Cici's apartment. I know Damian by accident, of course, but he doesn't know about us.

My mind is back to all the things that could be causing her from keeping her family from knowing about us. I'm falling in love with her, and the fact that she keeps me hidden hurts.

Does she feel the same way? Could she if she never wants to share the skeletons we both know exist?

I guess this is what it felt like for Garrett when Toni kept secrets and walked away from him to 'save herself.' I wonder if Toni would be able to talk to her. Make her believe that she can share anything, and I'll be here. Or does she need to find this out on her own?

Ritza is on her way over for another lazy evening in so I should focus on the here and now, like ordering food for dinner. Where's my wallet? Crap! I probably left it in the car. Walking down the stairs, I see Amelia's car pull up. Fuck! Not what I want to deal with today.

I stand next to my car as Amelia parks behind me. She didn't take a space, so I'm hoping that means she's not staying long. She exits the car and takes the few steps to stand in front of me.

"Hey," she says as she clutches her hands together in front of her.

"Hey," I respond, not having anything to say to her.

She looks around, and when she doesn't say anything, I ask, "Why are you here, Amelia?"

She bites the inside of her cheek, "I wanted to say sorry." She cocks her head to the side. "I was tired of living the way I had been. Tired of not making enough to survive. Tired of Eddie and his bullshit. Tired of going nowhere." She shrugs her shoulders.

"I saw y'all moving out and moving on. First Toni, and Alex keeping her away from me. Then Alex. And who would have ever thought Alex would make it out of the hood? And now you too. And I'm stuck there. I thought if you and I got together, I could get out too. I don't want to stay there. Be like my mom, working her whole life, for what? To still have nothing."

"You have to want to do it on your own. Yeah, we've had help, but we are working to make shit happen."

"I know. After that day at the garage, I realized I was acting like Toni's mom. Someone she hates. I couldn't be that person. Relying on a guy to save me. So I left the apartment. Luckily, we were at the end of the lease. I told you I broke up with Eddie. I'm back at my mom's, and I'm looking for a job I can balance while taking classes. I'm going to do it on my own. That way I can be proud of me. I just came by to pay you for fixing my car and to say thank you. You have been a friend. One I can count on. And I almost ruined it. And for that I'm sorry."

She comes in close hugging me. I wrap my arms around her, sorry she's hurting but knowing she has found her strength to do what she needs to. She pulls away and pulls some money from her back pocket.

"It's probably not enough for everything you've fixed on my car, but I'm trying to make amends." She hands me the money, then places her hand on my cheek. She surprises me as she tiptoes and places a quick kiss on my lips.

"Bye." She says, turning around to get in her car.

When I look up, I see Ritza's car stopped. I freeze knowing this scene could look all kinds of wrong. I need to explain and fast. She's watching me, but as soon as I move toward her, she peels out, speeding away.

"FUCK!" I yell my body tensing, wanting to punch something.

Amelia looks back at me eyes wide, "Was that her?"

"What the fuck do you think?" I reply harshly.

Amelia gets in her car and drives away.

I run back to my apartment, grabbing my phone and hitting Ritza's name.

Rings once and sent to voicemail.

"Bonita, come back please. It isn't what you think. It was a friend. Her name's Amelia, and she came to pay me for some work I did on her car. Please come back."

I hang up and call again. Ring and voicemail.

"Please pick up."

I wait a moment, hoping she listens to the messages, and then try again. Voicemail. She turned off her phone. Fuck. Fuck. Fuck. What the hell am I going to do now?

I grab my keys and head over to Cici's. Maybe that's where she went.

Her car isn't in the parking lot, but maybe she parked somewhere else to throw me off. I get out and knock on her door. No one answers, and there is no movement inside. To Damian's garage. I may get my ass handed to me, but I'll gladly take it if I can talk to her.

As I drive by, the shop is closing, and her car isn't there.

I don't know where she lives. She has purposefully kept this from me. Back to my apartment to continue calling and texting her.

————

A TWELVE PACK of beers and a few shots of tequila does not mix with the morning sun. My head is pounding. I look at my phone, and still no missed calls or texts from Ritza. I don't know how many I sent last night, but it was probably bordering on stalkerish.

The sound of the front door opening has me sitting up too quickly, and the room spins out of control, so I shut my eyes.

"Reinforcements are here." I hear Toni's voice.

Why is she here? I fall back onto my pillow, willing the room to stop spinning. Lola must be here too as I feel two people climb into my bed.

"Why are you here?" I mumble.

"Because you need us," Lola answers.

"Why do I need you?"

"Because you're hurting, and we know what that feels like."

Why in the hell did I call Alex last night? Of course, he was going to tell Lola.

"Just go. I'm fine." I roll over, placing my face in the pillow.

"We brought Gatorade for you. Figured you'd need hydration. Take some ibuprofen, and let's get the day started. We'll figure out how you can win her back," Lola says, too chipper.

"I told you Amelia was bad news. Didn't I tell you to stay away from her? You have this need to fix and take care of everyone. Some don't deserve it. You—"

"Let's not rehash old shit," Lola interrupts Toni's rant. "Nothing we can do about that now. Let's figure out what we *can* do."

I groan, knowing these two will not be leaving me alone. I might as well get out of bed now and make them take me to get some food. That and I have to take a piss.

CHAPTER 15

RITZA

I haven't left my bed in two days. Cici stayed with me all day yesterday. I made her turn off her phone because Javie also tried calling her. I just can't. Staying in bed hasn't helped much either, but what else can I do? It's not like I can forget about him by going out with someone else. I can't go to a bar and get drunk. I'm stuck. Again.

Each time I close my eyes, all I see is Javie with his arms around that voluptuous woman. The short shorts with her butt cheeks hanging out. The crop top with her midriff showing. Hair and makeup done to perfection. And then that kiss. The way they looked at each other. I was so dumb. I knew he had needs. I knew it, and I chose to ignore it. Live in ignorance. And all that did was make me look like a fool.

My chest physically hurts. Not like the panic attacks I was having. But an emptiness. A loneliness.

My door opens, and my parents walk in.

"Come on downstairs. Family meeting," my dad says softly.

"I'm not up for it," I respond, turning over and facing the wall.

"It's not up for debate. Get up," he says a bit more firmly.

"Fine." I growl, sitting up and throwing my blankets off. I grab a hoodie that's laying on the floor, pulling it on over my head.

I follow them down the stairs to the living room where Damian and Cici are already sitting on the love seat. I roll my eyes. *What is this? An intervention for an addict?*

"Cici has already shared what happened with us," my dad begins, "but—"

"Then what the hell do you need me down here for!" I shout.

"We want to know it from your perspective. So much has been going on that you haven't shared with us. You were dating someone. Going out. Spending time at his place. We were giving you time to process, but now we want to know everything." My dad continues, ignoring my interruption.

Tears begin to fall. After the past couple of days, I don't know how I could have any more.

"He's different. He's calm and strong at the same time. I feel safe around him. Like nothing could ever hurt me." I stop at that statement because he did. He has…had…the ability to hurt me.

"Keep going," my mom prompts.

"It started out small. Lunch at the garage. I was able to be around him and not panic. So then I invited him to our taco Tuesdays. When those went well, and I couldn't be the strange girl that could only go out once a week, we started eating at other places. Restaurants were always safe with him. And even if I felt an attack coming, somehow he was able to keep it at bay."

"What did he do?" Damian asks.

"Nothing. He doesn't even know what happened or that I have the attacks. It was just his presence."

"Why him?" Damian asks.

"I don't know." I shrug, not having an answer.

"Were y'all exclusive?" Damian continues.

"We hadn't had that talk, so…" I shrug again.

"There's more too." Cici jumps into the conversation. "She's met his family. She goes out with all of them too. She even went to that new venue that opened up, At the Corner"

My mom's eyes widen. "Really?"

I nod. Nothing to hide anymore.

"So you've been going out and meeting new people. That's huge," my mom says, smiling.

"Yes. But I've only been able to do that with Javie. If he's with me, I'm okay. I can feel the nerves, but if I have his hand or I can see him, somehow, magically the panic stays away."

"And he's seeing someone else?" There's an edge to Damian's tone.

"Yes," I say, as Cici says, "No."

"Well, which is it," Damian growls.

"I don't think he is. I don't know who that girl was, but why would he be calling and texting me nonstop if he didn't give a shit about Ritz?" She's shaking her head.

Damian fists his hands, running them over his legs.

"Just stop. It's my fault. I'm broken. I couldn't give him what he needs, and he moved on," I blurt out to protect Javie. My heart may be shattered, but I always knew in the back of my mind that it would end this way.

"That motherfucker." Damian shoots up from his seat.

"Enough!" my dad barks at Damian. "That's not going to help anything."

Damian sits back down, his jaw clenching.

"What do you mean, you couldn't give him what he needs?" my dad turns to me.

OMG, is he really thinking I'm going to talk about this with everyone in the room?

I stay silent, shaking my head.

"Can I?" Cici looks to me.

I know my family's stubbornness, and no one is leaving until the question is answered.

"She's talking about sex. Since she feels she can't or won't be able to go there with a guy again, he moved on to someone who would."

I keep my gaze low. I focus on Damian's arms tensing.

"They kind of talked about it. But she was never honest with him with what she's been dealing with," she finishes.

"Why wouldn't you just tell him what you went through? Not specifics, but just that you were raped and are learning to heal," my mom's soft voice questions.

"So he could feel sorry for me? Or disgusted? Or grossed out cause I'm tainted and damaged? Can't stop seeing her now because it would make him the asshole for breaking it off with someone so vulnerable. No thanks. He was never going to know."

"Baby, you're going to have to be honest about your past with the person you become involved with. You can't start a relationship on dishonesty. It won't last." My mom tries to guide me.

"Then I guess I won't be in one. I won't share that part of my life. Once I can deal with it, I plan on burying it deep down and never thinking about it again."

"You may feel that now, and you have every right to, but you don't know how you will feel three months, six months, two years from now. So please don't make a life decision when you are still riding on intense emotions," my dad says, the voice of reason.

"Fine." I pull my legs up and hug them to my chest.

"Now what?" Damian drops his head to the side cracking his neck.

"Now nothing. We let Ritza's heart heal, and then she continues the work she has begun," my dad answers him.

"I can't do the work anymore. I can't go anywhere. Not without him." I bury my face in my knees.

"Let's not think about that now. Meeting's over," dad says, so I instantly get up to head back to bed. That's the only place I want to be. The only place that's now safe. The only place I can avoid the panic attacks being around people cause.

I should have known it wouldn't be that easy. After a few quiet moments in bed, trying to figure out how to piece together a shattered heart, my bedroom door opens and Cici walks in with Damian.

"Sorry about the 'intervention.'" Cici air quotes with her fingers and smirks.

"No you're not," I throw back at her. "I'm pissed at you for not warning me. And what was that all about? Huh? It's been like two fuckin' days."

She shrugs. "Fine. You want the truth? I'm not sorry. I need my friend back! And I saw her again. I saw her coming back from the dead. I know she's still there, and I can't stand knowing you are getting in your own damn way!" Her voice increases with each word she says.

"Just get out!" I yell. I can't listen to her right now. She's speaking a truth I can't handle at the moment.

Damian sits on the bed and pulls me into his chest, wrapping me tightly in his arms. I'm shaking with fear, anger, confusion, and pain. I can't handle any more right now. My heart is the only thing that is shattered, but I'm close to crumbling completely.

"You know Cici and I don't always see eye to eye, but right now I'm going to agree with her. You have done so much. You have conquered a few demons. And I know you think it's him.

Javie. Maybe you drew strength from him… But *you* did it. *You* controlled it. You used him to keep you centered. But it was all you. You can't discount that. You chose to move along. To heal. To get stronger. You. You did all that."

His arms tighten around me, holding me together, making sure I don't fall apart.

They give me time. Time to absorb what they said. Time to process. Our deep breaths and the usual neighborhood sounds fill the room.

"What if I can't?" I say, barely a whisper.

"You start where you were before. At taco Tuesday. We go like we always do…then take it from there."

I pull away from Damian and look up to him. He just nods at me, agreeing with Cici.

"Want me to go with you?" he asks.

Do I? Indecision strikes me. I don't want to go at all, but if I do, will Damian there make it easier?

I shrug. "If you want." Damian eyes glance at Cici. I turn to look at her, and she has nodded.

"I'll meet y'all there." He nods at me then stands, leaving my room.

I fall back into my pillow, wrapping my mind around the excursion they are expecting of me tomorrow.

"You've got this, chica. Between the chihuahua and the pit bull, you're safe." She winks at me with a goofy smile.

Cici will follow me anywhere. She'd go to the depths of hell for me if I needed her to. The description of herself and Damian is spot on. She is full of bark but wouldn't hurt a fly, and Damian is calm until you mess with something he loves.

———

Back in my hoodie and jeans, I'm sitting with a large margarita in front of me. I don't want to be here. I don't want to be anywhere but my bed. Damian is sipping a beer, looking uncomfortable, and Cici is chatting about her classes and people on campus.

"If you are going to look this bored, why didn't you ask the guys to come babysit with you?" I say sarcastically. He shouldn't have come because I'm just feeling worse for ruining his evening. That's all I've been doing since…ruining people's lives.

"I'm not bored. Just…" He doesn't finish his sentence.

"Just what?" I raise my voice, frustration setting in.

"Can we talk, bonita?" His voice. My heart drops, and a heat floods my system. Tears collect in my eyes instantly.

I turn around to look at him and notice Toni and Lola standing with him.

JAVIE

There is more pain in her eyes than I've ever seen. She's usually swimming in it, but today, she's drowning. It guts me knowing I am the cause. I glance at the table and notice Cici smiling at me and Damian tense. I know he's only worried about her, and I would be acting the same if it was Lola or Toni on the other side of this misunderstanding.

I kneel close to her chair. "Hey. Don't cry. I'm here. I got you."

Her nostrils flair, as she shakes her head back and forth.

"I've got you." I place my hand on hers, which are laying on her lap.

Tears begin to fall. She stays quiet.

"Go on. Let him explain," Damian says gruffly.

She whips to look at him, and he nods his head to the front of the restaurant.

"We'll join you while we wait," Lola's cheerily announces.

Ritza stands slowly. I grab her hand, squeezing it. The

feeling of completeness with her close to me is undeniable. We walk to the doors, heading outside where there are tables set up for people waiting.

"Sit with me?" I ask, unsteady on how to begin.

She pulls a chair and sits down. Her gaze is focused on the table. How I wish she would look at me. I need her to look at me.

"I know what you saw the other day could look bad. I know that. And I'm so sorry you had to experience it. But know that it isn't what you think." I stop. It is bad. I have slept with Amelia. But I would never cheat and hurt Ritza on purpose.

"Then what was it? You kiss every girl like that?" she spits out angrily without looking up.

"Of course not, bonita. And I didn't kiss her, she kissed—"

"What the fuck ever! Semantics!" She stands abruptly.

I shoot out of my chair with her.

"I don't want her. I only want you." I plead with her to listen.

She looks up at me, and the venom she pierces me with is a shot to the heart.

"Please. I'll tell you everything. If you want to know."

She shrugs her shoulders, rolling her eyes.

"Sit." I point at the chair she vacated.

Her eyes dart, looking at everything except me, but she sits. She waves her hand at me, raising her brow. She still doesn't look me in the eyes, her gaze on my chest.

"Amelia is a girl I hooked up with before. She is an old friend of Toni's. I've known her since she was in elementary school. It happened during a time she was broken up with her boyfriend…They are always on and off. We were both in a bad place. It was before I met you." She still refuses to meet my gaze.

"I told her about you when she came to me again during another break from her boyfriend. I told her I couldn't because I was seeing you. She didn't interest me anymore because I only want you." Her eyes widen as she looks up. She swallows hard.

"I only want you," I stress. I continue with the story, leaving nothing out—even Amelia's performance in the garage—and ending with her paying me and apologizing.

"She's out of my life now. I can't have her destroying something I'm working so hard to build with you." I stroke her cheek, wiping the tears that have fallen. At least she's not pushing my hand away. She's quiet, watching me.

"Talk to me," I plead.

She minutely shakes her head, and my chest tightens.

"Talk to me, bonita." I grab her hand, which is laying on the table.

Her chest rises and falls. "I don't know what to say."

"Say you believe me. That you know I only want you."

She tucks her lip into her mouth then releases it. "Why? I've asked you before. Why bother with me when you know I'm…"

"You're right. I know there's something. I know you're in pain. But I want to be with you. I want to walk beside you while you figure it out."

"But I can't give you what Amelia did." She pulls her hand away tucking it in her lap.

"I don't care. I'll wait. I'll wait because you're worth the wait." I squeeze her knee. "I'll wait because I've fallen for you."

She watches me, biting her lip.

"And if I'm not mistaken, we did start having our own fun." I wink, and her cheeks fill with color.

"Are you sure?" Her voice trembles.

"Positive." I open my arms to her, and she gets up, sitting

back down on my lap and wrapping her arms around my neck. Her warm breath against my skin is welcome.

I run my fingers through her long, chocolate hair.

"I've got you. Will you please remember that?" I whisper to her.

She nods her head, not letting go.

"Come on. I'm sure your brother wants his time to kill me." A soft giggle tells me what I said is probably true.

She continues hugging me for a few more moments. I'm hoping she knows I'm the life vest she needs right now.

"I must look horrible now." She pulls away from me, her eyes a bit reddened from the crying.

"Never." I place my hand on her cheek, letting it glide down to her neck then pulling her close, her lips meeting mine.

As much as I don't want to, I pull away. "Time to head back."

She stands, extending her hand to me, walking back to the table.

When Lola sees us walking in, she taps Toni on the shoulder and points in our direction. They stand and move to the side of the table.

"You don't have to leave," Ritza says to them.

"Our work here is done. I figured it would be better if we came with Javie for moral support as opposed to Alex. You know how he can get, and there's no telling how they," Toni points at Damian, "would get along. Especially when it's family involved." She winks.

"They do seem to be cut from the same cloth." Ritza nods in agreement. "But Javie is not that different."

Lola laughs while shaking her head. "You'll learn. He may have the tendencies, but it's just the protectiveness that comes out in him. Now Alex is on a whole other level with his control-freak ways."

"It was nice meeting you, Cici," Lola gives her a small wave, "and you, Damian." She nods at him. "Javie's a good guy. I promise you can trust him." Lola pats my cheek, walking toward the door.

"Nice meeting y'all," Toni says walking away, then turning back to me. "I'll call you later."

I give her a quick nod, taking the seat she vacated.

"All figured out?" Cici starts.

I look to Ritza because she's the one in control here.

"Yeah. Javie explained what happened," Ritza answers her.

"Mind telling me?" Damian says with an edge to his voice. I figured it would be coming, but I thought I would be getting the threatening big brother call from him later. Later, away from Ritza, with no witnesses.

I look to Ritza for guidance. I won't divulge anything she doesn't want me to. This is between us. But I also won't shrink down to him either. Ritza shrugs her shoulders and nods once.

"Ritza saw an old friend kiss me. She came to say good-bye because we had a past." I keep it simple.

"Say good-bye?" Cici asks.

"I told her that we could no longer hook up the way we had in the past because I was seeing Ritza. She hadn't taken the news well before. She came to apologize."

"So you just go around using girls?" Damian fires at me his eyes narrowed.

"Not at all. But if that's what you choose to believe, I'm not arguing with you about it."

"Damian," Ritza says tersely. When he looks at her, she shakes her head at him.

"You know you can't use my sister like that. She's no—"

"Stop!" Ritza interrupts. "That's enough. What we do or don't do will be up to us. We're not talking about it here or ever. What happens between us will be between us." She waves her hand between the two of us. "We are going to go."

She turns to Cici. "Sorry to leave you."

"Go. I figured you might."

"Huh?"

"I might have confirmed it to Javie that we would be here. Why do you think I didn't argue about Damian coming? You really think I wanted him here ruining our fun?" A guilty smile spreads. "I have a friend waiting for me. I'll be fine." She rolls her eyes and winks at Ritza.

"I should have known…as much as you were defending him." She stands up, giving Cici a kiss on the cheek. "I'll call you later."

"You better."

I stand with Ritza, wondering where she wants to go but knowing I'll follow her anywhere.

I walk us to my car, unlocking the door and opening it for her to get in. Once I'm in I turn to her. "Where to?"

"My house. I'm guessing my parents knew about this plan of Cici's. They will either be waiting to console me or to be gossipy."

"I'm meeting the parents?" I tease her.

"Yes." A slight blush fills her cheeks.

"Before that happens, I want to make sure you know you are the only one in my life. I'm not seeing, talking, or sleeping with anyone else. It's you. Only you."

"Are you sure that's what you want?" she asks quietly.

"Absolutely. There is only you. I told you…I've fallen for you."

"Are…you…uh…sure?"

"No doubt in my mind."

She turns her head and looks out the passenger window.

"What's wrong?" My legs begin trembling at her lack of enthusiasm. I thought it would go much better than this.

Silence. I run my hand down her sweatshirt-covered arm. I feel her tense under my touch.

"Talk to me."

"What if you are wasting your time with me? You know I'm…" She doesn't finish her statement.

"I'm not wasting my time. And even if you call it off in the future, I won't regret it. I don't know what's going on, but I told you, I'm ready to listen to whatever it is when you're ready to share."

"Okay."

"Okay, what?"

"We're together. We're exclusive."

CHAPTER 16

RITZA

I HAVE A BOYFRIEND. A BOYFRIEND. SOMETHING I DIDN'T think I would ever have again. I'm not sure how long it will last, but for now…right now, I want it and need it.

We walk into my parents' house and are greeted right away.

"Hello. Welcome." My mom walks into the entryway from the living room. "I'm Maria and this is my husband, David. I'm so glad we finally get to meet you. Even though we only learned about you yesterday." She's too frank.

"Hi. I'm sorry about that. I'm Javier Martinez," Javie apologizes, smiling.

"The person who should be sorry is Maritza. But we'll let her off this time."

"Okay. You met. Since we didn't eat at the restaurant, we picked up some food. We're going up to my room to eat." Telling your parents that you will be up in your bedroom with a guy feels very high schooly. I will need to figure out how to move out of their house.

"We are headed to meet some friends. You will have to come to dinner soon." My mom smiles at Javie, giving him a hug goodbye. My dad shakes his hand and follows my mom out the door.

"Do they really have plans?" Javie asks as soon as the door closes behind them.

"Don't know. I don't keep up with them." But I secretly know they are probably giving me and us some space. "Come on."

I go up the stairs, and Javie follows behind me. I open the door to my room and am horrified. I forgot what a mess it was —bed unmade, clothes thrown about. All the things I had been ignoring while spending the last few days hiding.

"Sorry. I kinda haven't paid attention to cleaning the past couple of days," I tell Javie as he walks in.

He places the bag he was holding on the dresser and pulls me into a hug. "I'm sorry I hurt you. That you had to see that. And you had to go through that. If I could erase the last few days, I would."

Tingles run through me feeling his body flush against mine. I want nothing more than to get into bed with him and snuggle as close to him as I can.

"It was a misunderstanding. And if I would have answered your calls or texts, I would have known the truth sooner. I wouldn't have had to go through that." I pick up the bag, placing it on the bed, crawling to the middle.

He grabs a burger out of the bag and sits on the desk chair.

"You don't have to sit there. Come on." I pat the bed close to me. I sit on the edge my back against the headboard, then grab the remote and turn on the TV.

He comes and sits next to me, but he's stiff and uncomfortable. He takes a bite from his burger.

"What's wrong?" I ask.

"Nothing. What are we watching?" he asks, changing the subject.

"Something is. You're sitting there like a statue." I bounce on the bed. "If you're going to be weird around me…what are we doing?"

"We've always avoided the bed. I just…"

"I know. But…" I lift my shoulders and let them fall, "I'm fine with this. We could have stayed downstairs, but I like my room more. It's fine. I promise."

He grabs the bag, bringing it closer and handing me the other burger. He places the fries on the top of the large bag in between us. He leans back, lounging against the headboard.

I scroll though the streaming app, finding a comedy to watch.

———

"Bonita," I feel a tapping on my shoulder. "Wake up, baby. I should go."

I open my eyes and realize I'm tangled in Javie; my head is on his chest.

"What time is it?" I don't remember falling asleep.

"It's just after five in the morning." He kisses my forehead. "I'll call you later." He begins to roll me off him.

I fell asleep. Hard. I didn't toss and turn the way I have been. I didn't have a nightmare. I just slept.

He sits on the edge as I roll over closer to him. He brushes my hair away from my face and runs his hand down my cheek. He leans in and places a short kiss to my lips.

"Should I be worried about walking out and your parents?" A playful smile spreads.

"No. It will be fine."

"I'll see you later." He stands, walking out of my bedroom.

My eyes instantly close again.

———

"Well, well…someone slept in this morning," my mom teases as I walk into the kitchen.

"I did. I haven't slept that good in so long. Since I started counseling again," I answer her.

"Javie spent the night?" She knows the answer. I roll my eyes.

"You know he did. I don't even remember falling asleep. He just woke me up this morning when he was leaving. Thank God I didn't have any nightmares. How embarrassing would that have been?"

"Maybe you didn't have them because he's slaying those dragons." She finishes rinsing the last dish, placing it in the dishwasher.

"I was asleep. How would I even know that he was there?" The thought of sleeping peacefully because he was there is too good to be true.

"The brain works in mysterious ways. I don't know, but last night with him is the first night that you didn't have one. Not even a small one."

Could he be a solace to my troubled mind? The idea is absurd. Right? I grab a glass from the cabinet, pouring myself a glass of water.

Wanting to ignore that idea for the time being, I inform my mom I'll be going to the garage to get some work done.

THE DAY PASSES QUICKLY, and before I know it, Damian is quitting for the day. We have avoided each other all day. I'm not sure if he's uncomfortable with the thought of me and Javie. Me and sex. Me hiding my story. Whatever it is, he hasn't come into the office all day, which is a rarity. He is usually in and out all day while I'm here.

The door to the garage opens, and I'm expecting one of the other guys to come in as they have done all day, to cool off or grab drinks from the fridge. But to my surprise, Damian stands at the door.

"Hey. What were you working on today?" His jaw is ticking, so I know he's not here to talk about work.

"You don't want to ask me that. What do you really want to know?" I take a deep breath, knowing it's honesty with him and my parents from now on.

"Why did you hide everything that was going on?" He takes the couple of steps to the chairs in front of his desk.

Guilty of lying or, more accurately, omission of information, I squirm in my seat. "I… It was all too much, and I wasn't sure how to say it."

"Say what?" He leans forward, placing his elbows on his thighs.

"All of it." I bite the inside of my cheek.

"How did it start? Did he ask you out?" I can see he's having trouble with this. His forearms flex.

"No. I did." I point at myself, taking a second to gather my thoughts, "When I met him the first time when he came for the interview, there was just something about him. He didn't cower when he met you. He looked at me like he saw me. Not just some girl he wanted to pick up but *me*. Every guy since…you know…either ignored me or checked me out. He did neither. His smile was inviting."

"That's it? He saw you?"

"Kind of. But the more I saw him, the more I wanted to be around him. The day you guys tried to do your thing and establish dominance, he didn't falter. He took y'all in and had this who-the-eff-cares attitude. I have never met a guy who could look at me so tenderly but stand up to y'all at the same time. I'm not going to lie, I was intrigued. He did it again yesterday when you tried to pull your asshole-big-brother attitude. He sat there, never flinching, just answering you. He wasn't scared of you. I have a feeling if it came down to it, and punches were thrown, he could give you a run for your money."

"That's good to know. You like someone who could protect you if it came down to it."

"Yes. And you met his cousin and brother's girlfriend. They are a tight-knit family. His brother is pretty much a carbon copy of you and your tendencies, but he's a little scarier." I laugh knowing Damian won't find that funny.

He rolls his eyes at me, sitting back, extending his legs out.

"I don't know what's going to come of this, but I want to try. I need to try. He's the only one who has made me feel safe in my own skin. Even when the panic attacks begin, he brings me back, without trying."

"Does he still want to work here?"

My eyes widen. "You would be willing to hire him full time?"

"Yes. Especially if this place gets busier. I will need him here so you have your touchstone to keep you balanced."

"And what if things between us don't work out?"

"We'll cross that bridge when it comes."

I nod. "I don't know if he's looking. He's still working at both the garage he was at and doing welding jobs."

"I'll give him a call in the morning. Going over there tonight?"

"I wanted to."

"Give him the heads up, and tell him I'll call." He stands. "Ready to get out of here?"

In my car I send Javie a quick text.

Want company tonight?

A reply comes quickly.

Yes.

Be there in a bit.

CHAPTER 17

JAVIE

I yell, "Come in" when I hear a knock on the door. I'm busy browning ground beef for some spaghetti. I've never made dinner for Ritza and wanted to spoil her a bit.

"What are you making?" she asks, joining me.

I turn around, giving her a quick kiss, then answering, "Spaghetti. Nothing fancy. Go sit. I'm almost done."

"You didn't have to. We could have picked something up," she says, sitting in a chair after grabbing a water bottle from the fridge.

"I know. But now that we have formally established we are a couple, I thought this was the next normal."

"Thank you." A genuine smile spreads across her face, reaching her eyes. There is a lightness about her today.

It's easy and comfortable with Ritza. Talking about nothing and everything while I finish dinner. She asks about the engagement party planning.

"Now that we are a couple, you realize you are my plus one, right?" I say to her.

"I am?" Her brows pull together.

"Will you go with me?"

She hesitates before answering, "Uh…yeah…sure." Not the most comforting answer, but we can address it later.

I serve our plates and sit down with her at the counter.

"By the way…uh…Damian is looking to hire a couple of people full time, and he said he was going to call you about a job tomorrow morning." She smiles, taking a bite of her pasta.

"Oh. Really?" I was not expecting that.

She nods her head, chewing, eyes excited.

"I'm not really looking for full-time right now." My lips pull down, not wanting to disappoint her.

"I thought you were?" She wrings her hands together.

"I was, but now with Lola investing in a garage for Alex and I…"

"That's what y'all have been talking about? I didn't feel I had the right to ask anything about it then."

"Yeah. Her grandfather has the business mind, and we were running our model by him. Making sure we aren't wasting Lola's money."

"Oh." She drops her head a bit, and she begins playing with her pasta, twirling it around her fork.

"What's wrong?"

She doesn't answer, focusing on the food she's not eating.

"Nothing." She twirls up a noodle and places it in her mouth.

"Talk to me. This is only going to work if you talk to me," I probe.

She chews still staring at her food. I watch as she swallows, then, "It's just, I got excited about you being at the garage with me. Having lunch with you. It was dumb."

"That's not dumb. It sounds like heaven. Having you so close." She looks up at me, and I give her a sexy smirk. "But this is our chance. To have something of our own. You know we came from nothing, and we can make an honest name for ourselves with this business."

"I know. And I'm happy for you. I'm just disappointed for myself. Being a little selfish." She gives me a tight-lipped smile. I know there is more to her story, but I need to take my time for her to let me in all the way. Slowly, but surely.

We get through dinner and are watching some mystery series. Laying on the couch again. Her body flush against mine. My hand splayed on her stomach, feeling it rise and fall with her breaths. She squirms just a tad, rubbing her butt on my crotch and making my cock awaken.

"Javie?"

"Yes."

"Uh…will…uh… Will you…" She whispers, voice trembling.

"Give you another orgasm?" I smile into her neck, kissing it softly and letting my lips linger.

Her body trembles. I slide my hand up, cupping her breast, squeezing softly, letting my thumb rub over her nipple. I can feel it harden under the shirt and thin bra she's wearing. Her body responds to every touch.

"I need you closer," she says so quietly.

"Tell me how."

RITZA

I want to feel him. Right here, tucked into him, is not enough anymore. How? That's the big question. My pulse quickens, excitement zings through my body.

I place my hand on top of his and guide it down, then back up under my shirt. How does his warm hand on my bare stomach give me chills? His fingers graze my skin as his lips nip and kiss my neck.

"You are in control." His voice is gravelly and deep.

Control. I'm in control. That word gives me comfort.

"Keep going." My eyes close.

"You gotta tell me when."

A trail of heat follows where he slides his hand up to my breast. He pinches my nipple through my bra. A loud moan escapes my lips. He glides his hand down, and I automatically lift my leg, spreading myself for him. He cups my sex and a thrill shoots through my whole body.

I want more. I turn over to face him.

"Can we move this to your bed?" I run my palm over his scruffy cheek.

"If that's what you want." He kisses me, his arms tightening around me.

I stand and wait for him to follow me. His bed has always been the elephant in the room we don't speak of or look at. I stand at the foot of his bed with him in front of me. I grab the hem of his T-shirt and begin sliding it up. He takes over, sliding it over his head.

I place my hand on his chest and let it slide down, appreciating his ripple of muscles that lead to the V. I feel him shiver. I sit on the bed and scoot up. The desire in his eyes thrills me.

He crawls up the bed, lying next to me. I kiss him, the need becoming urgent. His tongue grazes my lips, and I open letting him explore. A clashing of tongues, sucking and licking. My body is burning like never before.

"I need you." My voice is hoarse.

"I've got you, mi bonita." He pauses then says, "Take off your shirt."

My heart races as I sit up, pulling it over my head. Can I go further than this? My nerves are clashing with the exhilaration. I turn around, facing him, and seeing him so relaxed eases some of the worries. One arm is tucked behind his head.

"You're going to have to…" He wants me in control, but I

need him to guide me. I need to follow him. At least right now. I freeze, not knowing what to do. Again, I'm not a virgin. I know how it all works, but I feel like I might short-circuit.

He sits up, placing his hand on my neck then slides it down to my shoulder. The small connection centers me.

"If you're a virgin, you need to tell me," he says casually.

I shake my head. "I'm not."

"I know intimacy makes you nervous. I don't know why, but I won't be the one who ruins it for you."

"You can't ruin it. If anything, you…" We are dancing too close to the truth. The room starts to spin.

"Stay with me," he whispers close to my ear. "You're about to leave me."

His voice, smooth and calm, tamps down the feeling of anxiety that was about to bubble out of control.

"I'm here," I say, not knowing if I'm making any sense, but not wanting to ruin what we began.

A trail of soft kisses on my neck relaxes me. "As soon as I feel you tense or leave me, we stop." He pulls back, placing his forehead on mine.

I want him to take control. I want him to take care of me. I need to say so much, but the words are stuck—fearing I may divulge something he can't ever know about.

"We aren't doing anything without your consent. We will lay here, and I'll hold you all night. I have no problem with that. But if you want something more, you need to tell me."

"I need you. I just…"

"Shhh." He places his index finger to my lips. "You don't have to explain. At least not right now. When you're ready."

His fingers slide down my chin to my throat, continuing down, stopping between my breasts. His lips come to mine as he guides us back down until his head hits the pillow. He has me on top of him as his hands roam my back, unbuckling my bra.

He rolls me over, holding himself on his forearm and looking down at me. His eyes roam my body slowly. With just the tips of his fingers, he begins trailing a line starting at my wrist moving up my arm until he reaches my shoulder. A couple of gentle kisses follow the line of his path. From my shoulder, he continues to the center of my chest and traces the curve of my right breast, gently kissing the flesh bulging out of my bra. He pulls my bra, and I let him slide it off my arms. The trail of kisses continues down to my ribcage to the flat of my stomach. His mouth exploring my body creates a hunger I didn't think would happen again.

I reach down to the band of my yoga pants and push them down. My panties slide off with the pants, and for a moment, I feel too exposed. Too open. Unprotected. I stop, not knowing if I can continue.

"Let's cover you up," Javie purrs.

Luckily his bed was unmade, so he's able to pull his sheet out from under me. Once I'm tucked in, I realize I miss his body next to mine.

"Get in with me."

He rolls over and tucks his legs under the sheet, placing his hand back on my stomach. He circles the area for a moment before asking, "Need help with your pants?"

I realize I hadn't finished taking my pants off when I suddenly felt overwhelmed. But now, concealed from imaginary eyes and with his hand moving closer to my mound, I work to remove them as gracefully as yoga pants allow.

I'm completely naked under this sheet. I'm trusting him with my mind and body right now, and he has no idea how significant that is.

He brings his lips to hover just over mine, gliding and barely touching. "You are beautiful."

His hand slides lower, cupping my center applying just a

bit of pressure. I squirm under his touch, raising my hips for more contact.

"Are you sure you want to go further?" he says, his breath on my lips.

"Please." My chest rises and falls dramatically with anticipation.

Wetness pools between my legs as he spreads my folds and rubs my clit. I groan, and he captures it with a heated kiss. I buck up, wanting more. Needing more. A finger is playing at my entrance. Rubbing. Circling. Then I feel it enter my body. A foreign but fantastic feeling. I was terrified of what I would do when something entered me again, but…

"Agh…" I let out a loud groan when I feel him fill me with another finger as his thumb circles the most sensitive spot.

He takes my nipple into his mouth and sucks, and when he releases it, he licks the hardened peak. He continues working my pussy and sucking and kissing my breast until I'm climbing, light-headed, tingly…until my whole body explodes.

His arm comes around me pulling me flush against him. Tucked into his chest I can feel the beat of his heart. I take a deep, satisfied breath closing my eyes relishing in the afterglow.

I can't believe I just had another extremely intense orgasm. Javie's slow and sensual motions, taking his time, prolonging the wait, teasing, created a whirlwind of sensations. And now he's holding me close with no expectation of me giving him a release I know he needs. *Next time*. Those are the two words he said. A next time. Just thinking about it sends a thrill between my legs.

I squeeze myself closer to him as I run my fingers up and down his chest. The warmth of his skin on mine welcome. I close my eyes, not wanting to leave the safety his arms provide.

———

I FEEL A SHAKE. "Bonita, you feel asleep. Do you need to go home?"

I was sleeping so soundly, it takes me a second to realize where I am. And the crazy thing is that I'm not even panicked or worried. Somehow, I know I'm safe here.

"Uh…" my mind races with wanting to stay but knowing I would worry my parents if I just didn't show up.

"Come on. I'll follow you home." He places a kiss on the top of my head.

I can't leave. I don't want to leave. I belong here. At least I want to belong here.

"Uh…" Why can't I find words or just ask for what I want? I never had this problem before. I did what I wanted. Asked for what I wanted. I wasn't always afraid.

"Wanna stay with me?" How in the hell does he always figure out what I want or need? That's his superpower. Predicting what I'm too scared to say out loud.

"Yes."

"Do you need to let anyone know?"

"Let me send a text to my parents." I begin to get up. The covers fall, exposing my breasts, and I realize I'm still naked. The light on the stove provides the only illumination.

"I got it." He kisses my shoulder and gets out of bed to retrieve my phone from his kitchen counter.

He hands me the phone, getting back in bed. I send off a quick text to my mom and lay back down. Again, this is not the first guy I have slept with. Slept, slept. Not wink, wink, we "slept together." Always feeling anxious, fearing a panic attack will creep up for no apparent reason is getting old. How can I fix my brain that's as damaged as my privates?

It has been nice orgasming again. I questioned if it would be possible, especially after the trauma I endured. What am I saying? I don't even know what happened. Javie would have no reason to want to…as much as I think I want it now. Sex. His penis in my vagina. Why would he want to go there with me if he knew I have no idea what has been inserted in me?

All the doctors and nurses could speculate was I had something hard, a foreign object, placed inside of me. With the number of tears and lesions, that is their conclusion. Suddenly my eyes fill with tears I didn't anticipate, which flow down and hit his chest. I wipe my eyes, hoping he has fallen asleep and didn't feel them.

CHAPTER 18

JAVIE

She trusts me—this I know. I have no doubt, but I also know that she doesn't want to share the ghosts she is trying to fight. Should I ask, insist she share? I'd risk having her get mad, possibly leave, because I pushed. Pushed her when she wasn't ready. Talk about rock and hard place.

"Why are you crying, mi bonita?" I timidly ask.

Her body tenses as she slowly begins to peel away from me. I wrap my arm around her tighter keeping her in place.

"Go back to sleep. We don't have to talk about it now."

I feel her chest expand and a long breath against my chest. I kiss the top of her head, breathing in her sweet shampoo. The lavender scent is becoming one of my favorites. She's here with me, and that's all that matters.

———

The sliding of fingers on my chest wakes me. I open my eyes to her chin propped on her hand. A bit of makeup remnants are under her eyes, and even then, she is the most beautiful woman. She walks through life not knowing the effect she has on the male population. Not one for attention and still receives it.

Her quiet strength is unmistakable. The storm she is weathering is huge, but she continues to move forward. And the change I've seen in her over the past couple of months is amazing. I have stood by her, proving she could believe in me. Hoping she gives me some of the weight she is carrying.

"I could get used to waking up to this beautiful sight."

She rolls her eyes with a laugh. "I'm sure I look just the opposite." She wipes under her eyes, not removing any of yesterday's makeup.

"Not to me." I smile.

"I should get up and let you start your day."

She pushes herself up, but I grab her and bring her back down to lay on her back.

"Never leave my bed without a kiss, please." I meet her lips with mine for a quick kiss, then rub the tip of my nose to hers. "Now you can get up if you must." I roll onto my back.

She hesitates, looking down at her bare body.

"I should go so I can shower and head into the shop. With all the work lately, I've had my hands full keeping up with their orders and inventory."

As she sits up, my phone rings. "Can you bring me my phone?" I ask.

She pulls on one of my shirts that's thrown on the bed and walks to the coffee table where I left my phone last night. She looks at the screen, and her eyes widen. She turns the phone so I can see who is calling—Damian. I can't keep the smirk of a smile off my face as she hands me my phone.

"Hello."

"Hey, Javie. It's Damian. Do you have a minute to talk?"

"Yeah. Sure."

Ritza is watching me, eyes wide.

"Well. First off, uh…about my…uh, sister."

Do I have the upper hand here? Mr. "I Try to Intimidate Everyone by Being an Alpha," sounds unsure. "What about Ritza?"

Her eyes practically pop out of her head when I mention her name. She sits on the bed close to me, no doubt to try and listen to what he's saying.

"She, uh…has been through a lot recently and…uh…I just want to make sure you…uh…"

"What are you trying to tell me?" I push.

"Nothing. Just you better treat her right." His usual asshole demeanor shines again. "And I mean it. She isn't someone you can just mess with and toss aside."

"Wasn't planning to," I respond, bored.

Ritza creeps closer, so I turn to her, shaking my head and smiling. Her cheeks heat up as she rolls her eyes at me.

"Well, since that's out of the way. About the full-time position you were looking for. We are looking to hire a couple of guys, and I thought of you. You did a great job on that Camaro."

"Thanks for the offer. I could maybe put in some part-time hours, but…" The only reason I'm giving in to a few hours when I don't need them right now is to see Ritza. I know deep down she needs me there. Not sure why, but she does. "I'm working with my brother. We are going to be opening our own shop closer to downtown."

"You are?" Shock fills his voice.

"Yeah. We are still a few months out since we just bought the property, and we've got to do renovations to the building. Alex can handle the majority of that, so I'm free for a few hours to help y'all out until you find all the guys you need."

It feels good to say that. I didn't know the pride I would feel talking about a secure job, one that is my own.

"Oh. Well, yeah. Can you come in today and we can talk more about it?"

We finish up the conversation while I'm watching Ritza watch me.

"You'll be at the shop today?" I'm greeted by one of those rare smiles that reaches her eyes as she asks.

"Yup."

"Well, I better go then to shower and change to see you later." She kisses me, then bounces off the bed. She pulls on her panties and yoga pants. Not like I can see anything—my shirt covers to her mid-thigh. She grabs her bra and shirt and shoves them in her purse.

"I'm taking your shirt hostage." She lifts her shoulders with a sly smile.

"Not gonna lie, you in my shirt is doing things to me."

She blows an exaggerated kiss to me and walks out the door. I quickly get up to follow her out. She is riding a high right now and isn't thinking that I'm not walking her to her car, which she usually needs me to do.

She's at the bottom of the stairs when I walk out my door. I walk halfway down where I can see her walk the rest of the way safely. Once she has driven away, I go back upstairs with a new sense of us. An us that means something. An us that is growing into something more.

———

THE MEETING with the contractor working on the garage went well. They estimated about three months' work from start to finish. Lola and her grandfather have a list of things for Alex and I to learn or consider/plan before opening.

Staring at all kinds of foreign paperwork on Alex and Lola's kitchen table, I begin tapping the eraser end of the pencil. Where do we begin? Can I do this? I barely have a high school diploma, and Alex just got his GED less than a year ago. The garage and fixing cars is the easy part. It's all the other stuff that's blowing my mind—from budgets to contracts to naming the damn place.

"Can you stop?" Alex sits back down across from me, placing a can of soda in front of me.

"Stop what?" I snap.

"The eraser. It's annoying."

I drop the pencil, grabbing the can. He grabs a paper filled with all the construction costs.

"So far we are under budget. As long as no unexpected crap comes up, we stay in the black for construction. Have some room to breathe." Alex says. I'm not sure if he's speaking to me or just thinking out loud.

He places the paper down and lifts another, glancing it over then looking at me. "I can't let Lola down. We have got to make this work." A slight resignation fills his words.

This is the first time I've ever heard my brother worried about anything. He is usually the epitome of confidence. Growing up in the barrio, he watched and learned and let his cocky attitude lead him. Starting a legitimate business was never on our radar. Was never something we dreamed of as children. Never something we prepared ourselves for. But it's here. He's engaged to a sorority girl and about to be a father. Life has a funny way of working out.

And me, I'm also chasing a college girl who I'm certain is way fuckin' smarter than I am. At least book smarts. Like Lola, living the suburban life may not have taught her anything about street smarts.

"I know. I'm two hundred percent in. This is our chance to show the universe we aren't destined for the hood life." This small taste of life away from the hood makes me never want to go back. "What are you looking at?"

"Before we can start marketing anything, according to

Lola, we need to name the place. She said once that is done, there is a company we'll start working with for our logo design."

"This is surreal, isn't it?" I look around. The normality of us sitting in a spacious apartment with new furniture is so strange.

"Yeah. Lola wants to buy a house. And the ones she has shown me are…" He trails off, eyes distant.

"Are?" I drag out the word, trying to get his attention.

"Knowing Lola and her lifestyle and what her dad's house looks like, what do you think?" he grumbles.

"Ah…that's what has you in this mood." I laugh. Alex can't always call the shots and be the person 'in charge' with Lola. He is adjusting to letting her take charge. It's not sitting well, but he's swallowing his machismo crap and playing nice.

"Shut the fuck up!" He drops his head to his shoulder, then to the other side, cracking his neck.

"You can try and fool someone else, but you forget I've got your number," I joke with him. "But if you really don't want—"

"It's not that I fuckin' don't want it. I do. I'd be living like a fuckin' king…but I can't do that. It doesn't sit right with me. I need to be able to provide for my family, or I'm not any better than our worthless piece-of-shit father."

I nod my head, understanding his dilemma. "If that's the case, then talk to her. You know she'll understand. Let her buy the house but get something smaller. Something she's proud of and something you feel comfortable with."

"Maybe." He picks up another sheet, glancing it over.

"And in a few years, when we have this place booming, you can purchase whatever house her heart desires. We'll succeed. We have to." These words aren't only for him, but maybe if I say them, I'll believe them too. Ritza needs a man who can take care of her, and I'm going to be that man.

We spend the next couple of hours going over contracts, designs, and potential names.

———

I WALK into Damian's garage excited to see Ritza. I walk up to the counter expecting her to come out of the office she's usually tucked in. But instead, Damian comes in from the garage to welcome me.

"Hey, Javie. Thanks for coming in."

"Sure." I want to ask where she is but decide against it. No need for Damian to know she's the only reason I'm agreeing to this.

He gestures for me to follow him into his office. Sitting on a chair across the desk from him, the formality of this meeting feels odd. I wait for him to begin. He shifts in his chair as he cracks his knuckles.

"To be honest, I'm not quite sure where to begin. I was surprised when you mentioned you and your brother were opening a garage. Has this been something you've been planning?" Damian begins.

"No. It's new. My brother's fiancé is investing in the business, and we're working with her grandfather," I inform him. I want to be honest for Ritza's sake.

"Oh." His brows pull together. "Well. Since you have starting a new business on your plate, are you sure you want to come in here?"

"Sure. Like today, I met with my brother this morning, did some preliminary work, and had discussions, and now I'm here. It will be fine for now, but I can't commit long-term. I don't know what it will be like a few weeks from now. I just didn't want to leave you in a lurch. Especially if y'all are that busy."

"I understand. And thanks." He glances down at the desk.

"I know Ritza trusts you, and it's nice having another someone she trusts and can rely on here. Especially being around only guys. I'm also looking to hire someone to help here in the office. Ritza is busy enough with all the finances and inventory."

In all his words, there's something he's not staying. Someone Ritza can trust and rely on. "Okay. So…" I drag the word out, hesitating to ask more. "I come in what, like twenty hours a week, give or take?"

"Sounds good. How about you come in on the days Ritz works." He says it too casually. The hairs on my neck rise. Why only on the days she's here?

"On the days she works?" I'm clarifying before I dig for more.

"Yeah. I'm sure y'all can work it out right?" He moves to stand.

"What aren't you saying? I know there's more. I know she's been hurt. I see the pain. I can feel her turmoil. What is it?" I keep my voice even.

His eyes widen just a fraction, as he sits back down. His facial features harden. It's something I'm very familiar with, and he won't intimidate me.

"I don't know what you're talking about. She's fine." The words alone may tell me something, but the strain as he says them says much more.

"You know exactly what I'm talking about. And if you don't, you may not know your sister as well as you'd like." I sit back, relaxing, placing my right ankle on my left knee. I'm pushing him. I want to get the rise. That's when men make mistakes. Never show weakness.

His eyes narrow, he knows the game, and he won't be easy to break.

"Tell me what you think you've seen." He tries to turn it

around on me. Little does he know, I back my shit up with receipts.

"The panic or anxiety attacks. Not sure which, but I've seen the beginnings of them. Her hesitation to go anywhere new." And now the bomb. "And the fact she's uncomfortable being with a man, even if she's not a virgin." BOOM.

What sane man would drop the image of sex with a girl's brother? Maybe not sane, but I need to go hard.

His head drops as he takes a deep breath. He shakes his head. "I can't tell you. She has sworn everyone to secrecy. I wish I could. I wish she…"

Confusion sets in. No push back? I don't know what I expected, but not this. When he looks up, I see the tears collect in his eyes. Whatever it is, it's huge and it frightens me.

"Fair enough," I concede. I won't have him break a promise to Ritza.

"I need more guys here. Ritza trusts you. You know things without knowing. I really believe you can catch her if she needs it. With all the new people here, I need you here at the same time. That's all I can say."

I nod my head and stand. He may not have said much but I've learned enough by what he didn't say. He didn't deny she has been through something. He didn't deny she has something she's keeping from me. His inability to share means, for her, it's huge.

RITZA

My phone pings with an incoming text. I pick it up to see it's a text from a number I don't recognize.

I need a more honest opinion about my dress. Can you come with Toni and me to the shop on Sat? We'll make the guys take us to lunch afterward. Not like I can go that long without food. LOL.

It's from Lola, and before I can respond, another message

comes through. *Sorry. Should have started with this is Lola.* <tilted-head laugh emoji>

I couldn't help but laugh out loud. I can imagine Toni there by her side making fun of her. I can't believe they would want me to tag along. They don't even know me that well. I'm guessing they're doing it for Javie.

Could I go? This is uncharted territory. I would like to try.

Where will we be going? I need to know the where to figure out if I could potentially handle it.

It's a boutique off Johnson Ave.

A boutique. I can handle that. Those are usually small and only women.

Sure. I'm in. I respond, slightly uneasy.

I'VE HAD a couple of nightmares the past few nights staying alone at home. Each time I wake is different. Once I was sweating and my heart was racing, but I don't remember the dream. Another time I was stuck, couldn't move, and when I came to, I practically leapt out of bed. At least these didn't have me reliving that horrid night.

My counselor, Josh, says it's a step in the right direction. He has pushed me, making me take the steps I was refusing before. He has encouraged me to talk. To look inside and feel. Something I never wanted to do. It's not like it has changed how I feel about telling Javie, but I'm feeling stronger. Leaving Josh's office, I don't feel like heading home, and I can't go to the shop because Damian is interviewing people and needs his office.

I send a quick text to Javie to see if he's free. After a few back and forths we decide on a movie. I haven't been to a matinee in forever and the thought of venturing somewhere new brings out the nerves, but the thrill overrules the fear. He insisted I meet him at his place so we can drive together. His ability to predict my needs would be creepy if I didn't depend on it so much.

"Butter on the popcorn?" Javie asks as we walk away from the concession stand to the theater.

"Is that even a question?" I look up at him confused.

He gives me a lazy, sexy smirk. "Let's butter it up."

As soon as we enter the darkened theater my heart begins to race. I can't stand that this is happening. I have been coming to the movies since I was a child, and now, as an adult, I'm frightened. Of what? The dark? Who's sitting in the seats? It makes no gawd damn sense! As I'm having this internal argument with myself, my heartbeat slows. The fear is subsiding as anger slowly grows. Why am I furious, or more accurately, who am I furious with?

The unknown guys that changed my life? Guys I can't put a face to? Guys whose voices I don't even know? Guys… How many? Guys…

No! I'm angry at myself. Why am I letting them win? Why am I cowering away from life? Why? Why? Why? So many whys for myself.

"M&Ms or Skittles first?" Javie nudges my arm with his elbow.

We are seated in big, plush, comfy, reclining seats. I was so caught up in my own head, I didn't notice we had taken our seats.

"M&Ms, please." I try and swallow; my mouth has gone dry. I pick up the drink between us, taking a sip.

He hands me the box. "You left me again, bonita," he whispers, running his fingers down the side of my face gently. "One day," he says in a hushed breath. I almost didn't hear him.

One day? I wonder what he means. He says it with no judgment or malice. Just an observation, letting me know he is aware. I hate that I'm hiding from him. I hate that I can't tell him what takes me away from him sometimes. I hate that there's a huge elephant that we don't discuss but see it every time we are together.

One day it will disappear. Fade away into oblivion. A day when I can go about life without the nagging feeling that something will freeze me. Is that what he meant? He knows and believes—one day. My heart thumps loudly against my chest at the thought of Javie considering us in the future.

———

THE MORNING SUN coming in through the opened blinds wakes me. Javie's arm is draped over my side, holding me to him. His body is flush against mine, and his deep breath passes over my neck and shoulder. I relish this quiet moment, a normality I had taken for granted. Not that I ever slept with a guy I had such strong feelings for. I dated, and I had fun, even had a few boyfriends sprinkled through. I can't even say I loved anyone before Javie.

Wait. Stop the presses. Love? Did I… Do I…love Javie? After yesterday and thinking about a future with him, it is so much more. I do. I love him.

"Buenos días, bonita," his warm, raspy morning voice says as he kisses my shoulder.

I lay my hand on his, squeezing it and hugging it tighter to me.

"Mmmm," he yawns, "my favorite way to wake up."

Javie's bed is the place I now feel safest. I'm surrounded by him here, his scent lingering.

"What time are you meeting Toni and Lola?" he asks, not letting me go.

"At ten. They said y'all are taking us to lunch after," I say with a smile.

"Of course, they did." I feel his smile against my bare

shoulder where his lips have taken up residence. "Did you bring a bag to shower and change?"

"Shit." I pull away from his embrace to grab a phone and check the time as he chuckles behind me. "Gotta go if I'm going to make it in time."

I turn around, giving him a brief kiss, which I wish was longer. But time is of the essence.

———

I WALK through an aisle of dresses following Toni, my hand grazing each of them like a child would do. I'm in awe of being here, enjoying their banter, soaking in the experience. This is a newer boutique I have never visited.

"Ugh…I hate everything I've tried on!" Lola exclaims rather dramatically.

"You looked gorgeous in all of them." Toni turns to her as she comes out of the dressing room. I nod in agreement.

Lola rolls her eyes, growling. That tiny blond-haired thing growled. I had to hold my breath to keep from laughing.

"They really did look great," I say cheerily backing Toni up.

"I just hate my stomach right now." She plops into a couch dramatically.

"You're preg-nant." Toni enunciates slowly, which has me giggling.

"I know, and I love it. But it's such an awkward stage. Can't he just grow already? It's too small for a cute baby bump, so I just look like I have stomach pudge."

"Then don't buy a fitted dress, narcy!"

My giggles turn into full-blown laughter at Toni's statement and her silliness of sticking out her tongue at Lola, who is still pouting like a child who can't have what they want in a toy store.

"Ritza!" Lola exclaims. "You're on her side?" Her face is tight as she tries to hold back a smile.

"On no one's side. But as an innocent bystander, I can honestly say you looked gorgeous in all the dresses you tried on. But if you want to know which I thought fit best…it was the blueish one you had on last."

"See! Someone can be nice." Lola widens her eyes, sticking her tongue out at Toni in retaliation. "What are you wearing?" She turns to me.

"Me?" My brows pull together.

"Of course. You are coming with Javie." The casual way she says it makes me feel like I belong. Javie and I are a couple now, and plus one invitations are assumed, but…can I? That's a bigger venue. More people. Eyes on me. Drinks. Mingling.

"Are y'all done yet?" Alex's gruff voice breaks me from the possible spiral I was about to fall into.

"I guess." Lola puffs out.

Hands on my shoulders startle me, but then I catch a whiff of his scent and automatically relax.

"Don't let her forget to buy a dress, Javie!" Lola shakes a finger at me.

"Maybe she has one already. Maybe she's not like you, who needs a new outfit for every occasion."

Lola turns back to him, her face scrunched as if she doesn't understand the words he's saying. She then shakes her head. "She's a girl!" She rolls her eyes and turns around to pick up the blue dress she had discarded on a rack.

"Can you speed it up, amor, we're starving, and you're already late!"

"Y'all go. Let me pay for this and we'll meet you."

———

AFTER HAVING a morning of shopping and a long, leisurely lunch, I'm exhausted. I used to be the extrovert that thrived on going out and being around people and now…now… trying to control potential panic attacks takes everything out of me. I can barely keep my eyes open on the drive back to his place.

We walk in, and he instantly grabs some clothes and walks into the bathroom to change. I strip off the jeans I'm wearing, exchanging them for a pair of joggers I brought with me. I sit on the couch, scrolling the streaming service for the show we had started watching, waiting for Javie to join me. The bathroom door opens, and he walks out in gray sweatpants and a white wife-beater undershirt. My heart skips a beat at the sight of him. I've gotten more comfortable around him, wanting him, completely turned on by him… But right now…this is a whole other level. Wasn't I just sleepy?

I squeeze my legs together, trying to tame the feeling. As he walks to the kitchen, I can see exactly what he's packing. And that tight tank against his chest. Is it possible to see stars just from ogling a guy? No, it's not. But I swear I'm close.

He notices me staring… Is my mouth open? He cocks a brow at me with a sinful smirk.

"Want something, bonita?" he asks huskily.

I lick my lips, knowing I do, but worried. He waits for me, taking a drink from a water bottle—his Adam's apple moving, the flex in his forearm, the twitch I just noticed in his pants… is too much. The urge is becoming overwhelming. I can't seem to squeeze my legs tight enough to lessen the arousal.

I nod my head. He crooks his index finger at me, telling me to come closer. I stand slowly, hesitating, knowing I need him to fill me. I want *him* in me. A few steps and I'm standing in front of him. He places his hand on my shoulder and skims it down my arm. A trail of goosebumps follows it down. He grabs the hem of my shirt and pulls it up over my head.

I'm exposed, but Javie's warm eyes gliding over me settles the unwelcome feeling.

"You're absolutely gorgeous," he whispers in my ear before claiming my mouth for a heated kiss. He pulls back and places his forehead on mine, he swallows hard. "How far?"

I'm lost in everything that is him right now. Can I?

"I want to feel *you*," I whisper, unsure of my voice.

"Are you sure?" His hands come up holding my neck.

"Yes."

He places kisses on each of my cheeks and brings his lips to mine in a sweet kiss that quickly turns desperate. His hands are roaming over me, the warmth of his hands welcome, somehow calming the nerves prickling at my skin.

Slowly, through kisses and fondling, each article of clothing is taken off. I didn't realize I was naked, my senses overloaded, until I was lying beside him. My hand snaking its way down his chest I feel the waistband of his sweatpants.

"These need to come off." A boldness I thought I'd lost suddenly comes out.

He cups my cheek, kissing me as his hand runs down my neck, then to my back. He separates us. "Let me grab a condom."

He gets out of bed and goes to his dresser drawer, pulling one out. He stands next to the bed then slides his pants down. Seeing his full erection has my core tingling and wet. He lays back down, holding himself on his forearm and using his other to graze my body with his fingertips. He kisses my shoulder, then trails kisses all over.

His hand makes it way between my legs, and I open, unashamed. His fingers tease my opening, sliding through the folds before entering me. I moan, wanting more.

"I need you," I cry out in a whisper.

He removes his fingers, tearing the condom package open and sliding it on. He rolls on top of me, his weight on his arms, his shoulders tense. He watches me before he positions himself at my entrance.

"Are you ready?"

"Please," I whimper, wanting and needing to feel like myself again.

He slides himself in slowly as I hear a soft growl in his throat. He allows me time to adjust. While I was ready, the fear that began to creep in made me tense.

Once he's in all the way, he stays motionless. He brings his lips to mine. "I've got you," he says through kisses. My legs spread a bit, believing in those words, and he begins to pull out and slide in gently.

He keeps this pace for a moment, but then a wave of desperation goes through me. Pleasure has taken over the fear. I spread my legs further and grab his rear pulling him closer to me, craving the fullness he's giving me. He speeds up his pace, pushing deeper into me. A sheen of sweat coats his torso.

His body stays against mine as he pumps in and out, rubbing against my sensitive nub. It doesn't take long to reach my peak, the stars I thought I saw earlier so much brighter now. He continues for a few more until I hear him groan out my name. My name.

He rolls to the side, catching his breath, and I watch him. He's beautiful. Calm and caring, yet fierce.

He turns to his side to look at me, bringing his lips to mine and kissing gently. When he pulls away, the most beautiful words fall from his lips: "I've fallen in love with you."

I can't deny it, and I can't hide it. Not from him. I place my hand on his cheek, seeing the emotion dance in his eyes. "I love you too."

CHAPTER 19

JAVIE

Ritza loves me, but the crazy thing is, I don't think I have all her trust yet. She's still hiding from me. Not telling me what holds her back. What scares her the most. I'm now obsessed with ensuring she stays in the present, not getting lost in her head as she does sometimes. The look of loss and confusion in her eyes when she leaves breaks my heart. I don't want that for her anymore. I want to be able to take it away for her.

I know she's taken a big step by having sex. I felt it. The way her body slightly stiffens before I can get her to relax again. It pains me to see her so lost.

She stayed at my place all weekend. I'm not sure what her mom and dad think of that, but she didn't seem concerned about it. All I know is, I would have her here permanently if she let me. I will keep her safe.

At dinner on Saturday night with Cici and a couple of her other friends, began discussing going to a new bar that opened by campus. Ritza said no, but they kept at her.

When she looked to me for help, I was at a loss for the correct way to answer. Did she want me to say I would go with her, or did she want me to say no we couldn't go? I saved the day with a vague, "We have plans, but maybe we could change them." Ritza has not brought it up since.

I'm headed in to Damian's garage. I'm on edge and my shoulders are stiff, not knowing what I'm doing there. I know he knows I can do the job, but the way he made it sound was, he wanted me to take care of Ritza. *How* is the question?

I walk through the front door like always, so I can greet her first. Damian walks out of the office, his face somber.

"Ritza's in here." He quirks his head toward the office as he walks out to the garage.

"Hey!" I announce as I stride in.

Her head is on her crossed arms laying on the desk. She doesn't look up to acknowledge me. I rush to her squatting by the chair, laying one hand on her lap and the other holding her arm.

"What happened?"

She stays frozen in place. The only thing moving is her chest rising and falling.

"Talk to me, bonita." Her arm shivers.

"I'm fine. I just felt a little dizzy. I skipped breakfast. I probably just need to eat." She raises her head, her gaze finding mine.

"Are you sure that's it?"

Her lips pull, giving me a fake smile as she nods her head.

I cup her cheek, coming up to place a kiss on her lips. "Let's go get you something to eat then."

"I have snacks here. Besides, I'll only be in for a couple of hours today. I'll eat when I get to my parents'. You have a job to do. I don't want to take you away from your paycheck." I have a sneaking suspicion I would still be on the clock if I took Ritza to lunch. But I don't press it.

"Okay. Come say bye before you leave." I kiss her again, this time firmly, wanting to get lost in her and her in me.

Out in the garage, there are three guys I don't recognize. I look around and only see Jaxson and Enrique. I walk up to Damian, who is bent over the front end of a car.

"What do you need me to do?"

"Help me here. I need to finish up the estimate for this car." The car doesn't look too bad, a minor accident, probably rear-ended someone.

We work side by side for a few minutes before he tells me to do a couple other estimates that are waiting. I spend the next hour looking over a car, inspecting damage and taking notes. This is all new to me, always being the one fixing, never the one inspecting and then making estimates.

"Hey." Damian strides over to me. "From now on, this is what I'll need you to do when you're here. Do the inspections and then sit with Ritza for part prices to complete estimates. She also has the labor guide for pricing too."

"Okay. Sure."

About an hour later, the door to the office opens, and Ritza walks out, eyes wide. She takes a second glancing around the area, finding me but still looking skittish. Her steps are slow and measured. Her eyes never leave one of the three new guys closest to her.

I pretend I'm still looking over the car in front of me, but I have her in the corner of my eye. She makes her way to me, and I notice she's trembling. I wrap my arms around her, bringing her close, wanting to be her safe space.

"What the fuck! You let that pissant fuck your sister? I guess he didn't follow your rule of staying away from her, huh?" The new guy she was staring at yells out.

My body stiffens, and I'm torn between bashing the fucker's face in and not wanting to let her go. He's a big guy, not gonna lie, but I've never backed down, and I don't plan on starting now.

"You're done. Get your shit and leave," Damian says evenly with a hint of menace. "Either of you want to follow the fucker?" He points in the direction where the other new guys are standing, watching the spectacle. They both shake their heads back and forth slowly.

"One comment that she's hot and you go ballistic and give me a long fuckin' lecture about staying away from your precious sister. And then this new guy walks in and what? He can fuck her and that's fine?" This guy doesn't know when to stop. He should have just packed up and left.

Jaxson and Enrique make their way in between Ritza and I and the new guy. I push Ritza back a bit, grabbing her chin and bringing her face up to look at me. "Go to the office please. I'm going to handle this asshole," I whisper.

She slightly shakes her head.

"Go on." I grab her hand, walking her to Jaxson. "Take her inside," I tell him.

He wraps an arm around her waist and guides her toward the door.

I turn my attention to new guy. "Have something you want to say to me?" I'm taking him in, studying. He's doing the same. Damian makes his way to my side.

"Fuck this. I'm out," new guy huffs, slamming the wrench he was holding on the ground.

We watch him, unmoving until he drives away. Damian turns to me, clapping a hand on my shoulder, "I was unsure about you with Ritz, but now, I know you can protect her the way she needs."

I tip my head a fraction, acknowledging his statement. I never doubted I am what she needs, but having Damian's blessing makes life that much easier.

———

EACH TIME the engagement party has been brought up, she has evaded committing to attend with me. Finally, she relented, and the night is here, and I'm on my way to pick her up from her parents' house. I wasn't sure what dress she had or bought. I'm not sure how she'll handle tonight; I've noticed the way she reacts around people.

Her mom opens the door and welcomes me in, giving me a hug.

"She's almost ready." She walks into the living room. "This is your cousin's engagement party?"

"Yes. They haven't set a date for the wedding. They are both busy in grad school right now."

"Good for them." Her smile is wide and bright.

"Hey." Ritza appears with her dad right behind her. I stand, shaking his hand, then kissing Ritza on the cheek.

"You look beautiful." A quick, genuine smile appears before it slides, and her usual mask is firmly in place.

"Let me take a picture," her mom says cheerily.

"Sure," she answers her mom as she takes my hand pulling me to the fireplace in the corner. This eerily feels like prom. Not that I went, but what TV portrays it to be.

By her mom's reaction, I know it's a big deal that she's going with me, and I'm not taking that for granted.

RITZA

I can't believe I'm about to walk into a barn full of people. Yup, you heard that right. A barn. But this is no ordinary barn; it was renovated to become one of the premiere event sites in the city. It merges elegance with casualness seamlessly.

I'm glad I listened to my mom and Cici about buying a new dress. We went back to the boutique I had been to with

Toni and Lola. When I was there, I saw a classic cocktail dress that I thought I would feel comfortable in. It is *Breakfast at Tiffany's* inspired with a black fitted bodice and an A-line full skirt that hits right above the knees. The bodice is strapless except for the lace covering that creates a sleeveless look. Thank goodness wearing heels is like riding a bike. Walking around wobbly is not the look I was going for.

I have not worn anything other than jeans, leggings, T-shirts, and hoodies for months. This would be the first time I wore something else and went out in public, exposed. Just the thought of people seeing me was enough to start my heart racing, but I know if I am going to stay with Javie, I need to be able to do this. Doing this gives me less anxiety than telling him the truth.

Javie is holding my hand as we walk up to a large wooden door. A gentleman stands to the side, opening the door for the guests each time they walk up. Javie releases my hand and places his hand on my lower back, guiding me in. He stops, looking around the vast area. People are mingling with drinks in hand while soft music plays in the background.

"Now what?" Javie looks at me.

"Let's find our table, I guess." I shrug my shoulders, waving my hand to the side where the seating chart was placed.

He cocks a brow and nods his head. "Lead the way."

I take the first step in the direction, and his hand comes off my back. I was about to freeze in place, but he grabs my hand, and my next foot moves. At the board, we skim the names and find ours with his family.

He guides me around the room looking for our table. When we find it, he pulls a chair out for me before sitting himself.

"I've never been to something like this before." He comes in close, whispering in my ear. "What do we do?"

I look at him, and his brows are furrowed, his forehead crinkled. The man who always seems so self-assured is out of place. I glance around the room and realize we are in a room full of wealth, and Javie did not grow up around this. While my parents are not wealthy like Garrett's and, I'm assuming, Lola's, we never wanted for anything. We were very comfortable. Javie lived a life much different than this.

I pick up the place card set on the charger plate in front of me. "It's cocktail hour right now." I speak low, not wanting anyone to hear me explaining this to Javie. "Drinks and appetizers while you mingle. That's why you don't see many people sitting at their tables yet."

"Oh. And if we don't know anyone to talk to?" A silly smile creeps on his face.

I have my hands full with this one. He's a quick study, and I bet would land on his feet no matter what. "Do you want a beer? Then we can say hello to your family who *is* mingling around the room. Then maybe we can take a quick walk outside. Until dinner is served."

"Sounds like a plan." He pushes his chair back, standing and offering me his hand. While he may not know the "rules" of upscale parties, he does have gentlemanly manners. I wonder where he learned them?

Drinks in hand, we make our way around the room toward Lola and Alex.

"Hi," Lola says with a smile, and Alex tips his head in acknowledgment.

"Hi," I respond back. My heart rate is fast, but manageable. I take a sip of the signature cocktail they created for the event.

"If this is the engagement party, what will the wedding look like?" Javie says jokingly.

"You got me," Alex puffs out. "All that money for…" His eyes scan the room.

"Oh, hush. This is the way it's done. It's beautiful. But I will admit, maybe Mrs. Anders and I went a bit overboard. But it's their only son," she says dreamily.

"Or maybe you are living vicariously through Toni." Javie winks at Lola and chuckles.

"Shut up!" She shakes her head but doesn't deny it.

"It really is gorgeous," I offer to Lola.

"I know!" She giggles with excitement. "How is the signature cocktail? I worked with the bartender to create it, and I can't even have one!" She frowns.

"It's good."

"After this, I think we're eloping in Vegas," Toni's voice says behind me as Garrett laughs.

"Sounds good to me," Javie agrees. "Do you even know all these people?"

"Don't ask me anyone's name. Mr. And Mrs. Anders have introduced me to the whole room. Don't remember a single one, except Sharie, because I loved her dress." She laughs at herself.

"I saw your mom's name on the seating chart. You invited her?" Javie asks quietly.

"Mrs. Anders insisted. But if she causes any trouble, please, please, help me." She looks to Alex and Javie.

They both nod, but I wonder what trouble she would cause.

"You know she'll probably come and use this time to try and find a new boyfriend." Alex states with a bite.

"That's what I'm scared of."

"Javie, how are you?" an elegant woman says, placing an air kiss on his cheek. She turns to me and says, "You must be Ritza. Nice to meet you. I'm Cheryl Anders. I'm so glad you could make it."

"Hello, Mrs. Anders. Everything looks beautiful," I answer. Garrett's mom is a beautiful older woman.

"And this is Garrett's dad, Robert."

I nod at him and say hello.

"Crap," Toni says out loud and everyone looks in the direction she turned.

A woman stands at the entrance, looking around.

"It'll be fine." Mrs. Anders places a hand on her shoulder. "Come on, and let's greet her."

Toni's head falls back dramatically before she rights it. Garrett whispers something in her ear, and she leans into him. Mr. Anders claps Garrett's shoulder, and they begin walking in her direction.

I want to ask what the big deal was but figure it isn't my business or the right time. I'll let them handle their own family issues. I have enough of my own.

The night progresses—dinner served, speeches made, and now a live band is playing. I am ready to leave now that the lights have dimmed, and the guests have become more bois-terous. But I couldn't ask that of Javie. My heart has raced, slowed down, raced, slowed down...the whole evening. Javie has my hand in his, as his thumb rubs up and down my wrist. Throughout the evening he would squeeze my wrist, which I found odd.

"One dance and then we can go," Javie whisper shouts in my ear.

"Uh." I'm stunned. I don't know if I can.

A slow country song begins, and he stands up, extending his hand to me. I fill my lungs with air, trying to build the strength. I place my hand in his, standing. Holding my hand, he leads me to the dance floor, pulling me close to his body. He begins a slow two-step, and I follow. His arm winds tightly around me, his body flush against mine. After a minute or so, I could feel my body's rigidity melt. Javie has me.

One song turned into three before the music changed to the obligatory pop music. Javie leads me off the floor back to the table but stays standing behind our chairs. Alex and Lola are speaking with Toni's mom.

"We're going to take off now. Can you let Toni and Garrett know?" Javie announces.

"So soon?" Lola pops out of her chair to give me a hug.

"Yeah." That's all Javie gives them.

"I guess it's time for my departure too since Alex won't stay off my ass." Toni's mom states crudely.

"If we thought you could act like a lady and not throw yourself on the men in the room, then we wouldn't have to babysit your ass," Alex responds in kind.

"Asshole," she grumbles.

Javie waits for her to stand and lets her lead us out of the venue.

Music from the radio fills the car. We haven't spoken since we left. The evening was perfect, even if I did feel like I was going to pass out a couple of times. Too many people crowded our table, wanting to speak to the couple of the evening. The crowd around the bar area left me light-headed, but each time Javie was magically able to distract me with a short kiss or a funny observation. It was enough of a distraction to bring me back.

He stayed by my side the entire night except the couple of times he excused himself to the men's room, and whenever he did, I had Alex and Lola right by me. And of course, Lola dragged me along to the ladies' room, which helped because I was at a loss for how I was going to pull that off.

"Your place or mine?" Javie startles me back to the present.

"Yours. If that's okay." I look at him.

"It's perfect." He smiles.

My mind wanders again… He has impeccable timing, almost knowing things he shouldn't. His way of commanding a room if needed. His smooth steps as he glided over the dance floor. My heart dropped when he decided to stand up to that new guy Damian hired. I had a weird feeling about him when I met him that morning. He gave me the creeps right away, even though he was a decent looking guy. His 'hot' comment that I overheard was what caused the mini attack that day. He was taller and more muscular than Javie. But when Javie called him out, I don't know which was greater—fear or arousal. I have this man. His hands have roved over my body. Is there anything he can't do?

Thinking of his hands, his kisses, his attention, a spark of excitement hits me between my legs, and my body instantly heats up. The way he transforms from grease monkey to hot guy to Mr. Sexy in a suit. Holy hell, I'm in trouble. My breathing picks up. I want to feel him again.

In his apartment, he begins to unbutton his shirt. "Grab a shirt from the drawer so you can get out of your dress."

"Thanks." I open the drawer, pulling one out and going into the bathroom.

I look in the mirror, watching myself. A thrill is traveling up and down my body, but also a hesitation. I want to be able to entice. To flirt. To lead. But what if I falter? I can't. Not with Javie. He'll bring me back, I tell myself. I unzip the dress, slipping my arms out and letting it fall to my feet. I'm wearing a black strapless bra and a pair of black boy-shorts, not the sexiest look, but it's what I have to work with. At least it matches.

My makeup is still impeccable, and I let down the few strands Cici had picked up for my hairdo. My heart slams against my chest. It's now or never.

I open the door to the bathroom, and Javie is shirtless and bent over, pulling on a pair of loose gym shorts. He stops and watches me with desire. Warmth and moisture collects between my legs. I scan his body, enjoying the view—his lean defined muscles, tattoos scattered down an arm and on his chest. He can be a bad boy with an edge or a handsome boy next door.

He stands, waiting for me to make a move. I take the few steps to stand in front of him. I slide a finger over his chest, letting it run down to the band of his boxer briefs. I lick my lips, then up on tiptoes I bring my hands to his shoulders for a heated kiss. He snakes his arms around me, pulling me closer. The kiss begins like all our others, cautious, but I lick his lips, and it turns desperate. Our tongues dance and explore each other. I feel his growing erection on my stomach. He pulls me up, and my legs automatically wrap around his waist. My core rubbing against his body sends more flares flying within me. I try and wriggle in his arms to cause more friction.

He pulls away, placing his forehead on mine. "Green light tonight?"

"I need to feel you in me." I press my lips back on his, not wanting to stop.

He begins trailing kisses on my cheek down to my neck, his hands are cupping my ass, holding me up. One hand slides up and unclasps my bra. I pull it out from between us, my nipples harden at the skin-on-skin contact. He bends down, placing me on the bed gently. He straightens up, watching me with hooded eyes.

I let my hand run down his chest, letting it slide further south, until I feel his erect penis in my hand. He lets out a low moan, so I rub him gently, his cock twitching against my palm. Wetness pools between my legs at the feel of his hardness. I'm safe with him.

"You're sure?" I can see how hard he's trying to keep it together.

"Yes."

He bends over, crashing his lips back to mine. The sensations flowing through my body are working overtime. He slides my panties down, kneeling between my legs. He's trailing kisses down my breasts before going lower.

My head is spinning in the best way. He spreads my legs apart kissing my inner thigh as his fingers graze my center gently.

"I'm going to taste you." He looks up at me as his fingers continue to explore.

I'm so lost, a yearning so intense taking over.

"Yes."

His tongue licks my clit, and I swear, I thought it would be my undoing, but he takes it away. He sucks and licks around my opening, then two fingers slide in easily. My body feels ready to clench around them.

"Not so fast, bonita," Javie growls, taking his fingers out kissing my mound then claiming my mouth.

It's so much, but not nearly enough. I pull away scooting up the bed, feeling exposed but thoroughly aroused. "I need you," I whisper.

"I've got you." His famous three words. The words that have come to mean so much.

He stands, grabbing a condom from his drawer and coming back to me. He watches me, lying naked in front of him, from the foot of the bed. His erection wanting to push through the boxer briefs he's wearing. He slides them down, sheathing himself before crawling up the bed to meet me. He positions his body between my legs, holding himself over me. He comes down for a kiss. "I love you," he says hoarsely. Then suddenly he flips us over placing me on top.

"You take control," he growls.

A feeling of exhilaration fills me. I sit up, straddling him and guiding his penis to my center, then lowering myself onto him until he's in to the hilt. The way he's watching me, the fire in his eyes, pushes me to start riding him. He caresses my breast, and my breath hitches as I feel a slight sting as he pinches my nipple softly. It hardens instantly. My nails are scratching into his chest. Euphoria fills my body as the beginning of my orgasm starts. He flicks my clit a couple of times and an explosion hits.

He flips me over quickly, pumping himself a few times, finding his release. After a few quiet moments, catching our breath, he gets up to throw away the condom and brings back a wet washcloth to clean me up.

He turns off the lights and crawls in next to me, pulling me to his chest. He hugs me tightly, placing soft kisses in my hair.

"Good night, bonita. I love you," he whispers as his hand rubs up and down my spine.

"I'm yours, Javie. I love you." I place a kiss on his chest, relishing in the feel of his stomach under my hand and the steady beat of his heart.

CHAPTER 20

JAVIE

Walking around what is to be our new garage still feels surreal. I was never supposed to have this. My own business. Growing up, the stars never seemed to align in our favor. Being dumped on a grandmother after our mother abandoned us was just the beginning of the struggles. But here I am...in a space that will be ours. Alex and I will make it. We both want to prove to the world we are more than the barrio we grew up in.

Lola is in the office area. She's full of big dreams. Her grandfather just left, and we decided to purchase the vacant lot next to us. He thought if we ever needed to expand, it would make it easier if we already owned the land. We didn't disagree, just followed his recommendation.

"We need a comfortable waiting area for the quick oil changes," Lola is saying to Alex as they come out to the garage area.

"We don't need anything fancy," Alex counters.

"I'm not talking fancy, but if you want repeat customers,

which you do, then you need to have something for them. Chairs that are a little better than fold-outs, for starters. Maybe a Keurig or coffee maker. Things like that. It needs to look clean," she pushes back.

They both turn and look at me.

"Uh…I've only worked at jacked-up places, and they had fold-out chairs if you were lucky." I shrug.

"Y'all are impossible. Just leave the indoor area to me," she huffs.

"Amor, as much as I love your input, we are staying within our budget," Alex says gently.

"I know. And I won't go overboard. I want this to be successful." She pats his cheek. "Now I have to go. I have class in an hour."

"Bye," I tell her as she walks out with Alex following her.

My phone chimes in my pocket. A text from Ritza.

Cici is bugging me to go to that new bar by campus. How about Friday?

I'm surprised she's saying yes, but if that's what she wants, then that's what she'll get.

Whatever you want, bonita, I respond.

See you later.

———

DRIVING TO THE BAR, I notice Ritza has her hands clasped in her lap. She squeezes one hand with the other, then switches. I reach across and place mine on top of hers. I need to feel how anxious she is. The tension she has in her hands and the rate of her pulse tell me what I need to know. She is so focused on herself, she has not figured out my little tricks to keep her in the present. Rubbing her neck calms her, but I can also feel her pulse. I hold her wrists when I slide my hand up her arm.

Her two pulse points confirm for me how she's feeling. I've learned the signs to watch for.

She's on edge, and we aren't even there yet.

"Do you want to stop to eat?" I give her an out or way to postpone before stepping into this new situation.

She doesn't answer me, still looking straight ahead. I squeeze her hand, trying to get her attention.

"Hey!" I say a bit louder while I turn down the radio. "Hungry? We can stop for something to eat."

She blinks a few times before turning her head toward me. "Uh…I'm sorry. I spaced, didn't I?" She plasters the fake smile on. "I'm not really hungry, and they'll probably have some apps there."

I tighten the hold I have on her hands. "Okay. Just checking." When I release her hands, she stretches her fingers out, opening and closing them into fists. This is another tell of hers, I've come to learn, when I know she's trying to calm herself.

The walk to the door of the bar is slow, I don't even think she realizes how slow she's walking. My hand is on her lower back, guiding her, but not pushing if she wants to change her mind. Her shoulders are bunched up tight, and I want to massage them down, but I know she needs to cross this hurdle before I try.

"Hey, Javie," the bouncer at the door calls to me. We worked together a couple of years ago at a club.

"Hey." We clap hands. "How's the place?" I ask to buy time for Ritza.

"It's cool. Nice gig. But you know college kids. Could get rowdy, but it hasn't happened yet."

I nod in agreement. College kids or not, mix alcohol and men's egos and the outcome isn't always pretty.

"Go on in," he says, not checking our IDs.

We walk in the doors to a compact bar with pool tables

and dart machines all around. I scan the area looking for Cici and their friends. For being so close to campus, I would've thought this place would be bigger. I spot Cici in a corner with their own pool table and dart machine.

I pull Ritza with me, hoping she relaxes because the grip she has on my hand right now is turning painful. I'll have to get Cici's attention soon and have her convince Ritza to leave. I don't think she's going to make it.

Once Ritza sees Cici, she loosens her grip a bit.

"You made it!" Cici rushes to Ritza hugging her tight. Ritza lets go of my hand holding on to Cici like a life vest.

Cici whispers something in Ritza's ear, and she giggles. Not long or real, but one to pacify Cici. I wonder why she's doing this when she clearly looks like she would rather be any place but here.

Cici lets her go and pulls her to the bar table, pointing at a chair for her to sit in. I follow her, then stand by her side, my arm draped over the back of her chair. Ritza keeps glancing around the space, nervously. Her fingers are tapping against her legs.

Cici grabs a couple of beers from a bucket and hands them to us.

"Thanks," I tell her, not knowing if Ritza will even make it long enough to finish one.

I recognize one of the two guys here from their Tuesday dinners. He takes his shot then comes up to us, saying hello and then asking if I wanted next game. I told him not yet, but maybe later. I can't risk leaving Ritza's side right now.

I take a long pull of my beer hoping it takes off the edge I'm feeling watching Ritza torture herself. I don't understand why. She takes a few quick sips of her beer placing it on the table. Her other friends come up to the table, saying their hellos, and she politely introduces me. Small talk continues for the next half hour.

One of the guys hands me another beer and offers one to Ritza, who turns it down. I notice hers is still half full.

"Come on," Cici calls out to Ritza, "you used to kick everyone's ass in darts before. Let's see if you still got it."

Ritza looks up at me. I haven't moved, standing right by her side to make sure she feels safe.

"Only if you want," I whisper, answering the question in her eyes.

She puffs out a breath, rolling her lips in and out of her mouth. She surprises me when she jumps off her stool and takes the few steps toward Cici. Her movements are slow and deliberate.

She takes the darts one of the girls hands her, dropping them from one hand to the other. She grips one in her right hand, tossing it up slightly and catching it. My bonita is a little hustler. She's testing the weight of the darts before she even takes her first shot.

"You got next game since Ritza's up and playing," the guy from dinner tells me. "I'm about to finish him off anyway." He cocks his head in the direction of the eight ball left on the table.

"Sure," I answer. Might as well. She's close enough to me anyways.

He knocks the eight ball in and begins racking the next set. Ritza has thrown a couple of darts, and they land on the board, but she seems disappointed by her score. She's rolling her shoulders and her head. She's getting into the game.

"Wanna break?" he asks me.

"Nah. You won the table, go for it," I tell him.

After a couple of turns, there are only a couple of balls left on the table; I'm behind him with three balls to his two. A loud, boisterous, girly laugh catches my attention, and when I turn around, I see Ritza doubled over her body moving with her laughter. A laugh I have never heard. A laugh I wish would happen more often.

As if she feels me watching her, she turns around, flashing a hypnotizing smile. Her eyes are dancing with amusement. My usually serious and sullen girl is having fun, and my heart explodes with joy for her. Whatever got her to laugh like this, I'll be forever grateful.

"I'm back!" Ritza shouts. I turn to see she is jumping up and down, and I notice she has hit the bullseye. She looks to me, so I give her a wink. She rolls her eyes and smiles before turning back to her game.

I break a new game after winning the last one. A couple of shots in, Ritza comes up to me with Cici on her tail. "We're going to the ladies' room."

"Okay." I place the pool stick against the wall about to escort her.

"I got her. Girl time." Cici stops me.

I look to Ritza. She needs to tell me what she needs.

"It's fine." Her lips pull out, and she takes Cici's hand.

I watch her walk away, much more relaxed than the way she walked in. I go back to my game, giving her the space she needs. I take a shot and miss, distracted with Ritza out of my sight. I watch as the guy takes a few shots, running the table. I scan the room and see them walking to the bar. Knowing she's still fine, I turn my attention back to my game.

"JAVIE!" I hear my name yelled across the loud bar. Busy focusing on the pool table, I missed what happened, but I look up to see Cici waving at me without Ritza.

My heart stops, and I drop the pool stick I'm holding and take off in a run toward Cici. As I get closer, I can see she's crouched over a passed-out Ritza.

"What the fuck happened?" I hiss at Cici before checking Ritza for any injuries. "Bonita, wake up." I say loudly, tapping her cheeks and gently shaking her.

"Carry her to the car," Cici says.

"What if she's hurt?" I roar, pissed she let this happen.

"She's not. She passed out from a panic attack. I've seen it before," Cici tries to explain.

Figuring she may be correct, I place my arms under her and lift her. Once I'm up, I notice people gawking. I weave my way through the crowd quickly, wanting to get her out of here.

In the parking lot, I run into a problem with Ritza in my arms and my keys in my pocket. She hasn't awakened, so I'm carrying dead weight.

"Let me help." Cici is running toward us. She's breathless as she asks, "What pocket are your keys in?"

"Left." My answer is clipped.

She places her hand in my pocket grabbing the keys and opening the back door for me. I slide Ritza in carefully.

"Get in the back with her. She needs to see you if she wakes up. I'll drive." She opens the driver's door, getting in and adjusting the seat. I squeeze in quickly, placing Ritza's head in my lap.

Once Cici is on the road, I pull out my phone and dial Damian's number.

"What's up?" he answers casually.

"Uh…" I hadn't thought it through. What do I tell him? "I was at a bar with Ritza, and she passed out. She's still out." It comes rushing out of me. I'm more worried for her than for myself. He can kick my ass if he wants. I would kick my ass.

"She was at a bar?"

As I'm rushing through the explanation, Ritza begins to squirm.

"Bonita. Talk to me baby."

"She's awake?" Damian asks.

"I'll see you at the house." I hang up on him, wanting to give my full attention to the girl my heart belongs to.

I cup her cheek. "Talk to me."

She opens her eyes, and she stares at me for a second before tears flood her eyes. She blinks, anguish marring her face. Silent tears stream down, hitting my hand. I wipe her face with my thumb, but more continue to fall.

"Come here, baby." I get my hands behind her to lift her to sitting. She covers her face with her hands, so I pull her closer to me. She turns around and straddles my lap tucking herself into my chest. The silent tears turn into uncontrollable sobs. I hold her to me, wishing I knew how to take away her pain.

Cici parks, and I see Damian's car in the driveway. Cici quickly jumps out of the car, opening the back door. Damian is walking toward me.

"Come on, Ritz," he says to her, placing his hand on her back, rubbing it up and down.

"I've got you," I whisper in her hair.

I turn my body, getting my legs out of the car. I hold Ritza close to my body with one arm and extend the other to Damian for help. He grips my forearm, and I grip his as he pulls me out. Once I'm standing, she brings her legs up wrapping them around my waist. Her arms clutch my neck.

I follow Damian into the house, and I go straight to her room, leaving Cici to explain what happened. I still don't know, but all I want to do right now is to make sure is alright.

I click on her lamp before sitting on the bed.

I hum, rocking her back and forth. Her grip on me never wavers. Minutes pass, and her sobs begin to lessen. A cough and soft knock at her open door announce her family's entrance.

"Want to tell us what happened, mija?" her dad asks.

She stays silent, but I feel her arms loosening.

"Has she said anything?" her dad asks me.

"No, sir."

"Cici said everything was fine, then all of a sudden, she went white and fell down," he continues.

"I'm not sure. She had gone off with Cici to the ladies' room, then I saw them head to the bar. I stayed behind."

"Why in the hell would you let her go anywhere by herself?" Damian says tightly, jaw clenched.

"Because I asked him to!" Ritza shouts hoarsely. She scrambles off my lap to stand as everyone watches her.

RITZA

This was the reason I should have never started seeing him. What the hell was I thinking? Everyone's eyes are on me. Concern, worry, pity…everything I hate. My back is to Javie, and I'm scared to turn around and see all of those emotions, and probably so many more, on his. I can only imagine what he's thinking.

My body starts to tremble… I'm dizzy.

"I've got you." Javie's arms come around me, holding me steady.

As much as I want him…need him…I can't have him. I'm scared to look at him. He'll want to know what happened tonight, and I can't tell him. As dizzy as I feel, I need to move away. I look to Damian, pleading for help.

I extend my arm in his direction. I don't know if I'm steady enough to stand on my own. He takes my arm, and I step away from Javie. I tuck myself into Damian's chest.

"You should leave, Javie," I say, my tone in conflict with my words.

"No. I'm not going anywhere," he argues.

"Leave."

"No."

"I don't want you here!" I yell, refusing to look at him.

"Son, I think it's time to go," my dad tells him.

A loud exhale then footsteps. Damian finally hugs me.

"Is he gone?" I whisper.

"He's gone."

I push myself away from Damian, looking around at my prison. I kick off my shoes and climb into bed. I pull the covers up high, pillows around me, cocooning myself away. As much as I don't want to fall asleep, terrified of the dreams that will follow, I'm exhausted. It's strange, an hour ago I thought I was going to be out, laughing and having a grand time. I thought I was going to become myself again. Or at least a small version of my old self.

I close my eyes, ignoring my family, who I know are watching me.

"Turn off the light." I don't look in their direction.

The light clicks off, but I don't hear my door close, the hallway light is still streaming through the door. Outside, the wind is dancing through the leaves of the trees. If only I could be swept up. Taken away from this hell.

I swear this guy has tried every cheesy pickup line known to man. He keeps talking and talking. He looks nervous, and I feel bad for the dude. He has no game.

"I think it's time for a blow job." A couple of guys, I'm guessing his friends, approach with the shots that are so crudely named. The guy that spoke wraps his arm around my shoulder. "How's Jakey treating you?"

"He's nice," I answer. I'm guessing he is trying to help his friend with his nonexistent game.

"For the eye candy." Crude guy hands me a shot.

I hope he doesn't think that works. New guy is just as bad as poor Jake.

"And your names are?" I ask grabbing the shot.

"Connor and Steven," the guy with his arm around me says.

They each grab a shot. They clink glasses, waiting for me. I clink theirs and follow their lead, downing the shot.

We continue talking, but each time I try to excuse myself to find my friends, they distract or beg me to stay.

A wooziness hits me, and I stumble.

"Why don't we get you some air?" *Crude guy places his arm around my waist to help me walk.*

Air sounds good. I think I'm going to be sick. I should go home.

The fresh evening air hits my face.

"I need to go home." I'm slurring. I can't focus.

"Where do you live? I can take you."

"Wake up! It's a dream." *Why are they shaking me?* "Ritza."

My mom's voice registers.

I sit up quickly, looking around my room. I remembered the night. At least part of it. My heart is racing; the shirt I'm wearing is drenched with sweat. My head is pounding.

"Why did you wake me?" I ask, knowing my dream. The sick fucks that took advantage of me, but this dream was not like any I've had before.

"You were mumbling nonstop. I thought you were calling to us, but you just kept talking and talking. Or more like mumbling. Then you started heaving like you were going to throw up. You kept moving your legs back and forth," my mom explains, her eyes sad.

"Oh." What else can I say? It's not like I'm going to share what I dreamt or remembered. That is just another piece I won't share.

"You want me to sleep with you?" Her voice is sleep filled as she yawns.

"No. I'm fine."

I wait until she leaves the room to get up to go to the restroom and relieve myself, change my shirt, then crawl back to bed.

———

AFTER A FITFUL NIGHT, sleeping and waking, I'm staring at my ceiling, not wanting to go anywhere. My stomach growled several minutes ago, but even thinking about food is making me sick. I can't tell if my throat really burns or it's all in my head from the dreams. I threw up so much that night. It burned from the spicy Thai food we had before going to the bar.

The pain, the sickness, the nausea, the fear... It's as if it just happened. It's all too much, and I can't focus. The tightness in my chest accompanied with the unsteady feeling won't leave me. I open my nightstand drawer and pull out a bottle of pain reliever PM. I pop four in my mouth and close my eyes, willing sleep to take me. A reprieve from the torture.

———

A STINGING PAIN on my cheek pulls me from the abyss. My eyes won't open. Am I awake? Where am I?

"Ritza, gawd dammit! Wake the fuck up."

Damian. He sounds so far away. I can't answer. Sleep is pulling me back under.

"I mean it, Ritza!"

My cheek throbs.

"Damian," I slur out as best I can without opening my eyes.

"What have you done? Wake up."

"I'm tired." The words feel slow to leave my mouth. My throat is still raw from throwing up. Wait...did I throw up?

I peel my eyes open to look at him.

"I couldn't sleep with the dreams. I took PM." I explain slowly, yawning and stretching.

"How many?"

"Four. Why are you waking me up?" The scratchiness in my throat bothers me.

"You let out a blood-curdling scream. You sounded like you were being murdered."

His bloodshot eyes stare at me.

"Oh." Again, I don't know how to let this go.

"Talk to me."

"Let me sleep, and then I'll talk." I buy myself more time and turn over, facing the wall.

Why did I scream? I don't remember anything right now. I wasn't dreaming. At least I don't think I was dreaming. Maybe that's the key…take PM to sleep. But I would need to live on my own, so I don't keep waking the whole house.

———

"THE KEY. I NEED THE KEY." I point to the plant and small gnome by my door. My secret key spot. The guy from the bar helped me to my door. That's sweet.

He gets the key from the hidden spot and unlocks the door, letting me in. He steers me to the couch with one arm around my waist, keeping me on my feet.

He places me down and says, "See you around."

Seeing double of him, I wave, my arm heavy. The door closes. I should lock the door, but I can't find the energy to stand back up. I'll lay back to rest a second, then I'll get up.

I can't breathe. I open my eyes, and the guy is back. I try and scream, but his hand is covering my mouth.

"Nuh-uh-nuh-uh…" I repeat over and over, moving to shake my head.

"Grab her leg!" I'm being stretched out.

"You're going to like this, I promise," he croons.

"Ritza!" I hear my name being yelled over and over.

I awaken to Cici sitting on my bed, her hands on my shoulders. I swallow; my is mouth dry. I have a slight headache, which is startling since I took pain relievers to sleep.

"What time is it?" I mumble, trying to produce saliva to moisten my mouth.

"It's four o' clock. You've slept for close to twenty hours." She keeps her voice even, almost robotic.

"Oh." I'm unaffected by that thought.

I don't think I want to wake up. I'm stuck in some sort of purgatory, not wanting to live but not wanting to die. There is nothing for me to live for. I'll continue with this cycle of memory torture. What can I possibly do? I can't tell them the truth. It will only make things worse than what they already are.

"Come on. Brush your teeth and take a shower. We'll go get you some food."

"I'm not hungry." I turn over, giving her my back.

"You have to eat." She pleads, "And please brush your teeth. You're rank right now."

"Then leave. You won't be able to smell me if you go." I can't make her life miserable too. I'm already destroying my parents' and Damian's lives.

"I'm not leaving." I feel her move and then hear footsteps.

She's not leaving but leaves? Okay. That makes sense. Maybe I'm still sleeping. I close my eyes, ready to visit dream-land again. As much as I don't want to know, now I'm curious. Like a gruesome accident, you tell yourself not to look, but you slow down to gawk anyways.

My vision blurs and goes black again. Peaceful until the memories begin to flood.

Clank, bang, clank, bang… What in the hell is that noise? I sit up, looking at the door. Cici is standing at my open doorway hitting a pot with a wooden spoon.

"Stay in bed if you want, but I'm going to continue to play my makeshift instrument. And if needed, I'll get Damian to bring his snare drum. You know how good I played that," she yells over the banging.

"Can you please just leave? Please! I don't want to get out of bed. I'm not ready. I don't know if I ever will be."

She pauses the clatter while I speak.

"Fine. At least take a shower and brush your teeth so you don't stink up the house." Leave it to best friends to tell it like it is.

"If I get in the shower, will you leave?" I bargain. I'll do whatever I can to get her to vanish.

"Sure. After you eat, too," she pushes.

"I gave you a shower and teeth brushing," I counter.

"Fine. But be ready for Damian to shove food down your throat later." She cackles evilly, doing a silly dance.

I stand, my legs weak from all the time I've spent in bed. I pass Cici without a glance and lock myself in the bathroom. My body creaks from the lack of movement. I twist the shower handle and strip out of the clothes I have been wearing since… No reason to think about it. I lost Javie, and that's all there is to it.

I step into the scalding hot shower, wishing I could wash off memories. Like the next morning getting home from the hospital. I didn't feel clean even after a shower so long, the water turned cold. I took several of them and never felt the disgusting film come off. Only time did that. Like a snake's skin that peels off when they are ready to shed. I shed the repulsion of that night when I was ready to let it go. When Javie came into my life. And since I have no more Javie, who knows if this layer will ever leave me?

My dreams have been a buildup. If guys didn't have to be such assholes and crude, maybe I never would have remembered that night. I could have lived in blissful ignorance. But no. One jerk-off, crude comment at the bar, and the flood gates to memories that should have stayed buried opened. Who in their right mind thought 'blow job' was an appropriate shot name.

The water feels good. I fill my lungs with air and hold it… one, two, three, four, five… Exhale slowly…one, two, three, four, five. I repeat a couple more times out of habit. I haven't needed or used this breathing exercise in so long. My peace, my serenity had become Javie. His gentle look and touch, his presence that could protect, the timbre of his voice, his scent… But now it's back to breathing.

Once the water begins to lose the heat, I quickly wash my hair and body, because I don't feel like freezing this time. At least there's that.

I grab the towel from the hook and step out of the shower. In front of the mirror, I have a flashback of me months ago. Vacant, dead eyes are staring back at me like the ones so many months ago. I glance down to the top of my breast, and the large hickey like bruise is there. I shut my eyes; it didn't happen again. It couldn't.

I open my eyes, and it's gone. My heart beats like I just sprinted a mile.

I quickly brush my teeth and head back to my room. Sweats and another hoodie to hide me from the world.

CHAPTER 21

JAVIE

I can't believe Ritza kicked me out. She needs me but dismissed me so easily. I would have fought to stay if it was only Damian, but how was I supposed to fight her dad? That would have been a real asshole move. I've texted and called all night. No response. None. Even Cici, who seemed to be on my side, is radio silent.

I fell asleep with my clothes on and my phone clutched in my hand in case she called. In case she needed me. She does need me; she just won't admit it and tell me why. I know it. I can feel it.

I sit up, looking around my apartment. I can't stay here. I'll go stir-crazy.

Any plans to head to the ranch today? I text Garrett.

No. Why? His response comes quickly.

You said riding clears your head. I think that's what I need.

Pick you up in 30.

Shit. Shower and change. I need to get out of here. My place still smells of her. Or maybe it's just in my bed.

———

THE FALL SKIES in Texas are the best this time of year. The heat of the sun mixed with the coolness of the breeze somehow is comforting. We drove up here, no talking, just the radio providing a distraction. I helped saddle up the horses, and we came out. I'll tell Garrett what happened eventually, but it's not time. Not yet.

My biggest regret is not following her to the bar. I got lax. I knew, know, she has trouble in crowds. I see it every time we enter a new place. The way her eyes dart around the room. The way her shoulders bunch tightly around her ears. I know, and I failed.

Fuck! How could I let her down? That's probably why she kicked me out. She doesn't think I can protect her. I know I can, and I think I'm the only one that can. How will she go into the shop now? Am I even welcome in the shop?

The few minutes are on replay. I saw her smiling and laughing with Cici walking to the bar. I saw her at the bar ordering a drink. I hit a couple of balls, and my name was screeched loudly. It felt like someone had their hand around my heart and was squeezing the life out of me when I didn't see Ritza. Seeing her on the floor, unconscious, was…is…a regret… Not being able to keep the woman I love out of harm's way. I just wish I knew what the harm was.

We ride until we come across a wide-open area, and I hear Garrett say, "Let's go." He nudges the horse with his heels, giving it a slap in the rear with the reins, and it takes off on a run.

I do that same and follow. The wind against my face, the feeling of handling the horse, and the exhilaration of the power under me places my thoughts on hold. All I concentrate on is the horse.

Garrett has made some sort of loop around, and we are

back at the barn. He has respected me and not asked any questions. Just small talk as we unsaddle the horses.

———

ON OUR WAY back to town, he pulls over at a small dive bar. Alex's car is in the parking lot. I guess the time has come.

I follow him in, and he walks straight to the bar, ordering a couple of beers. I look around, and Alex is sitting at a table in the corner. I grab the beer Garrett offers and make my way over to Alex.

I pull out a chair, sitting down. I take a long pull from the long-neck bottle.

"A ride?" Alex begins.

I shrug, not knowing how to explain what happened when I don't know myself.

"Girl trouble?" Garrett takes a drink, placing his beer on the table.

"Yeah, girl trouble, but I can't explain what happened. All I know is she passed out, I take her home, and she kicks me out," I grumble, each word increasing the anger.

"Back up. Passed out? You let her drink until she passed out and took her home?" Alex asks as his brows pull together.

"What the fuck? I'm not a fuckin' rookie. No, asshole. She was fine. Maybe had one beer. She went to the bar with her friend, and all I know is her friend starts yelling my name and she's passed out unconscious on the floor. She didn't wake until we were in the car on the way to her house. Cici and her family know something, know why it happened, and they aren't saying. She won't tell me. I try and protect her, want to be with her, and she fuckin' kicked me out. In front of her whole family."

Not gonna lie, that hurt. Stung the pride. Being asked to

leave in front of the whole family, kicked out like a stray dog nobody wants.

"You have no idea?" Garrett inquires.

"Nope. All I know are things I have guessed but never asked her about. She told me there are things she doesn't want to talk about. I just kept waiting for her to trust me enough to tell me. She's skittish around people, especially large crowds. That was the first time we have ever been to a bar. The time we met you At the Corner, I thought she was going to back out. Something happened to her to make her this way. She hasn't always been like this. She was in college."

"It has to be something big then," Alex offers. "Talk to her brother."

"He admitted there was something Ritza didn't want me to know and that he was sworn to secrecy. He won't tell me," I say, resigned.

The conversation goes nowhere so beer, a few shots, and a couple of pool games later, we head home.

———

IT'S BEEN several days and nothing. No texts. No calls. Nothing. I haven't given up sending her a good-morning and a good-night text every day. Lola wants us to go into the shop and check on the progress, then I need to start figuring out what inventory the old shop left behind and is usable before we start ordering everything we need.

A knock on my door startles me. Only a couple of people know where I live. I open the door to find a disheveled Damian. He looks exhausted, dark circles under his eyes, shoulders slumped.

"Can I come in?" His voice sounds pained.

I open the door wide, stepping aside so he can walk in. He

goes straight for the couch and takes a seat. He rests his elbows on his legs, his head down.

I close the door, then sit on the chair before asking, "Are you going to tell me what this is about?"

He takes a couple of ragged breaths. A few seconds pass, and I'm getting irritated. I want to know what going on with Ritza, and he walks in saying nothing?

"It's Ritza."

He pauses, and when he doesn't continue, I press, "What about her?" My agitation increases.

He looks up at me. "Look, man, I shouldn't be here. She doesn't want me here. She doesn't want you to know, but…" his head falls back down. "She's not doing well. We can't do this again. It's not the same as last time."

I watch as a tear falls to the floor. Whatever this is, it's big. I want to crawl out of my skin, worried about what he's going to say.

"What's not like last time?" I push. He can't keep me hanging like this. I know she's hurting, been hurting, but so am I. And they fuckin' won't let me help.

"She was raped," he blurts out.

My heart plummets into the abyss, and I instantly feel a rage I don't know how to contain. That was one of the things I had assumed, but hearing it said out loud and confirmed…is something else entirely.

"Who? I'm going to kill the motherfucker." I shoot up out of the chair fists clenched, body tense.

A strangled laugh escapes his lips. "Don't you think I would have done that already if she knew?"

All the oxygen has left. Did I just hear that correctly?

"If she knew?" I slump back into the chair. I've never felt as useless as I do right now. Someone stole Ritza's safety, and there's nothing I can do to fix it.

"Yeah. She was roofied. She hasn't shared much with us.

All we know is she was roofied and raped. Everything else she has kept locked up tight in her head." He finally looks up again. "That's why she came home. That's why she is working in the shop. It was the only place she would leave the house for because I was there. And the guys. After a couple of months, Cici was able to talk her into going out to eat every Tuesday."

He just handed me the puzzle piece I knew was missing. The picture becomes clear, and the pain coursing through my body is nothing compared to what she is going through. I'm wound so tight and have no way to release it.

He rubs the back of his neck then rolls it around. "Then you came along, and all of a sudden, we started seeing her again. The girl she used to be. But she didn't want you to know."

"Why?" I'm confused.

"She thinks she's damaged. Dirty. Who would want a girl like that?" His shoulders shrug.

I rub my face roughly, frustration with myself setting in. Was I not clear that I want her? That I love her? How could she not believe I would want her no matter what? I tried to show her.

Her hesitation with intimacy makes perfect sense now. I love her, but I failed her. I thought I was showing her how much she meant. I can't stop the tears collecting in my eyes. The horror she has been living and trying to overcome.

"I'm telling you this, but if she's right and you think those things, then I'll walk out now, and you can stay away." His hands clench and relax a few times. His jaw ticks. He's ready for a fight. Ready to protect her honor. What he fails to realize is I would do the same.

"Fuck you! I can't believe you could say that to me. I'm in. I've been in." I want to direct the anger coursing through me somewhere.

He tips his head at me. "Good."

A small glimmer of hope shines, so I ask, "Now what?" I cock an eyebrow at him. The need to be able to do something is eating at me.

"You can help us with her."

"How can I help? She doesn't want me." I sit back, body tense, ready to listen. He is coming to me, which means he thinks I can make things better.

"Go to her. I know my dad asked you to leave, but it was on her orders. Now we have agreed to have you come over. She isn't sleeping. Cici has had to come over and force her into the shower. I know, gross, but true. All she does is sleep and have nightmares. So she really doesn't sleep. She hasn't left the bed. All she's eaten is a bit of chicken soup. She's withering away." He says it all so quickly, like if he doesn't, he may not. "No one is sleeping in the house because the blood-curdling screams wake everyone. We take turns going in to wake her from the nightmares. She shoos us away as soon as she's awake but falls asleep again to do the same a couple of hours later."

"When?" I ask.

"When what?"

"When can I go over?"

"Now, if you want."

Pain and joy fill me. If there was a way for me to carry all her troubles, I would gladly do it. I stand, grabbing my keys, then opening the door. I hold it open for Damian, and I lock up.

———

I FOLLOW Damian into the house, and his parents are waiting in the living room.

No hellos, only, "Are you sure you can handle this, son?" from her dad.

I nod, knowing I can, if only she'll let me.

"Go on then." He tips his head in the direction of the stairs.

Her door is open, and she's lying in bed, covers all the way up, covering half of her head. Her long brown hair is in a tangled mess splayed across her pillow. Her soft, sleeping breaths are the only sound. I stand at her doorway, watching her for a couple of minutes. I don't want to startle her. I don't want to wake her if it's peaceful sleep. I step into her room, pull out her vanity chair, and sit. I'll wait for the right moment.

I pull out my phone and send Alex a quick message about where I'm at and that I will explain later. I can't worry about the shop right now.

Several minutes later, she begins to stir. I think she's waking up, but she's mumbling. Moving. I climb into bed with her, bringing her close to my chest, hugging her tightly.

RITZA

Pressure. I can't move. It's dark. Where am I? I'm having trouble breathing. Pain. A smoker.

I know that voice. Why is it so far away?

I can't scream. Pain pierces my boob.

"Wake up, mi bonita. It's only a nightmare." Javie's voice. I need him.

I mumble through the pain trying to call out to him. Save me!

"Shhh. Remember I've got you. Shhh. Mi bonita. *Nada te va pasar.* (Nothing's going to happen to you.)"

My eyes fly open, and as soon as I see him, I press myself closer to him. This dream is so much better. These are the dreams I need to be having. A few deep breaths and my breathing evens out.

Wait. Am I still in a dream? Where's the black that lulls me back under?

"Mmmmm…mmmm," Javie hums as he rocks me in his arms.

He's here. What's he doing here? I pull back, sitting up quickly. I blink a couple of times, making sure I'm seeing him. I pinch my arm to check if I'm awake.

"Uh…" No words are coming to mind.

He sits up and grabs my face in his large hands. "You can't get rid of me that easily." He kisses my forehead. "Come here." He lets go of my face and opens his arms wide.

I shake my head. No words, but I can't.

"Why not?" The concern in his eyes bothers me.

I can't explain why. "Please go." More tears collect in my eyes, falling freely.

"Not until you tell me why."

I shake my head again.

"Then I'm not leaving. I deserve an explanation."

He sits back against the headboard and crosses his arms. He watches me.

"I hate you. Leave!" I shout. Maybe that will get him to leave. It feels like the life is being squeezed out of me by saying that.

He shakes his head at me, a small quirk of his lips tugs a gentle smile. "You don't hate me."

Why is he doing this? I don't know how long I can keep this up. Where is Damian when I need him? He was so good at scaring guys away from me growing up when I didn't need it. Now that I do, he's lost. Not that Javie would scare easily. He doesn't. I've seen him stand proudly against Damian.

"I do." I cross my arms around myself protectively.

"I've got you," he whispers.

Fresh tears come with those three words. He doesn't. He can't. He doesn't know.

I shake my head yet again.

"I do. I always will. I love you." His voice is filled with emotion.

I continue shaking my head. "You can't."

"Why not?" His gaze sees more than I want him to.

"Because you can't."

"I told you. I'm not leaving until you tell me why. Why can't I love you? Why?" He licks his lips. Those lips that brought me back to life.

"Because." I drop my head, looking at my covers. I can't look at him any longer.

"I'm not going anywhere."

"Dad! Damian!" I yell. Someone needs to make him leave. I'm not strong enough.

"You think they can make me leave?" An edge to his voice grabs my attention. I look at him again. He has that strong persona on right now. The one that declares he's not one to mess with.

"No" flies out of my mouth without thinking.

"Tell me. You know I know there's something. We've talked about it. I was waiting for you to trust me enough. The time has come."

"I was never going to tell you. I made that decision from the beginning. You were never supposed to know how bad it is," I push back. I need to get angry, but all I want to do is crawl in his lap and let him hold me.

"Now I do. And now, I deserve the truth."

"No. I can't. No one knows. Only my counselor. He's the only one I've told."

"Why him?" His tone is curious, not hurt.

"Because I don't have to see pity or disgust in his eyes on a daily basis."

"Bonita, you will never, ever see disgust in my eyes. *Ever*. Or pity. You are strong. Resilient. I know it's bad, and you have trusted me to live again. That tells me you are stronger than you give yourself credit for."

He takes my breath away. How does he do this? How does he know the right things to say? No. No. No. I can't. He doesn't want a damaged girlfriend. He needs to leave. Now!

"I was gang raped!" I say it quickly, before I have time to process what I am doing. Once he knows, he'll leave. He won't want me after he knows the truth.

He doesn't move, but his lips pull down in sadness. "Come here." He extends his hand to me.

"I can't. You don't want me. You can't want me." The sobs that take over with my admission of what happened to me are too much.

"I do want you. I will always want you. I've told you over and over…I've got you." He creeps closer to me, pulling me into his arms.

He tucks my head under his chin and begins rocking me. I can hear his heartbeat and the vibration in his chest of his hums soothe me in a way I don't understand. A peaceful sensation washes over me, beginning at my head and floating down throughout my whole body. My breathing begins to even out. The tears slow.

I must look horrid. I don't even remember the last time I brushed my hair. I know I reek.

"I…" I know I should say something, but I'm not sure what.

"I'm not leaving." He squeezes me tighter.

"I should clean up." If he's staying, at least I can make myself look a bit more presentable. We should talk.

He loosens his grip on me, letting me pull back to look at him.

"Can I kiss you?" There's no disgust in his eyes. Some sadness, but no pity.

"After I brush my teeth." I move to stand. "You'll stay?"

He nods. "I'm going downstairs to get you something to eat. I'll be right back."

"Okay."

In the bathroom, I stare at my refection—red puffy eyes, a vacant expression, hollowed features. He's here. Robotically I move through the motions of showering and brushing my teeth. It all feels surreal, like any moment the rug could be pulled from underneath me.

By the time I make it back to my room, Javie is back with soup and toast on a tray.

"Is everyone downstairs?" I ask, knowing most likely they are.

"Yes. They are all worried about you," he answers honestly.

I'm wrapped in a towel, not having taken my clothes to the bathroom.

"Do you want me to step out while you change?" he offers when I don't move.

I shake my head. I take the couple of steps to my dresser, opening a drawer and pulling out a pair of panties. I bend over, pulling them up under the towel. Then grabbing a shirt from another drawer, I start to pull it over my head when the towel falls. I quickly pull the shirt down, embarrassed in my own skin. What is really going through his mind knowing what happened to me?

I look up at him, and the desire I see is surprising. I stare at him for a few seconds, then ask, "How could you want me?"

"How could I not?" he counters easily. "You're beautiful. Strong. Have a beautiful soul. I love you." He takes the few steps to stand in front of me. His hand cups my cheek. "Can I kiss you now?"

I nod my head. This is the first time since I woke up to him here that I've said yes to him. His lips meet mine in a gentle kiss. I close my eyes, wanting to get lost in him. Wanting my mind to settle from everything I've recalled about that fateful night.

A woman clearing her throat startles us, and we pull apart. I look to my mom standing at the door with wide eyes.

"You might want to put on shorts before your dad and brother come up."

I scramble to pull on a pair of shorts and get back into bed. Javie places the tray in my lap and sits in my vanity chair.

My family comes up, and we talk about things. They made me call my counselor and schedule a meeting with him for tomorrow. Javie sat and listened as they spoke to me, and at me. They had given me the time to wallow, but I couldn't stay there.

CHAPTER 22

JAVIE

I brought Ritza back to my place so her family could get a full night's sleep. I promised them she would be safe with me. Ritza quickly agreed to come with me. Her soft breaths and relaxed body tucked in my side feels natural. She belongs here…with me.

I can't sleep, wanting to watch over her. Wanting to slay the nightmares that haunt her. I'll be taking her to the counselor's tomorrow. I'll wait outside but be there to hold her when she's done. I sent a quick text to Alex earlier to let him know I was out of pocket for a couple days. He told me to take my time and he would handle everything.

She stirs a bit, but each time, I whisper to her, "I'm here. You're safe with me," and she stills. It's nice knowing even in her sleep, she believes me. Trusts me. I know we have so much to discuss, to work through. It won't be an easy road, but I know I can handle it. My life hasn't been easy.

FINGERTIPS LAZILY RUNNING up and down my chest wake me.

"Good morning, bonita," I say without opening my eyes. "How did you sleep?"

"Better. I think. I don't remember waking up in the middle of the night. Did I?"

"No, baby. You didn't. You stirred a couple of times but settled after I whispered to you." I kiss the top of her head, rubbing her back.

"Whispered to me?" She lifts her head to look at me.

"Just reminded you I was still here. You were safe. You would mumble a bit more, then you would doze off peacefully again."

She wraps her arm around my middle pulling herself tighter against me. I don't want to let her go, but I know she needs to learn to fly again. Trust herself that she can. I can't keep her in a bubble. I can only be there to catch her when she stumbles.

"What time is your appointment again?" I ask.

"At eleven." Her voice shakes.

"I'll be waiting for you wherever you want. In the car or waiting room. You tell me where to be, and I'll be there."

"Okay." She kisses my pec then sits up.

"I'll make us breakfast." I move to sit up, but she pushes me back down.

"Let me. I haven't left a bed since…you know. I'll fix us breakfast." There's a tremble to her voice, but she moves quickly to get out of bed.

"Sure?" I don't want to place too much on her plate right now.

She turns around and smiles at me. It doesn't reach her eyes, but it's a start.

I watch her as she moves around my tiny kitchen, pulling out some sausage and eggs from the fridge. She pulls out a pan and begins heating it up. I grab my phone from the nightstand and shoot off a quick text to the family group chat.

I'm with Ritza. She needs me now and I'll explain later as much as I can or as much as she'll allow me to share.

I love them, but I know for Ritza, they may be too much; we are all up in each other's business. I'm not sure what she will let me tell them.

Garrett is the first to respond.

Just let us know how we can help. T & L, I know you're already itching to ask questions. Don't. Patience.

I laugh out loud. Always the levelheaded one who will call it like it is.

"What are you looking at?" Ritza looks at me as she stirs the eggs.

"Just my family." I won't lie to her. She'll have to get used to them.

She drops the fork, eyes wide. "You told them?"

I shake my head. "No." I get out of bed and stand next to her. With my index finger under her chin, I tilt her head up to look at me. "I only told them you need me, and I would explain later. They are my family, and they are also protective of family. If you are with me, they will look after you too. I don't know what we will share with them. That will be up to you. But we have to let them in on a little bit. They want to help. I promise."

"Why did you laugh?" She pulls her bottom lip into her mouth.

"Garrett was calling out Toni and Lola. Those nosy girls are itching to ask questions." I place a kiss on the tip of her nose.

She gives me a tight smile. She's nervous, but it will fade.

RITZA

I don't know which is worse, knowing or not knowing. Before I recalled so many memories of that night, I wanted to know what happened to me. But now I kind of wish I never knew. It hurts to know the depravity of some people. I've seen my counselor three times in the last week. It's strange now because I can stay in the dreams, watching what happened, and not be scared. Now I'm more of a spectator than the participant. I don't know why or how, but every night that I sleep with Javie, he keeps the nightmares away.

We don't know and will never know if my dreams are actually what happened. They, of course, have pieces of the truth, but with dreams we couldn't know what is real and what my mind has skewed. Even the guys' faces have changed. I would like to say if I passed them on the street I would know, but I probably wouldn't. That alone gives me pause.

Javie has been patient, waiting for me to be ready for us to talk. He hasn't pushed, just being a quiet partner as I process and work through this. But Josh says it's time.

We are sitting in the living room of my house after my meeting with the counselor. I don't want to have to tell my story multiple times, so I called a family meeting, with Cici and Javie included. I will share what I can; some things are too personal. Those will stay between me and the counselor.

I curl up in the corner of the couch. At least the weather has turned cooler, and it doesn't look strange for me to be wearing a hoodie anymore. I pull the fabric over my legs and hug them. Javie is on the couch next to me, but I need some personal space to get through this.

I clear my throat, for no reason other than to hesitate. "I don't know where to start, so I'm just going to start talking." I glance around the room at the expectant faces. At one time this might have been torture, but now I'm just nervous.

"The reason I fainted, passed out, you know…at the bar with Cici and Javie was because of what a guy said to me. He was being a sleaze, and used a stupid pickup line," my hands begin to tremble, but I continue, "'Ready for a blow job?' The guys at the bar that night…the night of the incident, bought blow job shots, and one of them used that line. Just that line freaked me out. We all know I was roofied because I didn't remember anything. But now the dreams, they are me reliving that night over and over."

"What happened, mija?" my mom questions, leaning forward in her seat. I know she's itching to come hug me, but I asked them to let me get through this first.

I bite the inside of my cheek and press my fingernails into my skin to stay present. The little sting is keeping me in the here and now.

I just shake my head. "I can't. Not what happened during. Just know that I am talking about it. I am processing it." I didn't want to cry, but moisture collects in my eyes. "It's too much."

"That's all we ask," my dad says and places a hand over my mom's clenched hands.

"I've blamed myself over and over. I placed myself in that position. I shouldn't have been talking to strangers. I…" I drop my face in my knees and take a few cleansing breaths as everyone waits patiently for me. "But I couldn't know. How could I?" I mumble, repeating what my counselor has said to me over and over. I don't believe it wholeheartedly yet, but I'm working on it. I look back up, knowing I need to finish so we can all move on.

"The guys knew where I lived and how to get in because I told them. At least that's what I think I remember. They drove me home because I didn't 'feel good.'" I air quote with my fingers. "I was throwing up. It was awful, I didn't think I would stop. I must have told them where I lived. Wanting to go home after getting sick. And my key in the gnome is how I always got in my place when I didn't drive. They left after dropping me off, and I passed out. But they must have returned sometime later. I couldn't say when or how long they were there. I was out of it."

Cici is covering her mouth with her hand, tears in her eyes she's trying not to show.

"They?" Damian's body is so tense, it looks like if someone were to hit him, he might crumble.

I only nod. I don't want to get into the specifics of "they," —three. Their laughter as they had their way with me. Spreading my legs and holding them for another to "play." That's what they called it as they took turns. So many hands are rubbing me. My nipple hurts.

"Bonita, come back." A gentle squeeze to my hand brings me back to the present. My pulse is racing. I blink a couple of times to settle the thoughts and continue.

All I see are Javie's warm, brown eyes, full of admiration. The disgust and pity I was sure would be there once upon a time never appeared. There has been sadness and worry, but that's expected from a person who loves you. At least I'm listening to Josh and trusting his assessment.

"How do you know to call her back?" Cici looks at Javie.

"Her pulse. I've learned to check it, and when I feel it racing, I know she's about to leave me. I have always caught it, except that night."

"What?" Stunned, I look at Javie.

"When I rub your neck, I'm checking it. When I hold your hand and rub your arm, I'm checking it." He winks at me.

"Wha— How?"

"It was your eyes when I first noticed. Now though, if that's when I notice, I know you are gone. It takes a moment for you to come back. If I can feel it before I see it in your eyes, you stay with me."

It is amazing how in tune with me he is. Who knew calling him for an interview would finally bring me *beautiful serenity*?

"You love my daughter." My mom smiles, a twinkle in her eyes.

"I do. I really do." He nods as his hand continues to rub up and down my arm and wrapping around my wrist.

I bring my legs out from under the hoodie and move closer, snuggling into him.

"That's all I'm going to share. I can't...talk about..." I can't finish the sentence. "The pieces I've dreamt of are all scattered. I don't really know what happened other than I was raped. I didn't give consent." I needed to say that out loud.

I'm working with Josh on accepting what happened is not my fault. I did not give consent. I can flirt, talk, and wear whatever I want. No means no, and consent means agreeing to any sexual activities. I was not in the right frame of mind to consent. I did not do this to myself.

"That's fine. You have shared what you can and are working through it. That's all we ask." My dad stands. I stand up to hug him. He has been a silent strength behind it all. He knew about Javie and our secret before all the others. He trusted I was safe. He didn't push for more.

My mom follows and steps behind me, wrapping her arms around me. My father kisses my head.

———

"I can't believe you knew what I was going through the whole time and never said anything," I say to Javie as we are eating at his place.

"Not the whole time. But I caught on quick enough." He picks ramen noodles up with his chopsticks clumsily.

"You know, you can use a fork." I giggle at his attempt.

"I know," he says, slurping noodles into his mouth with a goofy grin.

It's quiet for a bit as we eat, then Javie asks, "Why did you ask me to have lunch with you that day? The day you ordered wings."

My heart thumps against my chest at his remembering our first lunch. "Truthfully, I don't know. It was a feeling, I guess. Most guys check girls out. I mean, I guess people do. Girls are guilty too. You know, that once over that sometimes turns into a gawk. I couldn't stand that look…after. I hid behind baggy clothes, but so many still… I don't know…looked. Like they were trying to figure out if I was hot underneath it all." I shrug, having trouble explaining. "But you didn't. You didn't scan me up and down. You greeted *me*. You weren't…" I don't even know what I'm trying to say.

"I couldn't look away from your eyes. I didn't want to make you uncomfortable. I saw the way you held yourself. Your arms crossed in front of you. The clothes. And most of all the fear and pain in your eyes."

"You saw all that?"

"I saw you." He grabs my hand on the table and squeezes. His hand rubs my arm, and I know he's checking my pulse. I don't say anything.

CHAPTER 23

JAVIE

I didn't know how hard it would be to let Ritza tell her story on her own terms. I know she needed her space to share the gruesome incident. All I wanted to do was hold her close. Stop the words. Not that I didn't want to know or didn't want her to share. I could see the pain and how hard it was for her to piece together those words. I wanted to be able to take that pain away. Carry it for her. Strip if from her so she never had to feel it again. But I couldn't. All I could do was sit there and watch as the love of my life hurt.

I felt useless in those minutes, watching her tremble, clench her fists, pinch herself, take shaky breaths. I wasn't built to do that. But that's something I have to learn. Stand aside so she can heal, and be there for her as she needs me. Let her dictate how I can assist in her recovery.

I can only imagine how hard it is for her, not knowing who did that to her, because it is like a stab to my chest knowing someone raped her, and I can't go out and beat him into a bloody pulp and chop his fuckin' dick off. I would gladly do the time. I would take it with a smile knowing that mother-fucker could never hurt another girl.

Rage fills me sometimes, knowing what I know. I've had to go to the gym a few times to release it on a punching bag. Alex and Garrett have gone with me, helping me work through these feelings so I never scare Ritza or make her uncomfortable. She doesn't need to see that. She needs me to be strong and in control to hold her hand on the journey.

———

I CAN'T SAY Ritza has officially moved in, but she has been here every day and night for the past month. Each day clothes of hers come and go, but the majority of them stay. She has taken over the closet and stuffed the drawers with her things. I like knowing she'll be in my bed each night. Any night when the dreams want to haunt her, I'm there to scare the ghosts away. It took several weeks, but now they only come occasionally.

The front door opens, and she walks in with another full overnight bag. We will be needing a bigger place when my lease is up.

"More?" I tease. Her wardrobe has been evolving. She's not trying to hide like she once was.

"Stop." She rolls her eyes at me. She throws her bag on the bed before coming to straddle me on the couch.

"Have I told you how much I love you?" I brush strands of hair behind her ear, placing soft kisses on her neck. She pushes into me. I want to show her every day she's not damaged or dirty like she wanted to believe. She will some-times try and pull away or hide herself from me, but I slowly bring her back. Show her she should be treasured. She is worth the love.

"Not since this morning," she says, breathless.

She's had a good day. On days like this, she is putty in my hands. Giving herself to me and trusting I will cherish her.

I kiss down her collarbone sliding my hands up the back of her shirt, unclasping her bra. She pulls back, her eyes filled with desire. She kisses me hard, opening her mouth for our tongues to mingle. My hands slide to her front, and I rub her nipples with the pads of my thumbs. They harden instantly as she moans in my mouth.

"I need you," she whimpers.

Her needing me is such a fuckin' turn on, and my dick stiffens, straining against the jeans I have on. I grab the hem of her shirt lifting it, separating our mouths momentarily. She rolls her hips, grinding. I pull on the cups of her bra, sliding her arms out. Her perky, full breasts stand at attention. Leaning over, I take one in my mouth, sucking gently.

I let it go, standing with her in my arms. She drops her legs, sliding down and lifting the bottom of my shirt. I grab the neck, pulling it over my head.

"Finish undressing for me," I say to her, sitting on the bed. I know she's still having trouble feeling confident in her own skin.

Her eyes dart around for a moment. Her chest expands in a deep inhale. She works the button and zipper of her jeans, pushing them down. She steps on the legs of the skinny jeans, working them off. She stands in her panties and covers her breasts with her arm.

I lick my lips and glance to her panties, reminding her she's not done. She hooks her fingers on each side and slides them down. She crosses her legs, bringing her arm back up covering her chest.

"Why are you covering yourself?" I touch the hand on her chest with my index finger, slightly pushing it down. She slowly drops it to her side.

My index finger slides down the curve of her breast to her

stomach, stopping it right below her belly button. I swipe it back and forth before dropping lower. Her breath hitches, and she moves one leg to open her legs just a tad.

"This…" I graze her torso softly, "is beautiful and never needs to be hidden from me. I will cherish it for as long as you allow me." Goosebumps follow the line I make on her skin.

She licks her lips, swallowing, then moves closer to me.

"Show me," she says, building her courage.

"Challenge accepted."

EPILOGUE

16 MONTHS LATER

RITZA

I can't believe life led me here. It's strange to think I was ready to give up, live with no one to love, no one to cherish, no one to walk through life with. The road to where I am was not easy, and I fell many times along the way. But Javie was always there to catch me or to lend me a hand to figure out a way to stand back up and try again. His love and patience allowed me to continue taking the steps. To choose the pace.

Slowly I came to realize I needed to be proud of myself for the work I was doing to move past the tragedy. I was doing it. I was finding the strength. I was moving one foot in front of the other. I did it with the help of the people who loved me. I did it with Javie helping me. He has corrected me along the way. Reminding me I am the strong one. He is only there to help me back up.

I'm supposed to be studying for a test, but my mind keeps drifting. It does that some days. I've learned to go with the flow and give myself grace. I'm back in college part time, and it feels nice to be back. To finish what I started.

Lucky for me, the test is next week, and I'll have Toni to tutor me this weekend. She has been awesome helping me through this dang accounting course. She's a mad genius when it comes to numbers.

A baby's cry breaks me from my thoughts, so I get up and go to the nursery to pick up the most adorable girl, baby Madeline, Lola and Alex's daughter. She sure did fool them. Lola had it in her mind she was carrying a boy for a while. This sweet thing has everyone wrapped around her tiny pinkie. To watch Alex, Javie, and Garrett cater to her is hilarious. Poor thing will have a time trying to date when the time comes.

I'm babysitting so Lola and Alex could go on a date. Javie is supposed to be joining me after he closes their shop.

I pick up the demanding baby and dance with her. A diaper change and bottle later, we are laying on the living room floor with toys scattered. They will soon need a baby gate around because she's crawling faster and pulling herself up to standing with the help of furniture.

The front door opens, and Javie yells at us from the foyer, "I'm here, bonitas!"

He walks in and sits on the edge of the couch close to us.

"I have a bone to pick with you!" I exclaim exaggeratingly.

"I haven't seen you since this morning. How could I already be in trouble?" He laughs.

"I thought I was the only bonita?" I pout, holding in my laughter. Each of us girls have had to get used to Madeline stealing the attention of our guys.

Javie laughs, shaking his head. "You will always be *mi bonita*. But you have to admit that little devil is fuckin' adorable!" He nods his head in her direction, and I turn around to her crawling away toward the kitchen.

I scramble up to catch her. She squirms, wanting to get down and explore.

I walk back with her and hand her to Javie. "Your turn to chase her." I laugh knowing he will let her crawl all over the house while following her. Watching him with her is hilarious, both crawling side-by-side.

He places her back down on the floor and kisses me briefly before lying down. Madeline decides climbing on Javie is a better idea. I watch him with her, patient and loving. Letting her explore while always having a hand ready to catch her if she fumbles. Just the way he is with me.

"You know, one of these days we are going to have one of our own too," Javie says, not looking at me.

"What?" I don't know exactly what he's talking about.

"One of these little devils!" He laughs as she stands using his face to steady herself and drool flops on his forehead.

"Slow your roll, mister!" I roll my eyes.

He lets out a soft chuckle. "No hurry. Just reminding you that it will happen."

"It will happen," I whisper to myself.

After everything and the slow progress to heal, this is his way of reminding me that we have a future together. A future I was unsure about. I'm ashamed of the time when I tried to push him away, scared I was holding him back. I should have known he wouldn't scare easily. He was up for my challenge, and I had to concede defeat. I'm so glad I waved the white flag.

The doorbell rings.

"Our food is here!" He picks the munchkin up, flipping her over as he makes his way to stand. She squeals and laughs, teething baby drool dripping on his shirt.

I go to the kitchen to get Madeline's baby food ready. He comes in, placing our bagged take-out on the table and pulling her highchair out to place in between us. He gets her strapped in as I bring her bowl and plates and utensils for us.

I give Madeline the first bite while Javie is unpacking the bag and serving us. Madeline has her hand clutched around something small. Babies will find every single choking hazard on the floor.

"Javie! Did you not notice Madeline has something in her hand?" I ask, shaking my head at him for not paying closer attention to her.

"Nope. What does she have?" He continues scooping pasta on each plate.

I pull her fingers up because she has Hulk strength when she has something she shouldn't. A shiny, drool covered diamond ring sits in her hand. My heart stops.

"Uh…" I stare at the beautiful solitaire sitting in the palm of her hand.

"You're going to let Madeline keep it?" Javie jokes, getting my attention.

I grab the ring from her hand, looking at it in awe.

"Mi bonita," he says getting my attention. "This is my way of telling you that I am in this for the long haul. *Para siempre.* (Forever.) There is no one else I want to do this life with. If you say yes, I will marry you tomorrow if you want or five years from now. When is not important. What's important is that you know, there will always be an *us*. Will you be my wife when you're ready?"

Tears have collected in my eyes at his short speech. "Yes. Yes…I will marry you." I lean forward, and Javie meets me in the middle for a short, baby-next-to-us-approved kiss.

"I love you," he whispers against my lips.

"I love you too."

For Women

The statistics are saddening, too many women have endured this traumatic experience. While I hope and pray no one ever has to deal with this type of healing, if you do, please get professional help. There are so many resources for those who need it.

Resources:
RAINN (Rape, Abuse & Incest National Network)
Get Help 24/7
CALL 800.656.HOPE (4673)

Rape Crisis Center
Most cities have a center.

SANE/SAFE Nurse
If you ever have to get examined at a hospital, ask for these nurses. They have specialized training working with sexual assault victims.

ACKNOWLEDGMENTS

Time for all my THANK YOUS!

As always, I need to thank my family. To my husband who will complain about my face in the computer again, but in the next breath tell me about a song he thinks could inspire a book. To my teen who thinks what I do is embarrassing. She'll soon pass this stage and realize chasing dreams is WORTH EVERYTHING. Even if others don't understand it. To my dad who continues to encourage and ask about my author life. Mom, you are always on my mind. 🖤

To my sister, Marisa, and sister friends, Susan & Stephanie, who are always a text or brunch (wink, wink) away to keep me laughing and sane.

Thank you to reader who turned into a wonderful friend, Andrea (aka, @chula.is.reading.romance). She read book 1 & 2 of the Graffiti Hearts series and began messaging me. I am so thankful she did! She has a beautiful soul and is a delight to know. She beta read Beautiful Serenity and with her help, made Javie shine brighter!

To my cover designer, Maria Ann Green. She is the best and is patient with me as she makes my covers SHINE!

Thank you Jackie for all your expertise in editing! Not only do you edit, but offer such sweet comments throughout or gems to help the story flow.

To the wonderful group of authors who I'm grateful are friends; Melanie A. Smith, Eve Kasey, Melissa Frey, Marla Holt, Ellie Malouff, Katie J. Douglas, Rose Croft, Andrea Nourse, Andrea Hopkins, K. Rodriguez & A. Marie. Y'all are always there for questions, support, to be an ear for venting, for a laugh or even a cry. Writing may be a solo endeavor, but it is the tribe that keeps us going.

And lastly to all the readers and bookstagrammers. Your support of sharing, reading and reviewing keeps me typing the words.

THANK YOU!

ALSO BY TORI ALVAREZ

Graffiti Hearts Series

Beautiful Collision

Tragically Beautiful

Novella

Love's Influence

ABOUT THE AUTHOR

Tori Alvarez is an educator by day and author by night. She spent her days daydreaming different stories and scenes so she finally took the plunge and began putting them down on paper.

She writes real, honest romance with a hint of steam. She is a sucker for happily ever afters, so you will always find them in her books too. She has five books published, Naive in Love, Graffiti Hearts series book 1, 2, & 3 and Love's Influence.

Tori is a Texas girl, born and raised. She lives in South Central Texas with her husband, teen daughter, dog & cat.

instagram.com/mstorialvarez

goodreads.com/torialvarez

facebook.com/MsToriAlvarez

amazon.com/author/torialvarez

bookbub.com/profile/tori-alvarez

twitter.com/MsToriAlvarez

A TEXAS SIZED THANK YOU!

Thank you for spending time with Javie and Ritza. I hope you enjoyed their story as much as I loved writing it.

Love the book? Please review!

As a small indie author, I appreciate any reviews. Reviews help future readers decide on the next book they will be picking up. Please take a couple of minutes to drop your review. Please visit Goodreads, Bookbub, and/or Amazon to leave your review.

If you post on social media, please tag me. I LOVE to see all the beautiful pictures and mentions.

Thank you, Thank you, Thank you!

 Tori

Manufactured by Amazon.ca
Bolton, ON